To Wade

I hope you enjoy the mystery of...

HIDDEN REFRACTIONS

MaryAnne MacCrone

HIDDEN REFRACTIONS

A NOVEL

MARY ANNE MACCRONE

TATE PUBLISHING
AND ENTERPRISES, LLC

Hidden Refractions
Copyright © 2012 by Mary Anne MacCrone. All rights reserved.

No part of this publication may be reproduced, stored in a retrieval system or transmitted in any way by any means, electronic, mechanical, photocopy, recording or otherwise without the prior permission of the author except as provided by USA copyright law.

This novel is a work of fiction. Names, descriptions, entities, and incidents included in the story are products of the author's imagination. Any resemblance to actual persons, events, and entities is entirely coincidental.

The opinions expressed by the author are not necessarily those of Tate Publishing, LLC.

Published by Tate Publishing & Enterprises, LLC
127 E. Trade Center Terrace | Mustang, Oklahoma 73064 USA
1.888.361.9473 | www.tatepublishing.com

Tate Publishing is committed to excellence in the publishing industry. The company reflects the philosophy established by the founders, based on Psalm 68:11,
"The Lord gave the word and great was the company of those who published it."

Book design copyright © 2012 by Tate Publishing, LLC. All rights reserved.
Cover design by Kenna Davis
Interior design by Nathan Harmony

Published in the United States of America

ISBN: 978-1-61862-820-6
1. Fiction / Romance / General
2. Fiction / Romance / Suspense
12.04.10

To my teenage boys, Colin and Tim,
who put up with a mom who wrote a romance.

To my husband, Craig, who supported and
encouraged me as I wrote my first novel.

And to God, who provided the ideas and
the tenacity to finish this book.

Chapter 1

"Hello?" Gregory Mason answered his cell phone.

"We need to talk." There was no greeting or introduction. The statement was short and direct. Creases dipped deep into the older man's forehead as the familiar voice registered with him.

"It's been a while since *you* called," Gregory said slowly, wondering what might have prompted this contact now.

"Meet me at the tavern near I-75. You know the one. Be there in an hour."

It was midmorning, and Gregory was alone at the store. Leaving now would mean closing. Trying to negotiate, he said, "I can't get away right now. It'll have to be later."

"Later won't work. I will meet you there in an hour." The phone line disconnected, and Gregory found himself listening to silence.

Regretfully, he closed the phone, locked the store, and left by the back door. He paused briefly after climbing into his car. With a deep breath, he started the engine and drove out of New Glory, Kentucky.

The taxi wasn't moving. Nothing was moving. Correction, pedestrians were making very good time. Alyssa shook her head. It was not a bad day for a walk, but fifteen blocks in heels didn't seem to be a reasonable solution. *Patience*, she reminded herself; this city was good for developing patience.

She opened her briefcase to review some documents that she had to make revisions to and began highlighting and making notes to save time later at the office. The first part of her day had been a meeting with a new client. It had gone well, but some interesting points had come up in their discussion, so she would need to reflect those in the business plan she had developed for them.

Alyssa Mason was a small-business consultant. With an MBA and a love for smaller enterprises, it had seemed a good fit for her when she finished her education. Signing on with Grayson & Associates, she had quickly proven her worth and was now well established in the field. Although she had some clients that were seeking recommendations on current operations, her specialty was setting up new businesses. For Alyssa, watching the small startups become established and, over time, successful was a thrill to watch. It was almost like watching one's children grow and mature.

The job had a single major drawback, however, and she was sitting smack in the middle of it: New York City. It was not exactly her idea of the perfect location to live. There were people who would never consider living anywhere else, and naturally, there were those that sought the big city lights for an exciting getaway. As far as Alyssa was concerned, they could have it. She had been traveling at the New York pace for four years now and most days felt like her fuel tank was down to fumes.

The taxi lurched forward, and they made limited progress toward her office building. With the business plan in front of her, she could focus on that rather than the annoying traffic jams and the questionable driving skills of her cabbie.

Finally arriving, she paid the taxi driver and hopped out into what could only be described as bedlam. It was coming up on noon, and the New Yorkers that wanted to avoid the midday crowds were already headed out for lunch. She wasn't sure if the pre-lunch multitude was any less chaotic than the high-noon frenzy. The main goal now was to negotiate a safe path to her building.

Meeting that objective, she found herself in the lobby of the quieter, yet still bustling, twenty-six-story office complex. She worked on the ninth floor; riding elevators was her life. Taking a moment to breathe and reorient herself at her desk, she pulled out her lunch. She checked her messages and made note of any that could wait but promptly returned the urgent calls before starting to eat.

The afternoon was hectic with meetings at the office and preparing business plans, which often took considerable research. It was incredible how many small businesses launched in New York, which made her job both easy and difficult. There was always information and trend data available to provide to interested entrepreneurs, but there was also significant competition to consider. It was her job to make any new venture stand out as unique in order to thrive.

Her cell phone rang just before she was ready to leave for home. Checking the caller ID, she was surprised to see the name June Mason display. It was odd to get a call from her during the day. She typically would call in the evening or on the weekends.

"Hi, Mom. This is a surprise." Alyssa's voice was cheery but cautious. The tone on the other end was sorrowful.

"Alyssa, your grandfather has passed away." Just like her mother, always direct. Her voice was faltering as she fought to hold back tears.

"Oh, Mom, what happened?" Alyssa's words were slow as she tried to process the news about her grandfather, with whom she had spent countless hours as a child.

"It was an accident, a terrible accident. Something went wrong with the brakes on his car. He was out on Highway 6, and when he came to one of…one of those really sharp turns, he…" She had stopped midsentence. Only her sobs were audible.

Alyssa felt control over her own emotions starting to fade. Memories began to flood back to her of her childhood and how much she had loved this man. She hardly remembered her father, who had died when she was just eighteen months old. It was likely more in response to her grandfather's need at the time than hers that Gregory Mason had become an important father figure to Alyssa, developing an especially close bond with his granddaughter. Alyssa and her mother were really all he had left. His wife had died the year before Alyssa's father, and Gregory Mason's only other child, Andrew, became estranged from the family around the time of Alyssa's father's death.

Trying to speak while she still could, she simply said, "It's okay, Mom. I'll be home tomorrow, and we can talk about it then. I'll fly into Lexington and drive from there." She ended that call and immediately booked the first available flight.

As she hurried home to her apartment, she made mental notes of what she would need to pack. She was unsure how long she would have to stay. The solution was simple. She would just take lots of clothes in case the visit stretched out.

Her apartment was her one refuge in New York, and each day when she returned there after work, she felt it calm her nerves. Today it was not having quite the effect that it normally did. She concentrated on packing but was interrupted when the buzzer in her apartment sounded, signaling she had a visitor. It startled her. She looked confused, and then comprehension settled over her as she glanced at her watch. It was seven o'clock, and she had a date she had forgotten about.

"Hello?" Alyssa waited for the reply on the speaker.

"Alyssa. Are you ready?" The familiar French accent flooded the apartment. Max Chevalier was born and raised in the south of France but had moved to the United States when he was twenty-one years old. Now, ten years later, he was an American citizen and spoke perfect English, but there was no losing that incredible French inflection and his European manners.

"Come on up, Max."

Max had been one of Alyssa's first clients four years ago. He had started a print service called Magic Copies and within two years had opened a second location. His enchanting personality gave the company its magic. Instead of assigning an impersonal identification to the distinct stores, he gave each a woman's name. He had named the original store Alyssa; he never tried to hide his smooth techniques of persuasive seduction, although they had been unsuccessful on Alyssa at that time. The second was Beatrice. His intent was to work his way through the alphabet by the time he was forty. Since those initial two stores, three more had opened: Constance, Daphne, and Esther. His love of women was paralleled only by his love of New York City, money, and his expanding print empire.

Alyssa had finally given in to his relentless invitations five months earlier, and his charm had kept her intrigued. She had chaste boundaries, though, and he had expectations, so it was uncertain how long this acquaintance would survive.

"Bonjour" she heard as he floated through the doorway. He quickly caught her in a tight embrace, greeting her the only way a respectable Frenchman would. When he eased back from her, he became still, noticing the luggage. "You're packing?"

Still regaining her poise following the passionate greeting, Alyssa sighed and began to explain. "Yes, I really am sorry, Max. I forgot we had plans tonight. My mother called this afternoon to tell me my grandfather died. I have to go home." Her face was apologetic, and Alyssa hoped that Max would not be too disappointed. He adored going out on the town, as had been the plan tonight.

"Hmmm. I am sorry about your grandfather." He paused, and then, brightening slightly, he asked, "How long will you be gone?" *Typical Max*, she thought. Everything was centered around him in his universe. That made Alyssa edgy, and her response was defensive.

"I don't know how long before I return. I have several projects underway right now, but they are all at a stage that I can handle remotely and over the phone. So there's no urgency regarding work."

Max nodded. "Is there urgency with regard to any other aspect of your life?" The point of his question was obvious, and he was starting to pout, a trick Alyssa thought very unappealing in a grown man. Normally she would never react to his suave manner with negativity. The circumstances were causing it, no doubt.

"Max, you are welcome to come to Kentucky with me, but I didn't think you would want to leave New York right now, with Esther having been open only three weeks." It was odd to refer to a printing and copying business by a woman's name; it conjured images of cloning women. She would give him credit, though; the nicknames eliminated any confusion about which store they were discussing.

"No, the timing is not ideal. When do you leave?"

"Tomorrow morning. They *have* cell phone service there. You *can* call me." She pointed out what should have been obvious. Then, softening her tone, she suggested, "Hey, would you like to order food in tonight? We can have dinner here, and I'll finish packing while we wait for the food to arrive." An hour later, they sat at the kitchen table over Chinese food.

The flight was on time, and although Alyssa was struggling to deal with her grandfather's death, she could not help but breathe a sigh of relief at getting out of New York City. She was really going to have to start working toward a long-term plan of relocating somewhere else.

Thoughts of her grandfather filled her mind on the plane. He had always been there for her. The earliest memories she had, included him, and she smiled, thinking back. He had been there for the typical father-daughter experiences like learning to ride a bike, coaching little league, and scrutinizing her dates. There were other events, though, that were unique to their relationship, and they made her grin.

Alyssa had spent hours after school and on Saturdays at her grandfather's store on Main Street in New Glory, Kentucky. He had been a lapidary, owning his own jewelry store for years. The small enterprise, called New Glory Gems, had been his world after his wife had died. Having Alyssa spend time with him there was simply a merging of the two most important aspects of his life.

When she was young, she marveled at the sparkling stones and pretended that she was a princess. She imagined her crown jewels were being cast into beautiful tiaras and pendants to set her apart from the commoners. The man creating these beautiful art pieces was a talented craftsman who cherished splendor as much as she did.

Her grandfather let her try on the pieces that he created. Some were custom made based on specific requirements of his clients. Others were his personal designs. All were exquisite.

New Glory Gems sold many engagement rings without the intended bride's knowledge, and that called for absolute discretion. On those occasions, only Alyssa and her grandfather had the required security clearance to be trusted with the information.

As she had grown older, she worked in the store with him, showing some of the pieces to prospective buyers. Alyssa learned to appreciate beauty, respect the choices of others, be responsible around valuables, and recognize the importance of being happy and content doing what you love. Perhaps that was why she had followed the career path she was on. It allowed her to help people realize joy and fulfillment while being successful, and that was satisfying to Alyssa.

The drive from the airport was relaxing and went by surprisingly fast. As she pulled into the drive of her mother's home, her stomach began to knot. She was not looking forward to the next few days. Although there was not a lot of family to mourn the loss, her grandfather had been a central part of the small community all his life and had many friends in the area.

"Alyssa, you're here." Her mother sounded much better now than she had on the phone, which was a comfort. After hugs and greetings, they went into the house and her mom filled her in on the arrangements for the funeral. She went over all who had been in to see her and what food the neighbors brought in. Her mother talked quickly, which was indicative of her anxiety.

"Mom, sit down and let me make you some tea," Alyssa offered.

"Oh yes, tea would be nice. There are scones in that blue container. Mrs. Francis brought those in. Oh, I probably already told you that." Alyssa smiled and, taking her mother's arm, guided her to a kitchen chair to sit.

"I will get the scones and the tea. Now just relax. Mom, you mentioned that something went wrong with the brakes on Grandpa's car?" Alyssa had cut the conversation short the day before and now wanted to hear all the details.

"Yes, apparently. There was another car on the road that saw the accident. He just went right off the road—didn't slow down at all. The coroner said it wasn't a heart attack or any medical cause. When they towed the car into town, Ted from the garage looked at it, and the brake line had leaked. The police ruled it an accident."

"What time did it happen?" Alyssa asked.

"It was just after eleven yesterday morning?" June was shaking her head.

"Where was he going? I would have thought he would have been working at the store at that time of day." Alyssa was still struggling to make sense of the accident.

"Normally he would have been. I wasn't working yesterday, but I from what I hear, the store had been open for a short time and then he closed and left." June's expression was thoughtful. "It is strange that he didn't let anyone know where he was going. That wasn't like your grandfather." Her mother suddenly looked exhausted.

"Were you able to reach Uncle Andrew?" The question was posed tentatively. The rift in the family had happened just after her father's death, and no one had ever shared the reasons of the disagreement. Alyssa had no idea where her uncle lived now or for that matter if he was even still alive.

"I didn't know how to reach him. The police said they would try to track him down for us. I haven't heard if they found him yet or not. Even if they do, I don't know if he will come."

"Mom, what happened between him and Grandpa?" In case her uncle did show up, she wanted to have some knowledge of the conflict. By the time she was old enough to realize she had an absent uncle, the reasons were never discussed.

"That was between your grandfather and your uncle. I never knew the cause." She shook her head, obviously saddened by the turn of events twenty-five years previous. It was possible Alyssa might never know the source of the conflict. Perhaps if the police were able to find him, she and her mother would be able to rebuild a relationship with him.

Midmorning the next day, the doorbell rang. Alyssa went to the side door and opened it to find a man she did not recognize standing there. His face registered surprise at the sight of Alyssa. There was little doubt that anyone arriving at their doorstep would have looked her over from head to foot. She had been away from New Glory for several years and had been transformed by the fashion sense prevalent in New York City. Alyssa was attractive by anyone's standards, but with her city persona in place, she gave off a sophisticated and often glamorous look.

Long dark hair, accented with matching chestnut brown eyes, framed a china doll face. She wore a rust-colored silk pantsuit, and the shade of lipstick and nail polish matched it perfectly. She paused briefly, taking in the handsome man on the doorstep. Finally gathering her composure, she smiled. "Good morning."

"Morning." The voice was low and smooth. Standing before her was a rugged-looking man, hardly the physical image she would have placed with that voice. He was not the polished Wall Street variety she was used to seeing. No, his appearance was, most certainly, a refreshing change of pace. "You must be Greg's granddaughter?"

"Yes. Alyssa Mason." She extended her hand and paused, hoping he would provide his name so they would be on equal ground.

A grin began on his face as he shook her hand. "You're older than I pictured." The smile widened. Alyssa frowned. She was twenty-seven years old. How old had he expected her to look? "Your grandfather told me about you on many occasions. In almost every story he told me, you were about eight years old."

Her eyes brightened. "Always eight? I must have reached my peak that year. And here I thought Grandpa found me irresistible my entire life." She feigned concern over her life failings. Her smile matched his, and she watched his eyes change as he took her in.

"Garrick. How nice to see you. I see you've met Alyssa." June moved in and wrapped her arms around the man. Alyssa narrowed her eyes.

"Well, actually, Mom, he's met me, but I haven't really met him yet." She shot a look at her mother to stress the need for an introduction.

"Oh, well let me do the honors. Alyssa, this is Garrick Samuels. He lives in the house next to where your grandfather lived."

"It's very thoughtful of you to stop by. There is visitation at the funeral home this afternoon." Alyssa thought that might have been a more appropriate time for him to pay his respects. Then again, the list of neighbors and friends that had been in before she arrived home was lengthy, so it really was not unusual.

"Yes, I actually stopped by about the visitation. June, I wondered if I could offer the two of you a ride over. One less car in the parking lot wouldn't be a bad thing."

That was very thoughtful, Alyssa thought. He probably did not bake, so this was his offer of support.

"That would be fine. Were you planning on staying at the funeral home all afternoon?" Her mother was obviously comfortable with accepting a ride from this man, so it was probably safe. Alyssa internally gave herself a small-town attitude adjustment. *Who couldn't you accept a ride from in New Glory?*

"Yes, I have some things to deal with this morning, but then I'm free the rest of today and tomorrow. I'd be happy to drive you ladies tonight, and tomorrow as well if you like." Alyssa's mother agreed immediately. "Well, I'll be on my way, then. I'll be back around one thirty this afternoon. It was a pleasure meeting you, Miss Mason."

Alyssa's face flinched at the formality. "Oh please, you know every move I made as an eight-year-old. I think you should call me Alyssa."

"All right, Alyssa, I will, as long as you call me Garrick." His stare was so piercing it caught her breath. That voice and his words seemed to knock her off balance. She forced a polite smile in return to acknowledge their deal.

After he left, she turned to her mother with her eyes narrowed once more. "What's his story, Mom?"

"Garrick moved here about eight years ago. You were off at school and then later working in the city. He bought the old Weston place that was right next to your grandfather's home. It had been vacant for several years. Everyone was thankful when he started to fix it up. It took some time, but he did a good job on it. At first he talked occasionally to Grandpa, but over time the two of them became quite close."

"Really? What does he do for a living?" Alyssa wanted to hear more, so a question here and there would help her mother cover the important points.

"He does odd jobs for the seniors in and around town. Monday nights he runs a seniors' program and considers that time his clinic hours."

"Clinic hours?"

"Yes, you know when he does triage to determine which repairs and upkeep items are the most important. It helps him plan his week. For instance, a broken step trumps a light bulb change and a light bulb change may trump a new coat of paint."

"Does that really give him enough income to live on?"

"Well, he worked at New Glory Gems with your grandpa almost every day too."

"He worked at the store?" Alyssa was trying to picture the man that had just left working with her grandfather. That had been her territory at one time. She felt a twinge of envy.

"They were very close, Alyssa. This has been quite hard on Garrick too. He was like family to your Grandpa and me."

"Apparently he was."

Uncle Andrew did not show up for the funeral. This was disappointing since the police had located and informed him that his father had passed away. They had tracked him down somewhere in Georgia. It was unlikely that Alyssa and her mother would ever see him again.

Following the funeral, June asked Garrick to drop her off at Mrs. Mabel's home. Mrs. Clara Mabel was ninety-six years old and had taught Greg Mason in school. She was recovering from a hip operation and upset that she had not been able to attend the service. "I'll just walk home from here. You two go on ahead. I'll see you later," June called over her shoulder as she got out of the car.

As Garrick drove Alyssa the remaining distance, she watched him out the corner of her eye. Oh, he did look good in a suit. It was not a designer cut, but it worked. Before he had gotten into the car, he had tossed the suit jacket in the back seat and loosened his tie and top shirt button. The muscles underneath the shirt were evident. She could not understand how he managed to keep a physique like that toned working at a jewelry store and changing light bulbs all week long. His jaw line was strong with just a hint of the shadowy stubble that would be more pronounced later in the day. She had caught those penetrating blue eyes of his staring at her a few times at the funeral.

Disappointment that she would allow herself to feel drawn to him was creeping up on her. She should not be feeling anything like that. After all, she had a relationship, if that's what you called it, back in New York City. *What would you call it?* she wondered. Max was handsome, charming, and successful, and he adored her. Yes, definitely a relationship—maybe. One eyebrow shot up in disapproval, thinking about the fact that she had been home for three days and Max had not called once. Well, she hadn't called him either.

She was staring straight ahead now, lost in the confusion over what her status with Max was. Not noticing that the car had stopped and Garrick had gotten out, she was taken by surprise when her door suddenly opened. He offered his hand to assist her out of the vehicle.

"Thank you. I guess I got lost in my thoughts. I didn't even realize we were home." Garrick would likely think her loss of focus was grief related. Her brows creased in confusion over why it wasn't grief related. At a time like this, it should have been. "Would you like to come in for a cup of coffee, Garrick?" Despite the exhaustion Alyssa was feeling, she did not want to be alone.

"Sure, I can come in for a few minutes."

They walked to the door together, and she fumbled with her keys when they reached the house. Pulling herself together once she got inside, she put the coffee on and then, trying to keep her voice light and conversational, asked, "So tell me, Garrick, what brought you to New Glory eight years ago?"

"Actually it was a girl," Garrick admitted with a half-smile curving up shyly as he moved over to where Alyssa stood and leaned his hip against the counter, crossing his arms. "I moved here because of a girl I had met, but it didn't work out and she moved away. I stayed." Garrick looked directly at Alyssa, his head tilted just slightly to the left.

"I'm sorry it didn't work out. What was her name? Maybe I knew her while I was growing up." She studied him, trying to assess his character, but struggled to focus given his extreme proximity to her and the fact that with his arms crossed, the muscles bulged against the shirt seams even more.

"Not sure if you would remember her. She didn't grow up in New Glory, just moved here with her mother when she was nineteen. Her name was Mary Emerson."

"Oh, so that would be Grace Emerson's daughter? I don't remember her very well other than I knew Grace had a daughter. Mary would have been a couple of years older than me."

He nodded. "I was probably just looking for an excuse to make a move at that time. She gave me a plausible reason to pick up and relocate. It didn't take long for me to discover that the New Glory community was fantastic and I didn't want to leave, so I decided to put down roots here. And I've been really happy with the life I've made for myself. Not the exciting life you probably have in New York, but it's enough for me."

"Believe me, it is *nothing* like New York, and I am thankful for that. I would much rather be here than there." She had turned back toward her coffee-making duties as she shook her head thinking of New York.

"What could New Glory have that New York doesn't?" The words were probing. He was obviously intrigued with her preference of small-town life.

Without looking at him, she said, "The question is really, 'What does New York have that New Glory doesn't have?' The answer to that is easy. New York City has too many people, most of whom have an insane amount of ambition, resulting in life being lived at an uncomfortable speed."

"So you prefer the slower pace of New Glory?"

"And the people. People here just have a different set of priorities built right into their DNA. *I* have a different set of priorities. It is just so difficult to find that small subset of New Yorkers hardwired the same as me. It can be lonely. All those people and you can still feel lonely."

"You don't feel lonely when you're here?"

Her eyes drew back to his at the question. "I don't feel lonely right now." She smiled. With her heels on, she was only a few inches shorter than him; having stepped out of them, though, when she had come into the house, she was forced to tip her head back in order to see his face. As their eyes stayed on each other, Alyssa felt her mouth become dry, and she swallowed hard. She unconsciously moistened her lips. He lifted his hand and traced his thumb over her cheekbone.

"You're beautiful, Alyssa Mason. I can't imagine you being lonely anywhere."

Her breathing stopped. Her reaction to him was disconcerting, and suddenly feeling awkward, she broke the gaze they shared. "I—I think anyone can feel lonely anywhere if they're not surrounded by people with similar interests and values."

She desperately wanted to know what he was thinking. In her line of work, Alyssa was a pro at analyzing markets, consumer needs, and preferences. Assessing her clients' abilities and drive was key to her being able to put together a business plan that would work for them. She could read people. Why couldn't she read Garrick Samuels?

"So are you a hermit in New York?" he asked with a smirk. That propelled her head around to glare at him.

"No, definitely not." It was time to turn the tables here. She was beginning to feel like she was the target of ridicule. He was developing a distorted image of her. "I'm actually seeing someone in New York—a past client, a very successful past client."

"And does he know you prefer small towns to the big-city life?" Alyssa was starting to feel very annoyed. This was none of his business, but he kept hitting all her hot spots, which made arguing about Max and New York pointless.

"No. We've never discussed my feelings about living there. Max moves easily at the New York pace, thrives on it." She hated trying to defend her relationship with Max Chevalier. Still, it was no surprise to her that he was not her ideal match.

"Why didn't he come to the funeral? Your grandfather died, Alyssa. Shouldn't he have been here to support you?" She closed her eyes and quietly sighed. He made a good point, another excellent point. If Max were here, their relationship would be obvious to Garrick, maybe clearer to her.

"He couldn't get away because of work commitments." What more could she say? It was a lousy reason, but it was all she had.

"I see. So you must be anxious to get back to see him. Will you be heading back right away?" Garrick's voice was calm and rational. It was impossible to hone in on his thoughts. Moments ago, he had gently caressed her face and sent her nerves on high alert, and now he appeared unfazed by the shift to discussing her involvement with another man.

"No, I need to stay and help Mom deal with some things before I go back. I haven't really decided when I will return to New York. I can accomplish most of my current work from New Glory, although the Internet connection speed is not ideal out here."

"Ah, New York does have advantages." He smiled, pleased with his ability to poke a hole in her proclamation against big-city living. Alyssa was relieved to have him joking now rather than asking more self-evaluating questions. "Looks like the coffee is ready."

"Yes. Cream and sugar?" she asked as she took out mugs from the cupboard. They sat with their coffee, and an hour later, when June returned home, Garrick and Alyssa were laughing together over childhood stories.

"Now it is time for me to leave," Garrick announced.

"I'll walk you out." Alyssa had completely relaxed with him. Their conversation had been friendly and light, a perfect balance against the solemn day. "Thanks for staying and talking." Alyssa said as the two walked toward Garrick's car.

Garrick responded with slow words. "I enjoyed it. Listen, I'm overstepping when I say this, but I'm going to risk it anyway. It seems that you and Max may have some issues to table for your relationship to be long-term material. When you figure out that Max *isn't* the guy for you, let me know." With that, he got into his car and drove off.

She watched him leave and closed her eyes, wondering why he had to be so incredibly insightful.

Alyssa decided to stay for a couple of weeks in New Glory. There were a number of items to deal with after a death, and she did not want her mother to have to deal with them alone. Meeting with the lawyer to attend to the will was one of the higher priority matters to take care of. Before her mother could even schedule an appointment, though, the lawyer contacted her. She had been listed as executor, which was not a surprise. He requested that she come in the Tuesday following the funeral to review the will, and he requested that Alyssa join her.

Alyssa tried to work as much as possible. Her projects involved a few meetings, but all could be handled via phone at this stage. She documented the meetings and any business plan changes and e-mailed documents that needed reviewing by other parties. She researched on the Internet and communicated with her various contacts in New York as needed. Generally, it was business as usual without the built-in rat race.

She considered herself fortunate that her projects were not in the initial phases where face-to-face meetings were much more critical. As her workload allowed, she helped her mom with whatever she could. There were thank-you notes to write to friends and neighbors who had donated to local charities in memory of Gregory Mason or sent floral tributes, and to the many thoughtful people who brought food to the house.

Her mother ensured that a general thank you appeared in the local paper to express their appreciation to everyone who showed their respect during the difficult time. Alyssa arranged for the headstone to be updated with her grandfather's date of death. She also took care of paying the funeral services bill and any other funeral costs that had come in.

Despite the focus on her work and all these necessary but regretful tasks that were taking considerable time, her thoughts kept coming back to Garrick. She could not explain why. The way he had touched her cheek, that comment about Max not being the guy for her—there was some sort of electricity between them that she did not understand, and she found herself helpless to fight it. Each time she envisioned him in her mind, she felt a flush come over her.

Finally, five days after arriving in New Glory, Max called. "Alyssa, ma fille spéciale. I've missed you." Romance with Max meant a mixture of French and English. She had been forced to pick up a few key phrases.

"Hello, Max. How are you?" She admitted it was nice to hear his voice.

"Well, I am disappointed that you are not home yet. When is your flight back to New York?" She had expected the question, of course, but not so soon in the conversation. He had not even asked how she was or how the funeral had gone.

"I have to stay here for a couple of weeks to help my mother, so I haven't booked a flight yet," Alyssa explained.

"Well, of course I understand, but perhaps you could come back for a few days and return to Kentucky later?" The pressure tactics were about to begin, and Alyssa had no interest in being coerced.

"Actually, Max, it is really much easier for me to stay here and finish everything up. Besides, I will have new projects starting up soon, and those will require me in New York, so it is easier for me to be away right now rather than later. Please, tell me what you have been up to while I've been gone." She desperately wanted to redirect the conversation to something other than her truancy.

"It is New York. Everything is happening. You cannot stay away, because you will miss too, too much. I wanted to take you to a new restaurant that opened in Manhattan this week. I will make reservations. Just tell me when you will be here, and I will arrange it."

She tried to ignore that he had yet again asked the same question from just a slightly different angle. "How is Esther doing? And when will you be deciding on your next location's store name?"

"Esther is my most successful location yet. It is astounding, so much so that I will be opening two stores in February instead of just one. I have decided on Genevieve for the seventh store, but I am undecided on the sixth store. Do you have any suggestions?"

"I like Faith," Alyssa spoke thoughtfully.

"I was actually thinking of Fiona myself. What do you think of Fiona?"

"Fiona is very nice. It will work well as a store name." Somehow, she knew that Faith would never be considered, and she was not sure why he had bothered to ask her. "I'm pleased that the stores are doing so well, Max. It won't be long and you will have to consider expanding outside of New York. Which city will you target first after you have conquered the Big Apple?"

"I expect Chicago, but I will hire someone to manage the opening of those. I love New York too much to leave. So let us get back to the reason I called. When are you coming home?"

Alyssa was silent for a few seconds. "So the only reason you called was to find out when I was coming back to New York?"

"Of course not, I wanted to hear your precious voice, ma chère, but naturally, I want to know when I will be able to welcome you back."

Alyssa's tone now changed. "Max, as I already told you, I don't know when I am coming back. And I don't intend to argue about it any further." She could be very forceful when she wanted to be, and it was much easier to be direct with Max when she knew he was in another city and she would not have to face him.

Her blunt statement was first met with silence and then Max's very abrupt response: "Very well, call me when you have a flight booked." The phone connection ended, and Alyssa was quite sure it was not a service issue. He had hung up on her.

Tuesday at 10:00 a.m., Alyssa and her mother sat in the reception area of Tyler, Lincoln, & Frost Law Associates. Sidney Frost had been Greg Mason's lawyer for thirty years. They were called into a luxurious office just a few minutes after arriving. Why was it that all law offices looked so ostentatious? "Mr. Frost will be just a few minutes. Please have a seat."

As promised, it was no more than five minutes before the lawyer entered the office. "Good morning, Mrs. Mason, Ms. Mason." He shook hands with both women before sitting down behind the large desk. "Thank you for coming in today. As soon as Mr. Samuels arrives, we'll begin." He shuffled through some papers on his desk organizing everything for the upcoming meeting. Alyssa glanced sideways at her mother, but June looked straight ahead.

Mustering her courage, Alyssa spoke up. "I wasn't aware that Mr. Samuels was attending the meeting today."

Mr. Frost spoke while he continued to arrange his work files. "Mr. Samuels is impacted by the terms of the will, so it made sense to include him in this meeting." Alyssa realized that her grandfather felt Garrick was like family, but she had not stopped to think that he would bequeath something to him. For that matter, she had not stopped to think that he might leave her anything either.

Garrick Samuels was shown into Mr. Frost's office. "Hello, everyone." Garrick's eyes immediately went to Alyssa.

What is he thinking? she wondered. Alyssa had returned to feeling uneasy around him and had no idea why.

"Have a seat, Garrick, and we'll get started." He sat in the chair next to Alyssa, and the sudden proximity to him sent a charge through her. She was acutely aware of his strong presence.

"Now, as you know, we are here to review the final wishes of Gregory Mason. Each of you has been named in his will as recipients of some token. Before I get to the distribution of assets, however, I want to inform you that Gregory Mason made one significant change to his will in 2008. Prior to that time, New Glory Gems was to be given to his son, Andrew. Due to circumstances surrounding the lengthy estrangement, which has been ongoing since 1986, a new last will and testament was written. At that time, Gregory Mason also formally documented the express disinheritance of Andrew Mason, his only remaining child." Mr. Frost paused, giving the three the opportunity to digest this piece of information. Then he continued. "I will read the distribution of property after debts and taxes.

"'To June Mason, I leave the sum of $50,000 and the princess-cut diamond ring that is stored in the main safe at New Glory Gems.

"'To Garrick Samuels, I leave the sum of $10,000.

"'To Alyssa Mason, I leave my home and all my remaining possessions including residual cash and investments with the exception of New Glory Gems.

"'I leave New Glory Gems in equal shares to Alyssa Mason and Garrick Samuels. As a condition of this legacy, the store is to operate for a period of one year and both parties must be involved in its day-to-day operations requiring local residency. If after one year either party no longer wishes to be a co-owner of the store, they are free to sell their share. If either party is unable to fulfill these conditions, the store is to be closed, all assets liquidated, with the proceeds evenly divided between the New Glory Elementary School and the New Glory Secondary School.'

"That is the distribution of the estate. There is also a letter addressed to Alyssa Mason." He handed her the sealed envelope and she automatically accepted it. "Do you have any questions?" There was silence for a moment. Alyssa's head was reeling.

"Yes, I have questions," Alyssa said breathlessly. "I'm not even sure where to begin. Just approximately how big are the residual cash and investments that you mentioned?" Alyssa had never pictured her grandfather as poor, nor had she considered him wealthy. She had never really given his financial position any thought whatsoever.

"I only have a rough estimate at this time, Ms. Mason. You realize that until we identify all of the debts and the required taxes are paid, we cannot fully valuate the estate. As an estimate, however, I would say it will be in the neighborhood of four million dollars." Alyssa just about choked. Was he serious? He looked serious.

"Ms. Mason, your grandmother had a sizeable life insurance policy in place when she died. That money was subsequently invested in some very lucrative stocks. Similarly, your grandfather had life insurance. Those two sources account for the bulk of the wealth that is currently being distributed." Alyssa nodded, trying to assimilate this information and add it to the astonishing revelation regarding ownership of her grandfather's store.

"For clarification, any dispute over the fulfillment of the conditions outlined in this last will and testament will first be managed by the executor of the estate—in this case that is June Mason—and if necessary, the courts. I recognize that the terms of this will have probably come as a surprise to you. It may take time to determine your next steps. What I suggest is that we meet again on Thursday and review plans on moving forward with distribution of Gregory Mason's estate." Mr. Frost left the office and silence hung in the air.

Alyssa was speechless. Her grandfather wanted her to leave everything she had worked for in New York and come back to co-own his business with a complete stranger.

Chapter 2

Alyssa stared at the envelope Sidney Frost had handed her in the law office that afternoon. She carefully unsealed it and hesitantly pulled the paper out. Unfolding it, sadness overwhelmed her. She had received handwritten letters from her grandfather over the last eight years. Here, she held the last letter she would ever receive from him.

> Dear Alyssa,
>
> I find it difficult to write this knowing that it will reach you when I am gone. I have known you all your life. Even though I surrounded myself with exquisite gems, it was you who added the real sparkle to my world.
>
> You loved being at the store as much as I did. You possessed a gift for recognizing beauty and assessing what would make our customers the happiest. My wish is for New Glory Gems to continue to serve our community. I know your involvement will make it a success.
>
> It will be difficult to understand why I have offered you conditional co-ownership, but I hope you will trust my judgment on this matter and accept this opportunity.
>
> No matter where you were, you were always in my heart and thoughts each day at New Glory Gems. I pray

that my presence lives on in the little store on Main Street for many years to come.
   With deepest love,
   Grandpa

Tears rolled down her cheeks and the sobs were difficult to control. How could she disappoint the man who had brought nothing but delight into her life? She was only now beginning to realize how much she had missed him since leaving New Glory.

Alyssa needed to get away and think. She borrowed her mother's car and headed for Lexington first thing Wednesday morning. She would shop, she would spend, and she would develop a plan. She knew how to shop, where to shop, and she most definitely knew how to spend money.

At first, the whole idea of dropping her successful career in New York and relocating to New Glory had seemed absurd. Who would ask someone to do that? Initially she had questioned if her grandfather was actually of sound mind when he wrote the will. The more she thought about it, though, the more she liked the idea.

The day her mother had called to give her the devastating news, she had been denigrating New York, as she did most days. On the trip home, she had consciously noted needing a long-term plan to relocate. Obviously, she had not planned on a move right now, but she knew life did not always follow a neat schedule. She just needed to be flexible.

Ultimately, the letter from her grandfather was responsible for her willingness to consider this transition. She had loved him and his accomplishments so much, and she too wanted to see the jewelry store continue to thrive in the small town.

As she drove to Lexington, she ordered her thoughts. If this were going to work, she would need to quit her job. Professional courtesy would dictate two weeks' notice. She would need to give notice on her apartment. Unfortunately, she would have to pay for next month's rent. Also, she would have to arrange to move all of her possessions to New Glory.

Since her grandfather had left her the house, she had a place to move into, which was convenient, and she would not have to impose on her mother any longer. There would be a certain amount of monetary inheritance. Whom was she kidding? It sounded like that could be in the millions since she was to get the remainder of the estate after the listed bequests, debts and taxes were paid. Financially, it seemed as if she could afford to make a career change.

Her business consulting would be useful and not wasted. Instead of providing a business plan and assisting someone else to restructure or start up their business, she would become the client, or rather, she and Garrick would be the co-clients.

Garrick would be the unknown quantity that would make this risky. She really knew very little about him. His background was sketchy at best, simply because there had not been time to get to know him well. What abilities, skills, and knowledge he would bring to the table were valid questions. What would happen if he decided midway through the year to default on the conditions? She would lose her half of the business and would have pulled up stakes in New York being left without a source of income. Again, her grandfather seemed to have reduced that concern through the extensive settlement from the estate.

Regardless, she would need a backup strategy. After the one year was up, she might want to walk away from it anyway. If that happened, she would definitely need an alternative plan.

It quickly became obvious that she needed to understand Garrick much better than she currently did. They would have to agree on everything to do with the business since his idea of what he would bring to the table might be completely different from what she was expecting.

Yes, Garrick Samuels was elemental to the success or failure of this venture. She would need a risk-mitigation plan. In the meantime, the shopping district in Lexington was drawing her attention with increased force, and who was she to resist?

By the time Alyssa had returned to New Glory, she had waged an assault on many of the higher end clothing stores in Lexington. Her credit card was nursing wounds from the aggressive attack made on it. She laughed silently at the sight she must have been to others. Her petite figure had carried multiple bags. She must have looked like a pack mule, a very well dressed pack mule.

With many soothing purchases in tow, Alyssa easily reviewed the various scenarios in her mind whereby she was willing to take on the challenge with which her grandfather had presented her.

The first scenario was her taking full control of the store. Garrick could sit back and be a silent partner for the year. This would be the least confrontational of the arrangements. It would also be the most work for Alyssa. She had years of practical shopkeeper experience, but she had been away from the precious-gems industry for several years and might not be as informed as she would need to be.

The second scenario placed her in the private partner role and Garrick taking full dominion. She couldn't live with that option. She needed to be involved, and from a small-business perspective, she had too much to offer to withhold it.

The third scenario was the one that her grandfather most likely had envisioned when he determined the conditions of the will. In this option, she and Garrick would have to share in the responsibilities, and decisions would be jointly agreed to. This was the most challenging, interpersonally, of the options however.

Alyssa had some bookkeeping knowledge, but perhaps for the first year, an accountant would be required. She obviously was equipped to work in the store as a salesperson. That skill was developed in her years before. There was budgeting, planning, and advertising to think of. All those business management processes were fine, but if New Glory Gems could not deliver what it advertised, it would not be in business long. Who would provide the lapidary skills that her grandfather had brought to the business? He had designed and created. She definitely did not possess those highly artistic and expert qualities.

She did not like the thought of having to bring too many others into the operation, but unless Garrick could provide the missing elements, she did not think there would be any choice.

When she arrived at her mother's place at 5:45 p.m., a car was sitting in the driveway. She had seen that car before. Garrick was here. As she walked through the door, she heard their voices.

Breezing into the living room with June in midsentence, Alyssa noticed she immediately stole Garrick's attention. That pleased her, and she was flattered. He sat comfortably on the couch with his right ankle resting on his knee, eyes now focused on Alyssa.

June was instantly aware she had lost center stage. Cutting her statement short, she turned her head slightly, asking, "Did you leave all your money in Lexington?"

"Let's just say the economy in Lexington hit an upswing today. Hello, Garrick."

Garrick nodded. "Alyssa."

Alyssa sat down, joining them. Her mother was a master of retreating discreetly. "You have excellent timing, dear. I have to leave to go meet Cheryl. We are having dinner tonight at The Quarters." Swiftly withdrawing from the room, her voice called back toward them, "It was nice visiting, Garrick. See you tomorrow afternoon at the lawyer's."

Garrick was laid back as usual. "Have you had dinner, Alyssa?"

"No, not yet." She was quiet.

"Would you consider joining me for a bite to eat? There's a new pizza parlor on Main Street. It just opened a couple of weeks ago. I haven't been in yet, but I hear it's pretty good."

"I could go for pizza. I guess we probably should talk a bit about the store before we get to the lawyer's office tomorrow anyway." He rose from the couch and outstretched his hand to help her up from her chair. She appreciated his abundant manners.

"Heard from Max?" he asked.

"Yes, I talked to him late last week." *Briefly*, she thought.

"You haven't told him about your inheritance then?" Garrick quizzed. Alyssa was silent. She had not mentioned it yet, of course. That was pointless until she knew what she was doing. Also, her last conversation had been cut short by the hang up, so she really wasn't in the mood to offer up any information to Max.

Finally, she broke the silence as they left the house. "No, I haven't told him."

The restaurant was homey. A mixture of red-checked and blue-checked tablecloths covered the tables, with Tiffany lights overhead. Dark wooden beams on the ceiling, matching wooden chairs, and some sections of wall accented with brick created a rustic appeal. Several tables were occupied, but it was not full, so Garrick and Alyssa quickly were seated and given menus.

After ordering drinks and then their pizza, both knew that the topic of conversation would have to move toward how they were going to handle Gregory Mason's wishes for New Glory Gems.

"Alyssa, I just want you to know that if you would rather not move forward with the two of us operating the store, I will understand completely. You have a full life in New York, and giving that up was probably not in your immediate plans."

"I am still astonished that Grandpa would have expected me to drop everything and return to New Glory for an extended time. Although we didn't spend as much time talking as we did when I lived here, I was certain he knew how important my degree was to me when I completed it."

"He did, and he was extremely proud of you too. You were not *only* an eight-year-old heroine in his tales. You were the success story that he loved to share with everyone. The idea of you succeeding in New York City was overwhelming to him."

"Then why would he have put a condition in his will requiring me to leave that life?"

"I said he was proud of you, not that he was comfortable with you living there."

"He was concerned?" Alyssa had never once considered that her family might be on edge with her living there. "I never felt like I was in danger."

"Greg mentioned the crime in New York, but his bigger concern was the influence that others might have on you. I don't see you as a follower, though—just the opposite. I think it would be you having the influence on them." The corner of his mouth drew up.

Alyssa chuckled to herself. New York was full of leaders. She would not influence them. "Well, I will take that as a compliment." Her eyebrows creased as she wondered if he had orchestrated the entire bequest just to get her to return to New Glory. Was he really that controlling?

"What's wrong?" Garrick had watched her expression become sad.

"It seems out of character for Grandpa to try to control me this way. I would never have guessed he would do that."

"There were two things that Greg loved more than anything else, Alyssa. One was the store, and the other was you. I suspect he never intended to control your life; he just wanted to bring the things he loved back together." Garrick watched her carefully. Their pizza arrived, and some of the tension released with the first bite of a slice of deluxe.

"If that is the case, why did he leave half to you?" Alyssa felt her question was valid, and she was curious to know the answer.

"Fair question, and I can only provide my impression since we don't have your grandfather to ask. I've been involved with the store for several years, and you haven't. In order to give it the best possible chance of succeeding without him, I can give it the continuity it needs."

Alyssa could not find fault with the reasoning there. So often when she developed business plans for ownership changeovers, continuity was a key to success. Garrick must have had either some business education or training along the way, because he seemed to be on solid footing.

"Well, regardless of his reasons, I thought at length about it today."

Garrick smiled as he enjoyed the food. "Between charge card activities?"

"Yes, shopping is very therapeutic when you are trying to work through a problem. Have you ever tried it?" Garrick just gestured that he had not. "I am prepared to stay in New Glory and fulfill the conditions of the will. I cannot help but recognize certain risks, though. Identifying and minimizing risk is part of what I do.

"The first risk I am concerned about is replacing the skills that Grandpa offered to New Glory Gems. Unless you are a lapidary, I think we are short a few key talents."

"Have you been into the store since you returned?"

"No. Why?"

"Perhaps after dinner we can walk over, and I can show you some of the pieces that we have for sale. You'll notice when we get there that although your grandfather never lost his touch, he was grooming someone to take over that part of the operation."

"Who?" She was anxious to hear about her grandfather's student and to see what kind of work they were capable of.

Looking down as his pizza, he quietly answered, "Me."

"You?" The question came out with a significant tone of surprise.

Garrick gave a self-conscious laugh. "That hard to believe, huh?" Alyssa was speechless. She stared at him, knowing he was not joking.

"So are you any good?" She had recovered from the shock and now teased him.

"My pieces were selling quite well. Your grandfather still handled most of the custom requests, but there had been fewer of those in the last couple of years."

"Well, I look forward to seeing your work, Mr. Samuels. This would be an ideal way to remove that risk from the list."

"But there are other risks?" Garrick questioned.

"At least one."

"And that would be?"

"You are a risk, Garrick Samuels." She studied him as his eyebrows raised first at the admission of staying in New Glory and now further when she cited him as a risk.

"Okay, how exactly would I be a risk?"

"I don't know enough about you. I have no guarantee that you will not pull out midway through the year. Until a moment ago, I had no idea that you had lapidary skills, and for that matter, I don't know how extensive they are. Are you knowledgeable in buying, or did Grandpa continue to do all that himself? There are lots of still unanswered questions."

"I need to rewind here. So you're saying that you are willing to stay even though I, your partner in this adventure, represent a risk? *And* you are ready to make this decision without discussing it with the man that you're involved with in another state?" Garrick narrowed his eyes, anticipating Alyssa to correct something in his comprehension of the situation.

She took another mouthful of pizza, not appearing to be ready to offer any clarification. Garrick leaned back in his chair and stared at her. "Look, I haven't said anything to Max because I won't be staying here if you are not prepared to take this on. Secondly, I was already thinking about leaving New York at some point. Although the timing is not quite what I would have mapped out for myself, it is an opportunity worth considering.

"You are a risk because I can only control my own contributions to this. If you decide midway through the year that you are leaving, I would lose the store and would have given up a career. So, yes, from where I sit, you are the risk, but risks can be managed."

Garrick laughed. "I've had women call me a few things over the years, but I don't think any of them referred to me as manageable."

"Well, I am not any of *those* women. I've said enough—your turn. Spill it. What are your thoughts?"

Garrick set his pizza down and looked at Alyssa. "I am not leaving New Glory. The reasons I came here initially are not holding me here. It's my love of this area and eight years living among these people. That's what is anchoring me. I won't leave midway through the year, and I have been working at that store for a while. I know exactly what I can offer in operating the business and where I think it would be wise that you lent your expertise. I don't think *I'm* the risk."

"The way you say that, it sounds like you think I might be a risk. Why is that?"

"Max. You're involved with someone that may insist on your return to New York."

"Max will not be a factor that you need to be concerned with." The statement was delivered without Alyssa's usual direct eye contact.

"Care to explain that?" Garrick's expression grew suspicious.

"Not at this time."

After dinner, they strolled down the street to New Glory Gems. The storefront had always been inviting. The oak arch front door was unique. Alyssa had always felt like she was stepping into some fairytale place when she walked through it. Perhaps that was where the whole princess fantasy of her youth had started. The storefront was rustic brick in varying shades of grey. Two rectangular windows with ivory-colored awnings flanked the front door. Overhead, the name New Glory Gems on an oak sign identified the store with pride.

Garrick unlocked the door, and they entered. The store was so similar to what she remembered. Even the smells brought back memories. It was spacious, tempting customers to browse the various showcases leisurely. Each case was in the same beautiful oak that the front door and sign were. Glass over each showcase was always polished to remove fingerprints, which inevitably appeared with little more than a glance from passersby. Tonight, though, a layer of dust covered them all.

With the lights now on in the emporium, Garrick headed to the back and came out with window cleaner. He must have read her mind. On the other hand, maybe he was just simply in tune with the importance of displaying the merchandise in the best possible setting. He started spraying the glass and handed Alyssa some paper towels. She was glad to help. She took much more time cleaning the cases, becoming absorbed with the beautiful treasures exhibited.

She wandered for a half hour, gazing in amazement, wondering how she could have stayed away from here for so long. "It's just as I remembered. It has a power over me, and I always tumble into an otherworldly realm when I am here. I expect Grandpa to walk out from the back at any moment." She ran her fingers along the oaken cases. "So which pieces are your creations?"

"Have a look at this case up here at the front counter." Alyssa moved toward that part of the store and peered down into the showcase. They were exquisite.

"So these are yours?"

"Actually these are your grandfather's. Everything else in the store, I did." Alyssa slowly moved her widening eyes in his direction. Everything else was Garrick's work. She was astounded. How could she have missed the mark so completely on him?

"Garrick, I'm impressed. You are very talented. I am beginning to think you are not a business risk after all."

After an enlightening tour of the store, the two walked back to Garrick's car. On the drive back to June's house, Garrick needed to bring their discussion to a conclusion since Alyssa shut down his final questions about Max. "We need to know what we are telling the lawyer tomorrow, Alyssa. I am willing to meet Greg's conditions. So I'm in. You are too?"

She smiled at him as he turned into the driveway then nodded as the car came to a stop. "Shall we shake on it, partner?" They shook, and Alyssa popped out of the car and headed for the house. Tomorrow they would meet with the lawyer, and they would put in motion the legalities of their decision.

June was already home, and after a quick update on their evenings, she told Alyssa there was a message for her on the machine. Surprised by that since she had not provided the house number to anyone, she went to listen to it.

"Alyssa, your cell phone must be dead. I tried to call it but could not get through. I will be flying to Lexington tomorrow and attempting to drive out to wherever it is that you are staying in New Glory. I would like to stay through the weekend and hope that you will return to New York with me on Sunday. I should be in New Glory about four p.m. See you then, my love."

Max. Well, she might well be heading back on Sunday with him, but it would be to resign, give notice on her apartment, and pack. Not really what he would be hoping for. "Mom, you heard the message already?"

"Yes. Will he be staying here, Alyssa?" June had not met Max, nor did she know exactly what his relationship with Alyssa was.

"I guess so. The motel in town is not his style. I'll sleep on the couch, and he can have the bedroom. Depending on what happens at the meeting with Mr. Frost tomorrow, I will likely fly back to New York with him on Sunday and make arrangements to move back here.

"Please don't say anything to him about the will until I have had a chance to tell him, Mom. He may not be very happy." Then rephrasing the statement for accuracy, she clarified. "He *will not* be very happy with my decision."

"You know, Alyssa, Garrick has a large home with ample space. Maybe Max could stay with him." Alyssa felt panicked. She did not want Garrick and Max talking. Why did she not want them talking? Was she afraid that Garrick would not like Max? That he would view her choice in men as poor and think less of her? Or was she afraid that Max would realize that there was chemistry between Garrick and Alyssa that was just simmering under the surface?

"I don't want to put Garrick out by asking him to play host to my unexpected guest."

"Oh, Garrick wouldn't mind. We'll play it by ear. Why don't you get to bed? It's been a long day, and I expect you up early tomorrow to show me all those purchases you made today!" Remembering her extravagant day, Alyssa beamed at her mother's comment.

"Good night, Mom."

The meeting the next afternoon went well. Alyssa had a sketchy, but feasible, plan to continue discussions with Garrick. Mr. Frost would begin the legal documents on the partnership and transfer of ownership. The store would re-open one week from Monday. They thought that would provide sufficient time to prepare. Alyssa intended to be back from New York on Tuesday, and that would give them time to finalize their roles and responsibilities.

"I am pleased that the two of you have agreed to accept the conditions and keep New Glory Gems open." Mr. Frost extended his arm to shake hands with Garrick and Alyssa. He nodded to June. "Always a pleasure, June. We'll be in touch concerning some other issues related to the will."

The three were exhausted after the hour-and-a-half meeting. They walked out of the law offices of Tyler, Lincoln, & Frost into a warm September afternoon. Alyssa was doing her best to keep her anxiety over Max concealed, but June knew it was there at the surface, ready to break through.

"I am sure you ladies would like to get home and relax, and I have some errands to run. How 'bout you come over to my place for dinner tonight? I'll cook. Alyssa, you haven't seen the house since I fixed it up. I think you'll like it." Alyssa's mouth dropped open. June let a smirk escape, and between the two reactions, Garrick was tipped off that he was in the dark about something. "What's up? Don't think I can cook? I haven't killed anyone yet."

Alyssa's throat seemed to have closed off. June looked at her for some sign that she should speak up. Finally, Alyssa looked at her mother and asked that she go on to the car and she would catch up. She watched her mother walk away, and when June was almost to the vehicle, Alyssa turned back to look at him. The tension had been mounting all day with the anticipation of Max arriving. Alyssa knew it must have been showing in her face and in her actions.

"Garrick, Max called last night and left a message that he is coming to New Glory. He expected he would arrive around four p.m. today." She glanced at her watch. "I need to talk to him and tell him about everything that has transpired regarding the will and my decision to move here. I certainly need to tell him before someone else in town lets something slip in front of him. I'll have to decline your dinner invitation. Mom should still join you, though. I will need some time to actually explain to Max, so a bit of privacy would be appreciated." Alyssa looked stricken.

"I understand. Will you be all right alone with him? I hate the thought of you having to tell him on your own." Alyssa, losing her battle to conceal her emotions, was unable to answer him. Garrick stepped closer, took her head in his hands, and angled it up toward his face. "Will you be all right?" he repeated.

She just nodded. Although she had examined what she was doing from all different directions, she still dreaded telling Max, and her eyes filled to almost overflowing.

"Is he planning on staying at the house tonight?" Garrick still held her face gently. He spoke the words so close to her that she could feel his breath.

"I expect so. I have not even talked to him. I told Mom I would just sleep on the couch. He said he was staying until Sunday." Now a tear did escape.

Instead of wiping it away, Garrick drew closer and kissed her cheek where the tear was streaking down and then whispered, "I want to see you tomorrow regardless of whether he is still here. For tonight, if you need to call me, please don't hesitate." Alyssa was spellbound. She had never been treated with such perception and sensitivity. She had never met a man like Garrick Samuels. They had only just met and yet she felt a connection with him that was astonishing.

Chapter 3

Alyssa hurried to the car, where her mother waited. A few more tears had trickled down her face, but all she could think of was the kiss on her cheek that had dried up the first tear. She had to pull herself together before she saw Max. She needed control, or he would try to convince her she was making a mistake. Max would only be able to picture her in New York. Now, more than ever, she could not picture herself there.

Alarmed by the tears, June questioned her on what had been said. Reassuring her mother that everything was fine, they drove away. When they turned onto June's street, Alyssa's eyes widened as she saw the rental car parked in the driveway. He had already arrived.

She took a number of deep breaths, trying to calm her nerves. As June turned off the engine, the driver's door of the other car opened, and Max stepped out. June's eyes grew large as she took in the sophisticated man who was walking back toward her vehicle. "That is Max?"

"Yes, that is Max. Wait until he speaks. The rest of you will melt, Mom. Please don't get sucked in by the charm." Her tone was pleading, and she hoped that her mother would be immune to Max's appeal: an attraction that drew so many women in, an attraction that finally overcame her too. Alyssa opened her door, and Max was there to take her hand immediately. "Hello, Max." She smiled tentatively.

"Ah, Alyssa. You look wonderful." Max stepped closer, taking her in his arms, and, with his usual passion, kissed her right there in the driveway.

Alyssa pushed him away and with a loud whisper, said, "Please, Max. The neighbors will see. My mother is in the car."

"No, she's not. Hello, I'm June. You must be Max." Alyssa felt even more mortified. Max still had hold of her but released her so he could greet her mother.

"I am Max Chevalier. It is a delight to meet you finally, Madame Mason." He took her hand and kissed it. Alyssa closed her eyes and shook her head at his endless European charisma.

"Please call me June."

She needed to regain control of this scene. "Max, how long have you been here? I'm sorry we kept you waiting." She was quickly shifting into the unemotional professional mode where she routinely dealt with challenging situations with fortitude.

"Ten minutes, perhaps. The drive was much quicker than I had expected." He was escorting June to the door on his arm. If Alyssa had brought him home to meet her under normal circumstances, she would probably have just stood back and been pleasurably amused by his tactics. She was not amused now, though.

Once June and Alyssa were inside, Max quickly dashed out to get his luggage. Alyssa sighed inside. The luggage. "Why don't you just leave your suitcase there in the entryway until we get things straightened out here? There are only two bedrooms. So I will sleep on the couch, and you can have the room I have been staying in once I get a few things out of it."

"The couch? No, Alyssa, I will not hear of it. Perhaps there is a hotel I could stay at?"

"You wouldn't be comfortable at the motel in town, Max. It's not what you're used to," Alyssa assured him.

"As I mentioned, Alyssa, maybe Max would be more comfortable at Garrick's place." June was determined to push this idea, and Alyssa had no idea why.

"Garrick? Is this another relative that you have kept secretly hidden from me, Alyssa?" Max was using his French accent to its fullest advantage.

"No. Garrick is not a relative—"

"Although, he is like family," June inserted. This suggestion seemed to put Max off balance. Alyssa had never seen him in uncertain territory. Even when he was first starting up his business, he always exuded confidence and knew his next move.

"The offer is very considerate. Does Garrick live close by? I want to spend as much time as possible with my Alyssa."

"It's about five minutes from here, but I haven't asked Garrick if you would be able to stay there." Alyssa was not sure how she would arrange that; although knowing her mother, June would handle it. And she was right. June hastily offered to call Garrick if that suited Max. Alyssa was not sure if she was losing her touch. Normally she could steer the direction of a discussion, but her abilities were dwindling with every minute that passed. Before she knew it, June was on the phone to Garrick and arrangements were being made.

"All set, I told him we would come over now. We'll have dinner in a while with Garrick. Max, you can settle in. The two of you can spend some time together over there this evening and then Garrick said he could drive you home later, Alyssa."

"Excellent." Max seemed happy. June seemed happy. Alyssa did not seem happy. "It has been a long ride. Would you show me where the restroom is?"

"Of course." June had him follow her to a hallway off the kitchen and directed him to the main-floor two-piece bath. Alyssa was on hold again. She would have to revise the plan. Garrick knew she needed to be the one to tell Max, so it would be all right. They would have dinner, and then her mother and Garrick would let them have the privacy she needed to explain her decisions.

Moments later, they were driving to Garrick Samuels's home. As they drove past her grandfather's house, Alyssa pointed it out to Max.

He commented on what an impressive home it was. "Yes, he and my grandmother lived there for many years, and he never wanted to leave even after she was gone. It is a large house, but he loved it."

When they arrived at Garrick's, he was at the door to meet them. Alyssa had been in the house a few times as a child but did not remember much about how it was laid out. She was delighted when she walked in. Garrick had done a spectacular job of updating it. It had all the charm of small-town living with every convenience possible. The kitchen had cherry wood cabinets and stainless-steel appliances. The countertops were granite. He must have come from money, because every detail screamed top of the line. He had only been twenty-three or twenty-four years old when he bought this place.

Garrick led them to the living room to relax before dinner. As he let June and Max pass by him, he stopped Alyssa and asked if she could help with something in the kitchen. He assured his other guests he wouldn't keep her long. Once out of view, his hand came to rest on the small of her back as he directed her to the other room.

"June was insistent that you both come over as soon as possible. Is there something I should know? I thought you wanted a chance to talk to him before he went anywhere," he asked.

"I don't understand what she is up to, so I have moved on to plan B, which is for you to occupy Mom after dinner so I can tell him what all has happened. During dinner, though, we need to fully skirt any conversation about wills, inheritance, the jewelry store—basically everything." Alyssa was frustrated.

"Hey, dinner won't be ready for a while. I will get June out here to help me, and that will give the two of you time to talk. How does that sound?"

"Good. Thanks, Garrick." Putting on an expressionless face, she returned to where June and Max were talking. When there was a lull in the conversation, Alyssa spoke up. "Mom, Garrick was hoping you might be able to help him out in the kitchen."

"Absolutely. That will give you two a chance to talk." June sent Alyssa a knowing glance.

Now that she had the privacy that she had requested, she needed to scare up some courage to get this exchange rolling. "How was your flight?" She began on neutral territory and posed the question quietly while still standing.

Max watched her, and as he spoke, he rose from his chair and moved toward her. "It was fine. Flying isn't as exciting for me as it used to be, but it got you back in my arms, so it was worth it." He reached out and touched her hair. "You seem troubled, Alyssa. Is it the loss of your grandfather, or is there something else?"

"Max, we need to talk."

Max let out a puff, which was not like him. "I never like conversations with women that start that way. Should we be sitting down for this talk?"

Alyssa licked her lips and realized she needed something to drink. "I'm thirsty. Would you like something?" Alyssa was stalling, and she knew it. She feared that Max realized it too.

He asked for coffee. She escaped to the kitchen, where she knew Garrick already had coffee ready, and taking two mugs fixed the way she and Max preferred, she returned quickly to him.

Sitting in the comfortable living room with their coffee, she began choosing her words slowly and carefully. "Max, it was extremely kind of you to travel here to see me. There have been a number of things for us to sort through here because of Grandpa's death, so it just wasn't possible for me to return to New York earlier. We met with the lawyer on Tuesday morning and he shared with us the details of the will. Grandpa left me a few things, which was extremely thoughtful of him."

"I am very happy for you, Alyssa. Of course, you always spoke so highly of your relationship with him. I am not overly surprised that he would leave you something. Tell me, what have you inherited?"

"Well, he left me his home and most of his possessions. There were a couple of monetary bequests to Mom and Garrick and a special ring for Mom, but beyond that, it was pretty much left to me."

"Ah, so you have a property that will need to be sold. I can see why you felt you had so much to do. I expect a Realtor can handle the sale without you staying here, though."

Alyssa bit her lower lip to keep her focus. "I'm not going to sell the house immediately, Max. I'm going to keep it."

With some surprise showing on his face, Max set himself for a debate over her decision. She had expected he would object to her keeping the house. If he only knew the rest of the decisions, he might not be so quick to pick this one as the one to argue about. "Alyssa, if you keep it, you will have expenses and worries that you don't need. Tenants can be a challenge even if you are nearby. With you in New York City, I would be afraid that much too much pressure would be left on your mother to shoulder."

"Actually, Max, I am not going to rent it out."

"It will be difficult to insure if no one lives there. You really should sell it, my sweetheart."

"It won't be empty, and I am not going to rent it out, Max. I am going to live in it." There she had cast the first critical piece of information. Now the real opposition would start.

"I don't understand. You are not returning to New York City with me?" The illogical path the conversation was taking confused Max.

"I will likely go back on Sunday if I can get a flight. I need to give notice at the apartment and pack all my things." Alyssa knew it was best to filter this new reality to him in very small chunks.

"You are giving up your apartment in the city and relocating to New Glory, Kentucky? Are you planning to work full time from here? You meet with so many clients face-to-face. How can you manage it from here?" Max was starting to show some irritation now, which had been expected.

"No, I will actually be giving notice at Grayson Monday morning as well."

Max said nothing for a seemingly endless time. Then finally he said, "How much money did your grandfather leave you? Are you suddenly independently wealthy that you can quit your job?"

"Max, I will be taking over my grandfather's business here in New Glory. That is what he wanted, and after thinking about it carefully, it's what I want too. New York City is too big for me. I am much happier here. I am so sorry, Max. I know your life is in New York, and I won't be there." She paused looking down at the floor and then back up and into his eyes. As gently as she could, she suggested, "Max, it wouldn't be fair to you for us to try to continue dating. I think under the circumstances we should stop seeing one another."

"You've decided all this since Tuesday when you spoke with the lawyer?"

"Yes, it's all I've thought about. I put together a draft business plan and met with the lawyer again this afternoon to file the papers transferring ownership of the business. The store will re-open a week from Monday." Alyssa carefully avoided any mention of the partnership and the conditions of inheritance.

"Why don't you first request a leave of absence from your job? Give this a few months' trial, and then if it is not what you want, you could return to your role with Grayson. I don't see the point of quitting your job when this might not last."

"I am committing to a minimum of one year at the store, Max. I am not prepared to ask for a leave of that length. The decision has been made, and I'm going to see it through."

"Alyssa, what is this really about?" Max pressed.

"What do you mean?"

"Are you running from New York City or from me? Are you looking forward to opening up your grandfather's store, or are you looking forward to spending time with Garrick?" The tone was accusatory and the words cutting.

"I don't think I am running from anything, Max, and I am not sure what you are suggesting with regard to Garrick."

"Is he an old flame?" Alyssa was not used to jealousy from him. Her forehead creased in confusion.

"No, I just met Garrick when I came back for the funeral. Why would you think he is an old boyfriend?" She was cautious, trying to anticipate where this line of questioning was coming from but, more importantly, where it was going.

"You work quickly then." Disgust was seeping out of his words.

Now the innuendos were irritating her. "Enough, Max. Spit it out. What are you talking about?"

"You and Garrick…the kiss on Main Street this afternoon as I drove through town. It didn't look like you were pushing him away like you rejected my kiss in the driveway of your mother's home." His voice had gotten louder now. He waited. Finally, Alyssa broke the silence.

"I can't explain what is happening between Garrick and me. What you saw was simply a comforting gesture because I was anxious about telling you my decisions to live here. Max, nothing else has happened. I am not involved with Garrick."

"But you will be. I noticed the way he looked at you. It's what he wants." Nodding in resignation, he said, "Well, I think after this revelation, I should leave now. Is there a taxi service in this town?"

"I'm sorry, Max. One of us will drive you back." Alyssa felt horrible that she had hurt him and was basically agreeing that he should leave, but there was a component of relief mixed in that was promising genuine peace, and that gave her some comfort.

Alyssa asked her mother if she would mind driving Max back. She would have driven him herself, but she was uncomfortable with the thought. Garrick offered, but he had no idea the accusations that had been made, so she did not want him to be blindsided. June prepared to drive him back to pick up the car while Max phoned for the next flight home to New York City.

By the time June had delivered Max to his vehicle, a migraine had closed in on her, so she called Garrick to let him know she would not be returning for dinner. "Don't worry about Alyssa, June. I will drive her home later this evening. You get some rest."

Alyssa had been quiet since Max and June left. Her relationship with Max had been nothing more than a friendship really. She had never imagined it becoming more, but ending a friendship was painful too. She felt disheartened but then smiled, remembering how much energy Max put into everything he did. He was special and would be the ideal man for some other woman.

The dinner that Garrick prepared was simple but delicious. He had been on his own for a long time and obviously had developed some quality domestic skills. Alyssa felt like collapsing once she finished helping Garrick with the dishes. It had been a stressful couple of weeks, but the last two days in particular had been draining.

Garrick put a movie in. His collection was extensive, but they decided some action might be a good distraction. With a 1980s action flick loaded up, they settled in for the needed diversion.

"It's getting late, Garrick," Alyssa said when the movie finished a couple hours later. "I really should be getting back to Mom's. If I had already moved in next door, I could just walk over." She smiled. It seemed easier now to visualize how her life was going to be.

"I'll drive you home." He stood and, as usual, offered her his hand in getting up off the luxurious leather sofa.

"Garrick, you have a wonderful home here. I don't think I ever got around to saying that earlier. You did a terrific job with it, and the furnishings are so extravagant. You didn't spare any expense, did you?"

"Thank you." She suspected he had heard what she said, although his thoughts seemed to be drifting quickly away from house and home decorating topics. "It was a difficult day for you, Alyssa. Tomorrow will be better."

"I know." He had not relinquished her hand after she had stood, but now his fingers slowly traced up her arm from where he released his hold. Without thinking, Alyssa's hands moved up and pressed against his chest while her eyes continued to gaze into his. She could sense his heart rate increasing with her touch. "Garrick, I'm not sure this is a good idea." Her voice was breathless and soft. She was uncertain of these reactions. This was so incredibly fast to be feeling what she was feeling.

"This?" he asked simply.

"Yes, this—" she swallowed—"this closeness."

"Is that what we're calling it—closeness?"

"What would you call it?"

"I haven't decided yet. I'll drive you home." With that, he took her hand, and they headed for the door.

Friday, Alyssa arranged to travel to New York at the end of the following week to pack. She called her employer, giving them the two weeks' notice she felt obligated to provide. She also called her apartment complex to see if they had anyone on a waiting list that might sublet her place while her lease ran out, and finally she scheduled movers to coincide with her trip to New York. Things were falling into place.

Alyssa spent time over the next couple of days at her grandfather's house. She arranged for workers to come in and do some minor repairs before the movers delivered her things. She went through her grandfather's personal belongings and dealt with the items that had to be disposed of. Knowing that there would be more involved with going through his office, she opted to leave that room untouched until later.

Needing a short break on Saturday from the work at the house, she looked up a friend she had known quite well before she had left New Glory. Laura Simmons had been Alyssa's best friend during high school. She had attended Gregory Mason's funeral and Alyssa had been pleased to see her. Her husband, Mark Wilson, had not been able to attend, but in the few minutes that Alyssa had to chat with Laura, she learned about their marriage, heard about their four-year-old son, and promised to call to get together. Looking up the phone number, she dialed, hoping that Laura would be free.

"Hello?"

"Laura? It's Alyssa Mason."

"Oh, Alyssa, hi."

"I was wondering if you might have time to meet for coffee?" Her voice had an anxious tone. Although Alyssa needed to start reacquainting herself with the New Glory natives because of her new business role in the community, this contact was born out of personal necessity. This was exactly what she needed right now, a little girl time.

"Yes, I could get away. I will have to bring Jason, but if that's okay, I would enjoy getting together."

"That's fine. How about we meet at the café on Main Street in about thirty minutes?"

"We'll see you there."

Alyssa, Laura, and a very talkative Jason arrived at almost the exact time at the café. Alyssa had never been in this establishment. It was new since she had left town, and she was just starting to scout out everything that New Glory had to offer its inhabitants. The café was busy. Laura pointed out that Sarah's Café was owned and operated by a girl who had been in the year ahead of them during high school. Alyssa vaguely remembered her, but given the café was just two doors down from New Glory Gems, she knew they would become very well acquainted in short order. They ordered lattes for themselves, and Jason got apple juice.

"So how long are you staying in New Glory?" Laura had always been easy to talk to, and they fell back into that comfortable interchange she remembered. Laura was blonde, taller than Alyssa, and absolutely gorgeous, the typical head cheerleader. Her high school days were spent dating football players and other jocks, but Alyssa did not know what the years after high school had been like for her.

"Actually, I'm staying. I'm surprised you hadn't heard. I thought this was a small town, no secrets, everyone knows everything, you know, the stereotypical small community," Alyssa teased.

"You're staying? No, I hadn't heard. Yay. Did you hear that, Jason? Mommy's friend is staying for a while." Laura's enthusiasm was encouraging, and Jason was caught in the excitement, expelling a joyful squeal.

"Yes, Grandpa left the store to me and to Garrick Samuels. So we've decided to re-open and continue to operate it."

"So you will be working with Garrick? How intriguing." Her voice had shifted straight from pure innocent glee to sinful accusation.

"Why do you say it that way?"

"No reason." Laura shot the sarcastic remark out to Alyssa. "Garrick is probably *the* most eligible bachelor in all of Kentucky, and you will get to corner him in the store room on a regular basis. Girls everywhere are going to be heartbroken."

She feigned sniffles to which Jason sympathetically patted her arm. "It's okay, Mommy." Both women smirked and shared a glance of utter enjoyment.

"It doesn't seem as if Garrick is involved with anyone. Or is he just really good at concealing his personal life?" Alyssa probed, not letting on the intimate moments that she had shared with him over the last few days.

"He's been in New Glory almost as long as you've been gone, and I don't remember him ever seeing anyone for more than one or two dates. He seems to be content to live here, but it is not because of a love interest. I think he is fantastic, though. He introduced me to Mark. He and Mark were friends from college, and he brought Mark out to a community dance about seven years ago. We were married eighteen months later, and then Jason arrived about a year and a half after that." Laura looked lost in memories but quickly pulled herself back. "So I am a big fan of Garrick's."

Alyssa smiled. Garrick had a fan club, and Laura was obviously president.

"What is his degree in? Do you know?" Alyssa was interested, considering his creative abilities.

"Actually he was in a criminal justice program, but then when he moved here, he got involved with your grandfather and followed in his father's footsteps. Garrick's dad died probably about ten or more years ago, but before that he was a lead designer of jewelry for Cartier."

"Really? I have seen some of Garrick's pieces in the store. He is very gifted."

"Yes, well, apparently it must be in the genes. Come on. Give me the dirt. There isn't anyone special in New York City who is stricken with your decision to move to small-town America?"

"Well, I was seeing someone, but it wasn't going anywhere. He was not crazy about my decision, but he'll deal with it. New York City was closing in on me. I was quickly coming to the realization that I would not be able to stand that life for much longer. This just set in motion a future plan in a more immediate timeframe."

"Well, if you are available and Garrick is available…" She let the comment hang.

"You haven't changed one bit, have you?" Alyssa shook her head, pleased to engage in this female chatter.

He opened the newspaper to the obituary section and pulled out a cigarette. He scanned the names on the list, stopping when he saw it. Raines, Jeremy—near Lexington, KY, as a result of an accident… He didn't read any further. He smiled, closed the newspaper, and lit the cigarette.

Chapter 4

Garrick poured himself a cup of coffee while he waited for the toast to pop up. With his breakfast and coffee in hand, he moved to the table to sit down in his kitchen nook with a view of his backyard. The nerines were just coming out in full bloom now, and the mix of color was impressive. He didn't get enough time to enjoy his spacious yard, so Sunday morning was the perfect time to make up for the rest of the week.

Even though the store was closed, it had been a busy week. He had spent two days at Mr. Jeffries's house doing various repairs and general maintenance. Mr. Jeffries was coming up on eighty-two years old, and although he was quite capable on many levels, his children preferred that he keep to floor level. They had made it very clear to him that no ladders or chair climbing were to be in his present or future, and since so many tasks that needed to be accomplished at his house required that extra height, he had enlisted Garrick's assistance.

Two visits to the lawyer, Monday night seniors' program, and several requests from neighbors for help with winterizing their homes before the fall season progressed any further had put Garrick on the move every day.

He had not seen Alyssa since Thursday night, even though it appeared she had spent long days at Greg's house next door both

Friday and Saturday. He had debated going over to see her but knew it would be best to let some time pass. He would make a point of running into her today, though. Sunday was the perfect day for more relaxing activities. Alyssa was one woman he was interested in exploring some of those relaxing ideas with, and he was hoping to convince her that she agreed with him.

Reasons evaded him as to why he was feeling this way about her. He was thirty-three years old and had been dating since he was seventeen. That amounted to approximately sixteen years of experience. He had never in all those years been put so far off balance so quickly and so completely by any other woman as he was by Alyssa. Garrick typically became moderately intrigued, and that stage consistently and quickly waned into disinterest.

The local coffers of new eligible and interesting women to spend time with had been fully depleted by Garrick already. Garrick spent most of his time in New Glory Gems, which catered to wealthy older people and young couples. Very few single women came in to the shop to purchase expensive jewelry for themselves. That made a jewelry store not the ideal location to meet available and appropriately aged females.

Perhaps it also didn't help that he ran a seniors' program, limiting his social circle one evening each week to people that were sixty years of age and older. Sincere as they were, their matchmaking choices had ranged from approaching social security to illegal.

Then there was Mrs. Sinclair who each week, without fail, would try to set him up with her granddaughter Amy. Garrick had dated Amy briefly a few years ago, but despite repeated reminders to Mrs. Sinclair, she would arrive each Monday evening enthusiastically suggesting that she introduce him to Amy. "She's a lovely young lady. You two would be perfect together. Have I mentioned she is a schoolteacher? First grade. She loves children, you know." Garrick often wondered if he was really the only man to whom Mrs. Sinclair did this. Perhaps she spoke of Amy's virtues to several of

New Glory's residents. Regardless, he got a kick out of the attention that this dear elderly lady paid him.

With his current social circle, he had begun to think the idea of a serious involvement would not become reality until he hit his sixties when the selection would be a variety of spinsters and widows. Rarely did anyone ever leave or move to New Glory. Therefore, by the time he was in his sixties, he probably would have already dated all the spinsters and maybe even most of the widows in their younger years.

Alyssa's appearance in New Glory, however tragic the reasons, had changed his outlook. He thought about his first glimpse of her in that silk pantsuit. Closing his eyes, he drank his coffee, and the image of Alyssa became more vivid. Although the picture in his mind was of an attractive, classy lady, there was another dimension to her. That other dimension filled him with wonder: her sense of humor, her capacity to love deeply, and her sense of adventure.

He was still amazed that she had decided to stay here. She was big city from head to toe, and he could not help but think that she would grow bored with New Glory sooner than he would want, sooner than she expected. The pace and excitement she thought she wanted to leave behind was a drastic difference from the pace in this small town. Would she really be able to adjust to that dramatic a change? Only time would tell.

He had almost crossed the line with her a couple of times, and he needed to keep his guard up for several reasons. After all, they would be working together and needed to maintain a professional relationship. Unbiased decisions would be necessary. Staying neutral and unaffected by what the other wanted or thought would be a challenge if they were to get involved. Worse yet would be the awkwardness if a relationship began and then ended badly.

In addition, she had just come off a relationship, and he didn't need the whole rebound angle working against him. It was clear to him that Max had not been right for her, but regardless of that, she needed time to heal.

She was managing so much change in her life right now she did not need anything more. The death of her grandfather, relocating, changing jobs, and ending a relationship put her high on the stress meter. Starting up a new involvement, especially the kind that Garrick was beginning to realize he wanted, would be demanding. It really wasn't fair of him to introduce even more emotion into her life.

Maybe most important, she was just too tempting for her own good. If he let himself act according to what his body was suggesting, he would end up thwarting his own values. It would be best to keep a safe distance, as much as he disliked that conclusion. Maybe those relaxing ideas that he was thinking of including her in should be postponed. Yes, definitely better to postpone them. Now if he could only get his mind and his heart and his body to do just that.

Climbing into his CTS, he departed for the 11:00 a.m. church service at New Glory Community Church. It was the largest church in the area, and Garrick had attended there ever since moving to town eight years earlier. Both June and Greg had been regular parishioners throughout their lives, and Alyssa had attended before leaving for school. He wondered if she would be there this morning.

It was cooler out today than it had been but was still sunny. As he turned into the church parking lot, his gaze fell on her. There she was, walking into the church with June, wearing a form-fitting red knit dress. No one else in New Glory dressed like that for church. He shook his head and concentrated on parking safely before she distracted him completely.

He caught a glimpse of the two of them once he was inside. Alyssa nodded, acknowledging that she had seen him. He was acutely aware that she was tracking his movements. He liked that. He found a seat in the sanctuary and waited for the service to begin. Garrick decided that a lunch invitation for both ladies after church might work. June would likely bow out, leaving them alone. However, it would be easier to keep that safe distance he had just talked himself into, if June chaperoned.

Just as the service was about to begin, Alyssa slid into the seat beside him, followed by June. She smiled at him, and the muscles clenched in his stomach. She leaned in and simply whispered, "Hi." Her scent was exquisite. Whatever the fragrance was, it was trouble. Garrick didn't think he had ever sat through such a long sermon, and the message was lost on him. The pair of legs that were crossed next to him beneath that clinging red dress was fragmenting his focus.

Finally exiting the church, he casually touched Alyssa's lower back and murmured into her ear, "Lunch?"

She turned, smiled, and nodded. "Where?"

Garrick chuckled to himself, realizing that neither of them had used more than a single word in each exchange since arriving at the church. Not wanting to break the pattern, he just said, "Quarters."

"Now?"

"Yes."

"Sure."

"June?" Garrick asked Alyssa, feeling obligated to include her mother in the invitation.

"No." Alyssa's answer was unwavering.

"Fine." He didn't say anything more, just directed her toward his car. Alyssa glanced around at June, who stood talking with other ladies from the church. She motioned that she was leaving with Garrick. June beamed, obviously pleased with the thought of the two of them spending time together. The communication was subtle and succinct. He drove in silence to the restaurant, and when they arrived, he opened her door for her and helped her out. He was determined not to be the one to change the rules of the unspoken game.

Inside they waited to be seated, and when the hostess approached them, Garrick said, "Two." Alyssa was smirking at him.

He held out the chair at the table for her, and when he pushed her in, she responded with "Thanks."

The waitress appeared at their table and said, "Drinks?" to which both Garrick and Alyssa broke into laughter. Alyssa gave in and explained to the waitress the evolution of the morning's single-word dialogue, and the waitress's unsuspecting entry into their game was the source of their laughter.

After they had ordered their drinks, they slipped into an easy conversation while they perused the menu and then waited for their meals to be prepared. Once their orders arrived at the table, Garrick looked at Alyssa, carefully assessing the relaxed expression on her face. "You look great today, calmer than dinner on Thursday night." He wanted to broach the subject of Max but wanted to avoid directly mentioning him.

"I feel like a huge weight has been lifted, a couple of huge weights in fact. The decision to not return to New York City was weight number one, and the second was acknowledging that my relationship with Max was never really a relationship." She paused and then said, "I've been focused on me enough over the last couple of weeks. Could we please talk about you?" A challenging look in her eyes gave Garrick a tinge of disquiet. "Tell me about your parents. Do you ever see them?"

"My parents. Well, my father passed away in 1999. Car accident. He and my mother divorced about five years before that."

"I'm sorry about your father, Garrick. How old were you when he died?"

"I was twenty-one then. After their divorce, I lived with him, but not long before the accident, I moved out. I left for college. He was living in New Jersey and commuted into New York City each day. There was a multicar accident, and he was one of the casualties. So when college was done, I felt free to settle anywhere and with some shortsighted encouragement from that girl I mentioned, ended up here."

"What about your mother? When was the last time you saw her?"

"I haven't seen her since 1997." He noticed her forehead crease in concern. He wanted to drop this conversation and get back to a safer topic. "Not everyone is as lucky as you when it comes to mothers."

"Does she even know where you live?"

"I hope not." He looked around the restaurant, scoping it out for a convenient escape route. Returning an unsteady gaze to her, he said, "Alyssa, change the subject, please." He had grown very uncomfortable discussing his mother.

"Okay. Tell me about college."

She had complied, but she had not shifted the conversation far enough, from his perspective. He couldn't dodge every topic, so he would talk about college and just avoid too many details. That would work. "It was great. What twenty-year-old guy doesn't like college life?"

"College was where you and Mark Wilson met, right? His wife, Laura, and I reconnected. She was my best friend back in high school. She thinks very highly of you since you introduced her to Mark. What did you study in college Garrick, the art of matchmaking?"

Garrick felt the trepidation grow now. Mark and Laura were the only two people in New Glory other than June that knew much of his personal history. "I didn't realize you knew Laura that well."

"Yes, we were inseparable when we were teenagers. We met for coffee yesterday. Well, we had coffee, Jason had juice." Her smile was captivating, and he felt the uneasiness draining from him. "It was great catching up with her, and she seemed pleased when I said I was staying and that you and I would be operating Grandpa's store. She mentioned that your father had worked for Cartier. He must have been very good at what he did. Not just anyone can work for them."

"Yes, he had a gift."

"Guess I know where you come by your talent." She grinned at him. He had successfully kept his history in the background for the eight years he had been in New Glory. Now in a matter of days, Alyssa was drawing out more details of his past than he was ready to divulge. He was not sure if that was a wise idea. Maybe protecting his own past was another reason he should be keeping his distance from her.

After lunch, Garrick took Alyssa back to June's place. She changed into comfortable shoes, jeans, a t-shirt, and a warm sweater, and they went for a walk. The leaves were turning, and the colors were beautiful. Each street had so many different types of trees, and each tree had its own mix of color. The blend was breathtaking. It must have been inspiring since they talked about color as they wandered. They talked about the color of cars, favorite colors, and gem colors. They even wound the discussion around to paint colors for both Alyssa's house and New Glory Gems. However, it was color as it related Alyssa's wardrobe, which had proven to take considerable time to do justice.

At first, Garrick kept his hands in his pockets. He remembered all the reasons he should keep his distance from this alluring woman. When the conversation got embroiled in the entertaining world of her wardrobe, however, Garrick forgot all about the "keep your distance" rule and took her hand. Eye color had naturally followed, and not wanting to take Garrick's word as to the shade of blue his eyes were, Alyssa turned in front of him and tried her best to look him in the eye. Standing on her toes in her flat shoes did not give her the height she needed, and laughing at her antics, Garrick lowered his face so she could clearly see his eyes. Even in doing that, she lost her balance, wobbling slightly, and he secured her by wrapping his arms around her.

He did, she agreed, have eyes that were violet blue tanzanite with perfect clarity. Garrick lost track of his thoughts as their eyes held the gaze. Then his lips touched hers, and eyelids slowly closed as the kiss intensified. She tasted of the crème brûlée they had enjoyed at the restaurant.

When he finally pulled his mouth away from hers, she seemed unsteady and her breathing was choppy. "Garrick," was all she said and laid her head against his chest.

"Alyssa, you've just ended a relationship, and we're going into business together. This is not a good idea, but I can't seem to focus on that when I'm around you. I'm sorry if I'm crossing a line." Alyssa lifted her head and looked at him thoughtfully.

"We've already crossed that line, Garrick, and I'm right where I want to be." He studied her for a time and then kissed her again.

Monday morning was overcast. It would be a good day to work in the shop. Alyssa had indicated that she would be there midmorning, but Garrick planned to be in by 9:00 a.m. He would have to leave by 5:00 p.m. in order to prepare for the seniors' program that night. He thought about asking Alyssa if she would like to join him at the program but decided that he would leave an invitation like that for a few weeks. He wasn't sure she was ready to be scrutinized by his overprotective guardians, as they liked to think of themselves. They would love her. After all, she was one of them, but he wouldn't subject her to that just yet. They would be together the majority of the day anyway. She would likely be ready for some time alone by evening.

Garrick opened up and did a quick clean. He knew they would want to do a complete inventory of everything and suspected that would be the first order of business. After cleaning the showcases and sweeping up, he moved to the back storage rooms. He had been back there for about fifteen minutes when he heard the front door of the shop open. There was a built-in bell to alert them when someone entered. It helped at times when only one person was there. Looking at his watch, he surmised that Alyssa was early, so he didn't rush to return to the main showroom. Then he heard, "Hello?"

Not Alyssa after all. The voice almost sounded familiar, but he couldn't quite place it. He moved back into the front of the store and froze as his eyes landed on the woman. His eyes narrowed, and the silence inside was absolute set against the irregular passing of vehicles on the street. He was staring at a tall woman, slender build, dressed well. She had dark hair, probably dyed, and her face was showing the effects of age and a hard life, although makeup concealed some of the evidence of timeworn skin.

"Garrick?" the voice questioned.

"What are you doing here?" Garrick's voice filled with contempt. "How did you know where I was?"

"It took a while, but I was able to find you." She was not looking at him anymore. Her eyes were surveying the room they stood in. As she digested the surroundings, her eyes took on a distant stare. She moved toward the closest case, holding several very valuable pieces of jewelry. "I should have guessed your father would have had a profound impact on your life's direction." Glancing at him from the corner of an eye, she said, "Do you miss him?"

"What are you doing here, Jillian?" Garrick pressed again.

"You already asked me that, dear. And please don't call me that." Her voice was calm and polite.

"You didn't answer me the first time, so I am asking again."

"I missed you, Garrick. It has been years since I've spoken to you or seen you. I wanted to see how you were doing. I can see that you have found a way to surround yourself with wealth and objects of beauty." Moving to another area of the store, she traced her fingers over the oak frames on showcases, acting as if she were in a trance.

"The store is not open right now. You should leave."

"That's too bad. I was enjoying browsing. I've decided to stay at a bed and breakfast just outside of town, so perhaps we could get together and catch up."

"Can't imagine what you would have been doing for the past decade that would interest me." The words and the tone matched perfectly, both cold and insensitive.

"Well, you would probably be interested to know that I've changed quite a bit from all those years ago."

"I doubt that." The reply was immediate and curt.

"You'll soon see. I'm a new woman." The statement was made with self-assuredness. Although Garrick was enraged at the sight of her, he was now also becoming concerned that he would not get her out before Alyssa arrived. He did not want them to meet.

"It's time for you to leave."

"All right, but we'll be in touch. Take care, Garrick." She gracefully turned and floated toward the exit. Before stepping out, though, she glanced over her shoulder, and the look set Garrick on edge. "I'll be back in to examine the assets." With a sly smile on her face, she disappeared through the door.

Garrick ran his hand through his hair. She was in town, and she would be up to no good. In her universe, she viewed trustworthiness as a nonessential. Ethical and moral boundaries did not exist for his mother.

He quickly went through what he had last heard about her. The last time he had seen her was three years after she had divorced his father. The memories he had of her were locked away deep but still accessible. He remembered the arguments between his parents. His father had threatened to quit his job, take Garrick, and disappear. His mother was horrified, not by the thought of Garrick being taken from her, but by the idea of Lawrence Samuels quitting his prestigious employment with Cartier.

So much of Jillian's attachment to Lawrence had been the Cartier job. She would make special trips into the city to see him at work. At first, it wasn't obvious why or what was happening, but it had finally dawned on his father the reason for the frequent visits. The divorce quickly followed.

Garrick had not been aware of the reasons at the time, but a series of events soon started to uncover Jillian's activities. By 1997, police had her in custody pending a trial. She had been arrested, along with others who were alleged to have been responsible for a number of home invasions in wealthy neighborhoods. The plunder in each case was expensive jewels. Although they were linked to a much larger jewel-smuggling ring, those associations were never proven. As a first-time offender, Jillian's guilty verdict had won her a five-year prison sentence.

With probation, she had gotten out in 2000. Garrick was unaware of any attempts she might have made to get in touch with him at that time, and she had never reached out to communicate in any way with him while she was in the Bayview Correctional Facility. That had been fine with him.

However, in 2001 he was alerted to the infamous trail she was blazing. She had stepped up to armed robbery but still had an eye for gems. By late 2001, she had been incarcerated for a second time and this time was given room and board for fifteen years at Bedford Hills Correctional Facility.

Now she was in New Glory.

Garrick grabbed his cell phone, pulled up the stored numbers, and dialed.

"Brown, Spencer, Albany, and Scott."

"Hello, I need to talk to Ted Brown please. It's Garrick Samuels." Ted had been the lawyer he had dealt with after his father's death. In addition, Ted had kept track of his mother's round one release from prison.

"One moment please."

After a few lengthy seconds, the line opened again, "Garrick. It's been awhile. Is everything okay?"

"Not sure if everything is okay or not. I just had a visit from Jillian." Garrick waited for a response.

"Aren't you still in that small town in Kentucky?"

"Yep, I am, and now so is she. I don't know how she tracked me down here. Can you find out when she got out, Ted? I let my private investigator license lapse, so there is only so much I can get access to."

"Sure. It might take some time, though. Give me your cell number, and I'll let you know what I find out." After providing the cell phone information, Garrick thanked Ted and ended the call. He stood leaning against a showcase, head down, wondering what havoc his mother was about to cause. Up until now, she had not involved him in any of her illegal antics, but he did not have a good feeling after her announcing her presence.

Chapter 5

Alyssa woke up later than she had planned Monday morning. Sleep had been broken for her. Each time she had awakened, thoughts of Garrick and the eager kisses of the afternoon before filled her mind and made falling back to sleep impossible. Regardless of how tired she was, she was anxious to get to work at New Glory Gems and, with a sigh, admitted that she was anxious to see Garrick. She quickly showered and grabbed some breakfast.

Her mom had obviously already left for Flourishing Flowers. She was back to work for the first time since Greg's death, having taken two weeks off to try to deal with everything.

Alyssa left the house and climbed into her new car. She had picked it up late last week. New York City life had discouraged her from having a car, but for small-town existence, it was more essential. Standing back and admiring it when she had first brought it home, she decided the brand new Barcelona Red Metallic Toyota Prius looked very nice in the driveway. It would take some time to get tired of this ride. Smiling, she drove toward downtown.

Garrick was already there she noticed, spotting his car as she pulled up in front of the store. It was no wonder. She was late, and he had probably arrived early. She hurried and just before opening the door into the store, she caught a glimpse of him talking on his cell phone.

Probably calling her at the house to see what was taking so long, she thought. He had hung up, putting away the phone just as she walked in. Garrick stood, leaning against the showcase holding their expansive selection of pearls, located near the back of the showroom. She got an uneasy feeling seeing him deep in thought, although she had no idea why. "Hi, Garrick." She moved toward him, but he said nothing.

"Sorry I'm late. I overslept."

"No problem," he said without any emotion, "I just did some cleaning and organizing. We probably should start an inventory and decide on any touchups that we need done before re-opening. I could work on them while you go to New York later this week." Garrick was not even smiling.

"Are you all right? You don't seem like yourself."

"I'm fine."

Even though she was unconvinced, she thought it best not to push the issue. "Okay. I brought my laptop. I thought we would track the inventory on that if you and Grandpa didn't have an inventory system in place. I couldn't remember Grandpa having a computer." Her voice was lacking the usual assertiveness typical of her in business situations, not wanting to insult Garrick if their tracking process was much more advanced than she expected.

"No, there isn't a computer here. We should probably consider getting one for the business. If you don't mind us using yours for now until we get underway, it would be helpful."

"Great. All right, why don't we start with the pearls then?" She realized it was going to take time to inventory everything. What would significantly slow them down was matching each item against the records her grandfather had kept. Several filing cabinets holding the documentation sat in one of the backrooms. The pulp-and-paper industry would have had great admiration for that man.

Agreeing to first inventory everything and then work on matching the pieces against the vast number of records as a second phase, Alyssa and Garrick started.

The work was slow and tedious, but that did not bother Alyssa. What did bother her was Garrick's continued emotional distance. He offered no explanation, and she didn't ask for one.

Over the next two days, the two new proprietors inventoried all the pieces on display. Garrick's impersonal detachment continued, and, after Sunday's fervent kisses, Alyssa found she was confused and disheartened. Perhaps he was just making every effort to keep his professional and personal life separate. If that was his intent, he certainly had the professional side perfected. There had been no kiss as he left on Monday, no easily interpreted touch or even a suggestive glance. Tuesday had been the same, and getting together outside of work had not been mentioned. It was as if Sunday afternoon had never happened.

Alyssa was finally getting into the groove and was at the shop by 7:30 a.m. on Wednesday. Fortunately, the previous day, Garrick had extra keys cut so she had her own now and could come and go as she pleased. She dropped off her laptop, locked up, and went to Sarah's Café for coffee and a bagel. She recognized most of the faces in the restaurant, and that gave her a sense of security. *Knowing the people that surround you is comforting*, she thought.

"Hi, Alyssa. What can I get for you this morning?" Sarah was at her café each morning when it opened and handled the early crowd personally. Her outgoing and friendly nature was perfect for this type of venture. If she was assisting Sarah with a small-business startup, this was exactly what she would recommend.

"Hey, Sarah. Coffee, please. I'm not used to being productive at this hour, so coffee is definitely required. Also, one your multigrain bagels, toasted."

"Sounds good." Within minutes, Alyssa had her order and handed over a twenty-dollar bill.

"Is Gems still scheduled to re-open on Monday?" Sarah asked as she handed the change back to her customer.

"Hope so. Things are moving along. I have to go back to New York tomorrow for a couple of days, but Garrick will be doing some painting and some last-minute work."

"Lots of people talking about coming in next week. Feel free to send 'em on down here when they're done shoppin' at your place." Sarah smiled and winked. Apparently, Main Street vendors tried to support one another, and that was fine with Alyssa.

"Okay. I'll be back in later this morning. I'm meeting Laura for coffee. Bye."

As Alyssa walked back up the street, she cringed at the day's mission. Behind the main showroom were four rooms. There were two large rooms and two small, in addition to a restroom. One of the large rooms contained several filing cabinets and a large vault secured by a combination lock. Mr. Frost had provided the combination to this vault, along with the instructions on how to change the combination, which they had done promptly. The second large room was a workspace with tools and equipment for the lapidary work.

The first of the two small rooms was an office space with a desk, leather chair, and lamp. A few unopened letters had sat on the desk, and those would all need to be dealt with. Alyssa had opened them to assess the urgency on each.

A door similar to each of the other rooms closed off the second small room; however, this one was locked. No key had been provided, and Garrick was not aware of any key. His duties at the store had never required him to enter the small room, and he was not even aware that there had been a lock on it.

This small locked room would wait, as there was an abundance of other things to sift through that were accessible. If Garrick had not needed to go into the room, then it was fairly certain that the day-to-day operation could be handled without whatever was hidden behind that last door.

However, the daunting task of the filing cabinets loomed on the agenda for the day, and that was what was making Alyssa skittish.

Just as she reached the store, her cell phone rang. With expert stacking and balancing skills, she placed the keys on top of the bagel, which she put on top of the coffee. She dropped her purse on the ground and then, grabbing her phone, hit the talk button.

"Hello?"

"Alyssa. It's Garrick. Listen, I'm sorry, but Mrs. Simpson just called, and she's got a plumbing emergency. I need to head over to her place and help her out before I come in." Alyssa groaned silently at the thought of attacking those filing cabinets alone.

"No problem, Garrick. Plumbing emergencies trump paper sorting. Good luck. Just come in whenever you can make it."

"Thanks. I'll be there as soon as possible. Bye."

Garrick had assured her when they left the night before that her grandfather was meticulous with his paperwork. In fact, it was so important to him that he never allowed Garrick to get near it. "Your grandpa used to say, 'A solid record-keeping system needs to be consistent. Two people will always have some distinct way that will detract from that consistency,' and then he would gruffly follow it up with 'stay out of my records.'" She smiled and shook her head as she adopted her grandfather's approach to handling administrative duties. *Doing it alone will definitely be better*, she thought sarcastically.

The next two hours flew by. Taking a small pile of files into her grandfather's office and sitting at his desk, she began the tedious matching process, capturing the details on her laptop. Her grandfather really had done a great job of documenting everything. This was turning into a simple process of transferring paper records to her digital tracking system.

By ten thirty, she was ready for a break. Garrick hadn't gotten there yet, so she just left a note for him to come down to the coffee shop if he arrived before she got back. Locking up again, she went to meet Laura.

Her coffee date had already arrived by the time Alyssa got there. She joined her at the table for two by the front window. "Where's Jason?" she asked when she saw that Laura was by herself.

"Pre-kindergarten. He attends in the mornings, so I have to go pick him up at eleven forty-five. He loves going. It makes him think he is very grown up since he has somewhere to go, just like his dad." The waitress came over and poured them both coffees. "So how is the work going at the store this week?" Her friend was so enthusiastic that it made Alyssa smile.

"It's going well. I think we will be on schedule to re-open on Monday, unless Garrick thinks we should wait for some reason. I will be leaving for New York tomorrow and back on Saturday. The moving company will have my things here in New Glory on Sunday. So much has happened in the last couple of weeks it makes my head spin."

They chatted on for about a half an hour about old friends, new friends, and special interests, and of course, Laura wanted an update on how Garrick was and if he had put any moves on Alyssa yet. Laura was very direct in her questions, and although Alyssa should have been used to it, she had been away long enough that it was still taking her by surprise. She considered confiding in Laura about her confusion over Garrick's actions but instead decided to put the issue in someone else's corner to explain. "Why don't you ask him yourself?" Alyssa was looking past her now at Garrick, who was approaching the table.

"Ladies, good morning." The corner of Garrick's mouth curved up, and the grin that resulted was intoxicating.

"Garrick, pull up a chair and have a seat." Laura was thrilled to see him and as directed, immediately threw the question at an unsuspecting Garrick. "I was just asking Alyssa if you had put the moves on her yet, and she suggested I go to the source and ask you." Laura's teasing eyes widened in anticipation of some witty retort. Garrick's amused expression shifted toward Alyssa and then back to Laura.

"Is this what you two discuss when you get together for coffee?"

"Not if Jason's with me, but he's at school right now, so no censoring required, Garr. Go ahead. Don't hold back, give me all the details."

"Laura, is it a description you want, or are you looking for a demonstration?" Garrick asked with a shake of his head. Alyssa's eyebrows shot up, and her eyes opened wide. Laura spotted her friend's reaction and was delighted with the lively banter.

"Oh, Garrick, would you demonstrate? You know you probably shouldn't because that would draw more business in here and Sarah really can't handle any more."

"Ah, I see. You're using Sarah as an excuse. Are you sure it isn't you that can't handle it?" Garrick was in full tease mode now. He obviously knew how far Laura would push this and was confident he could play along with it.

"Hey, I can handle it, but *unfortunately* I have to leave to go pick up my boy." She put down some money on the table for the coffee and, looking at Alyssa, said, "Next week—same time, same place?" Alyssa nodded, and Laura left with a magnificent smile on her face.

"Ready to head back to the store?"

"Were you really prepared to demonstrate for Laura?" Alyssa's look was playful.

"Great, I just got rid of one tease, and now I have to deal with you?"

"You're avoiding the question."

"Yep, as long as Mrs. Van De Laar is sitting behind you, I am going to dodge every question possible. Good morning, Mrs. Van De Laar." Garrick leaned to the side to speak to the aging lady. The older lady smiled demurely at Garrick and politely greeted him in return.

Alyssa took some money out to leave on the table to cover her coffee and said, "Time to go."

They made good progress over the remainder of the day, although Garrick had moved right back to his distant behavior once they were out of the café. Alyssa was not prepared to go off to New York the next day with nothing more than that morning's Laura-induced teasing. "Garrick, how about we have dinner together tonight?" She proposed the idea as nonchalantly as possible and was surprised by the response from Garrick.

"Sure, come back to my place. I have beef stew in the Crock-Pot, and I'll make some biscuits. I'd like to spend some time with you away from Gems." There was more invitation in the gaze that followed than the words had suggested. That made Alyssa's heart swell. "I can drive and bring you back to pick up your car later."

"No need. You don't need to come back downtown if I bring my car. I'll drive. Besides, I like driving my new car."

"Are you going to take me for a ride in it soon?" he asked as they walked to their cars.

"Well, I will be moved in next door to you on Sunday, so I expect we could carpool on Monday if you'd like." He nodded.

The beef stew and biscuits were a perfect meal on a cool fall night. Alyssa was conscious of the time since she wanted to do a little more work at the store and get home to pack before it was too late. Regardless of her ideal time schedule, she did not want to rush the time with Garrick. She found him interesting and easy to be with. They were comfortable together, and that was a different feeling than she had experienced in any recent relationships. "Dinner was great, Garrick. I will have to cook for you once I have the house together." Alyssa had helped with the cleanup and was thinking she should leave.

"Do you have time to stay and watch a movie with me tonight?" He had moved in front of her and looked down into her eyes, waiting for her response. He was back to being the warm man she had walked with on Sunday afternoon.

"I really don't have time tonight, Garrick. Would you be available Saturday night? I should be back from New York by about eight p.m." He didn't answer right away. The palm of his hand cupped her cheek, and he leaned in to gently kiss her.

"If that's all I can have, then Saturday night it is." His voice was deep and rough.

"Garrick, I know we are working together, but you don't have to act so distant from me at the store."

"I know. I'm sorry about this week. I needed some time to adjust to our working relationship, I guess."

"It's all right. I had better leave now. I'll see you when I get back on Saturday."

Alyssa returned to the store. She decided she would just work for a couple of hours and then call it a night. *It's surprising how much work I can get done by myself,* she thought. She had gone through several files, inputting the details against the inventory. She guessed she had time, or maybe it was just energy, for one more small stack of files. Returning from the filing cabinet with the new folders, her cell phone rang.

"Who could that be? Hello?"

"Hey, Alyssa."

"Laura, I didn't expect to hear from you tonight. Is everything all right?"

"Oh everything's fine. I just got Jason off to bed, and I really wanted to finish our conversation from this morning." The chipper tone never seemed to ebb. Alyssa marveled at it. "So what's the deal with you and Garrick? Anything juicy to report?"

"Laura, someone who didn't know you so well might think you were a busybody." Alyssa's comment, although based in truth, was nevertheless delivered with all the love of a best friend.

"Yes, well, you do know me *and* you have had all day to decide how to answer the question, so unveil all there is, honey."

"Laura, there isn't that much to tell." Alyssa was dragging her feet and moaning at the knowledge that stalling was just a useless delay. Laura would not let her off this phone until she had the whole story.

"Ah, 'isn't much to tell' means there is something to tell." And she waited.

With an audible sigh, Alyssa began. "We had lunch after church Sunday and then went for a walk in the neighborhood."

"And?"

"And he kissed me." Alyssa could not believe she was so uncomfortable divulging a simple kiss to a friend.

"Excellent. What kind of a kiss?"

"What do you mean 'what kind of a kiss?'" She might as well just give up on the stalling tactics and tell all.

"You know what I mean."

"Okay, I was trying to see exactly what color eyes he had, and I sort of lost my balance while stretching up on my tiptoes. He caught me, and then he kissed me. It was a sweet, gentle kiss at first, and then it changed."

"Really, so are we talking about a steamy kiss?"

Alyssa laughed aloud. She might as well write an article for the local paper so that none of the important details got missed. "You don't give up. Who, what, when, where, how…Garrick and me, passionate kiss, Sunday afternoon, Peartree Crescent, his arms around me and my knees weak. I am not giving you anything more than that. Are we done, Laura?"

"Whew, why didn't you just say so today at the café?"

"Honestly, this morning I wasn't sure what was going on between Garrick and me. Sunday was wonderful, but then Monday and Tuesday, he treated me as if nothing had happened. I was confused. I was actually hoping, when I saw him walk in, that he might explain to both us what our relationship was."

"But that was this morning? Are you feeling on more solid ground tonight?"

"Yes, we had dinner together, and he said he is just trying to adjust to balancing our work and personal connection. We're going to see each other Saturday when I get back from New York."

"Awesome! So you'll have an update for me next Wednesday. I will try to get a more discreet location so you can talk easily." She sounded like a spy setting up a clandestine meeting to exchange secret information.

"I can't promise anything juicy, as you like to phrase it. Hey, I have to get going. We'll talk next week." The call ended, and Alyssa knew that her friend would sleep much better tonight knowing there was a romance brewing.

The interruption had shifted Alyssa's focus away from her paperwork. She sat quietly in the office, considering a possible relationship with this man. There was obviously a strong attraction. It had surfaced the first time she saw him. Thinking of it made her blush. However, she felt there was some sort of imbalance. Garrick knew details of her life that she might have trouble remembering. He was perceptive, almost able to see inside her soul.

What did she know about him, though? He offered very few details, even when asked, about his personal life. Laura had told her more about Garrick in a couple of minutes than Alyssa had been able to find out during several conversations with the man.

The distance he had put between them at the store also seemed to be more than just an adjustment to a new working relationship. That left Alyssa feeling uncertain. A couple of days away from New Glory might be good. She quietly laughed as she realized that as confusing and private as Garrick might be, she was intrigued and wanted to know more about him.

She shook her head, trying to redirect her thoughts. She needed to complete this final pile of folders before leaving. Thoughts of Garrick would have to wait until later. She dove into the stack of papers. She was about three folders into the pile when she came across a shipping receipt for a relatively large number of gems received in February 2009. There were no other documents in the folder, no record in the inventory that matched up with the specifications on the shipping receipt. A notation was on the paper that indicated *Vault B*.

Alyssa was perplexed. Every other folder she had gone through had an order receipt, a shipping receipt, a diagram and description of how each gem had been used, and where a sale had already been completed, the sales slip.

There were no outstanding orders that she knew about. Everything her grandfather had authorized the purchase of had been received. Details on gems that had been ordered and received but not used in any jewelry had the first two pieces of documentation, and they had inventoried them in the vault. She was at a loss to explain the missing documentation.

Also, she had not seen any reference to different vaults until now. Garrick had not mentioned another vault, and the lawyer had not mentioned another storage location for New Glory Gems property.

Her grandfather's desk was unusually tidy, she noted, but was pleased that it was. She placed this mysterious folder in the bottom drawer of his desk and would discuss it with Garrick next week.

Thursday morning, Alyssa loaded her car with her overnight bag and left by 6:00 a.m. She would drive as far as the airport in Lexington and then take the usual flight into New York. The movers would arrive by 8:00 a.m. Saturday and would likely take no more than two hours to load everything. She would be on an afternoon flight out of New York for the last time and back to Kentucky and, she hoped, to Garrick's arms by Saturday evening. She smiled at the contented feeling that image gave her.

Chapter 6

He could not have been in a more awkward position when the phone rang. Perched part way up a six-foot ladder, balancing a full tray of paint and already wearing a good portion of the Ripened Fig shade himself, he looked over at his cell phone, which sat on the counter. It was 10:05 a.m. and he was so close to finishing the first coat of paint on the walls, but in case it was important, he should answer.

"Garrick here."

"Hello, Garrick. It's Ted Brown. I have that information you were wondering about."

"I'm listening."

"Jillian was released on early parole three weeks ago. She must be a real charmer during those parole hearings, or else she has the best lawyer imaginable."

"Did you manage to find out anything about her conditions of parole?"

"That's the most interesting part. She is supposed to check in weekly with her parole officer in New York. She checked in the first two weeks but was a no-show last week. She is not supposed to leave the state. So she has at least two violations as I see it."

"Do you have an obligation to report her location?" Garrick was hoping that Ted would be required to since he was an officer of the court.

"Already done. I told them the name of the place and that she is supposedly in some bed and breakfast outside of town. That was just this morning, so it may be a day or two before they get someone out there to bring her in. Kentucky doesn't allow bounty hunters, so it will have to be handled by a peace officer."

"She must be smart enough to know that missing that parole meeting would bring out the hounds. I wonder if she is still even in the area. I'm guessing she will have to move around a lot to keep off their radar."

"I think she's smart. I think being caught that last time was a mistake she will do everything possible to avoid repeating. Keep your eye out, and if you see her again, let me know."

"Sure. Thanks again for the update." Garrick ended the call and stood for a moment, thoughtfully pondering why she had come to New Glory to begin with and why she would stay. He certainly did not have the answer and probably never would. He glanced at the new wall color and was impressed with Alyssa's choice. Ripened Fig was a muted grape color. The trim would be an off-white called Sandcastle. Whoever came up with these names was a creative genius as far as Garrick was concerned.

He would leave the naming selections to someone else and the parole-jumping captures to a trained individual, and he simply would focus on finishing the painting.

It was a bit past noon by the time Garrick was finished. He had done two coats of paint and would come back the next day to touch up anything that needed it. For now, he was ready to head home and have some lunch.

Just as he was ready to walk out the door, June peeked in the entryway that he had propped open to keep fresh air circulating. "Hi, Garrick. Wow, look at this. You must have been here at dawn."

"It was pretty early." A grin crept over his face. "I wanted as much of this done today as possible, and I'm satisfied with what I accomplished."

"You should be. I think Alyssa will be pleased when she sees the color. I'm anxious to see Greg's house once she gives it her decorative flare."

"Me too, and that was one reason I was trying to have this pretty much wrapped up today. I was hoping, if you don't think she would mind and you would let me in the house, I would try and get a room or two done for her before she gets back." Garrick was eager and intent on surprising her. "What do you think?"

June considered her daughter's reaction if she let Garrick in without her knowledge. "I expect it will be fine. I still have one key. You can use it. Which rooms were you planning to start with?" she asked.

"Well, I have never been a fan of sleeping in a freshly painted room, so I thought I would start with the master bedroom. If I can get it done by noon tomorrow, it should have time to air out, and it won't be as much work now as it would be after the movers bring everything in. Then I figured the living room would be the other place quite a bit of her New York furniture would end up, so that would be the next one to tackle." Garrick gave June an approval-seeking look.

She smiled, as June often did when there was really nothing to add. She dug in her purse and found the key to the big house. Handing it to Garrick, she looked at him with searching eyes.

Garrick was not one to miss details, and this didn't escape him either. "What?" A suspicious frown formed on his face.

"Garrick..." She paused briefly. "What are your intentions regarding my daughter?" Her face was serious, and her chin slightly lifted to be able to peer up at him.

"Intentions." He tipped his head sideways as if to give careful consideration to how he would answer such a question. "Do you mind me asking you a question first, June?"

"Of course not, go ahead."

"What makes you think I have *intentions* toward Alyssa?"

"Oh please, it's obvious to everyone." She laughed as the words came out.

"Who do you mean by everyone?" His tone had taken on an annoyed and angry edge. Garrick could not believe that in the short time that he had known Alyssa and the few times they had been together that anyone could be doing anything other than purely speculating. He had to remind himself that it was a small town after all. Gossip reigned supreme in this culture, and fast-spreading news came in many forms. The type that traveled the fastest was naturally scandal, but running a close second was rumors of the romantic variety.

June began to smile widely, and that deepened Garrick's concern. He did not like to gossip, and he really hated being gossiped about. "Garrick, you don't really think that an attractive eligible bachelor like yourself would escape being the subject of speculation when someone like Alyssa moved to town, do you? Especially since you sat together at church on Sunday, had lunch with her afterward, and then went on a walk where, might I point out, you were observed kissing her on Peartree Crescent in front of Dave and Marie Overton's bungalow." She was enjoying this, and the over-enthusiastic disclosure was alarming to Garrick.

His head dropped as he stared at the floor. The whole town would have them married off before Alyssa got back from New York if the grapevine wound its way through New Glory at the pace it normally did. "What do you expect me to say, June?" There was a pause as he briefly pursed his lips and looked around the store, trying to avoid eye contact. "I would like a relationship with her, but she is just coming off that breakup with Max and we're working together. We need to take it slow." He looked at her now, worry creasing his forehead.

"Garrick, I am not opposed to the two of you seeing one another. You don't have to feel guarded around me."

"I just don't like being talked about."

"The talk will die down unless you give it reason to flare up. It should be easy enough to be discreet when you are living side by side. Hey, listen, I didn't stop in here to give you the third degree about Alyssa." A soft laugh escaped her. "That was just a bonus. I was going to ask you to come for dinner Sunday night with Alyssa and me. Perhaps given our conversation you won't want to, but the invitation is open."

Garrick grumbled quietly but said, "I'd be a fool to pass up one of your meals, June. Of course I will come."

"Great, the other reason I came in is because I just left the lawyer's office." Now her expression shifted from light to uneasy, and with a sigh, she continued. "Yesterday we sent out notification to Andrew of his disinheritance. The courier's tracking system indicates that he has received it. I have made comments to Alyssa that we will probably never hear from Andrew again, given there hasn't been any contact and he didn't show up at the funeral, but I'm afraid that the letter that just went out could invoke some hostility."

"Alyssa is not aware that there has been contact over the years, so she would have no reason to suspect Andrew could cause trouble."

"I know, and I had hoped to keep it that way. The contact that was made was not something we wanted publicized. I keep telling myself that Andrew never actually acted on any of his threats, but when he finds out he is getting nothing, it could be the final blow."

Garrick nodded, recognizing the potential danger Andrew could emit. "Thanks for alerting me."

"Be careful, Garrick." He nodded again.

On the drive back to his place, Garrick thought about the situation that could bubble up with Andrew. He was relieved right now that Alyssa was out of town. He needed to sift through all he knew and could remember of the man, see if he could piece together what the lawyer's letter might ignite in him.

He knew there had been several calls throughout 2001 asking for money, which Greg had adamantly refused. Giving in to such requests wouldn't have solved anything. A taste of the money would have only encouraged Andrew to ask for more. When his requests were turned down, however, they had escalated to threats in 2002, just after Alyssa had left for school.

It was in response to those threats that Greg had sought out Garrick's assistance. He had been able to ascertain a few things about Andrew. He had a criminal record and had done three years in a New York State Penitentiary, receiving early parole in 2000. The conviction had been on a robbery charge. He could have been having trouble getting a job, and that could have prompted the desperate calls.

Almost immediately after Garrick had arrived in New Glory, though, the calls from Andrew stopped. He had never quite figured that out. The threats before Garrick arrived had been specific—both physical assault and property damage. Then they just stopped. Garrick, with all his resources as a private detective and contacts in law enforcement, was not able to track him down. It was as if he had vanished. No record of him back in jail, no record of any kind.

The disappearance had lasted about five years. Garrick had suspected that he either had gone underground or had been put underground in a final gesture by some disreputable associate. Then, out of the blue, another call came. Greg's answering machine had recorded the message, nothing more than "Dad, it's me, Andrew." Garrick immediately activated the call trace that he had setup on Greg's phone all those years earlier. When a second call came in, the machine again picked up. Having a recorded voice speak before Andrew was able to leave his message gave the trace extra time to search. Although it was not able to pinpoint the exact origin of the call, it had uncovered something quite alarming. Andrew Mason had been calling from New Glory.

The reason for the call had not been clear to Greg. It was cryptic. Andrew had said something about, "I'm getting things planned out so that I can enjoy life, but I'm not plannin' on waiting forever." The tone had been irritable and abrupt. That was it, and there were never any more calls. Again, an attempt to find an address on Andrew came up empty. Sometime between then and the time of Greg's death, he had come back on the radar, because the police were able to locate him to notify him about his father.

Garrick pulled into the driveway and sighed. Andrew was out there and was a potential powder keg.

Friday morning started on a high note but plummeted with such speed Garrick felt dizzy. The weather was as promised. So Garrick had headed next door, to get the windows open to air out any paint fumes in the bedroom. He also wanted to begin painting the living room. He entered the backyard through the gate at the side of the house. The key that June had provided was for the door into the kitchen nook off the deck.

Alyssa's new home had a spectacular backyard. It was large, and Greg had brought in professional landscapers to create a beautiful getaway. The perimeter provided complete privacy with various shrubs and flowering bushes. Along the rear property line stood tall deciduous trees, which provided shade in the morning. Situated in front of the trees, which were in full fall colors now, sat a large oval, red-cedar double-roof gazebo.

The house itself had great character with a front covered porch, two rear decks, and a curved, sweeping covered porch facing the lush backyard. The rustic feel of the home was accentuated with timber trusses, grey fieldstone, and oversized doors and windows. A wall of windows in the family room provided a glimpse out to the scenic expanse.

Taking the steps up onto the deck two at a time, Garrick dug in his pocket for the key June had given him. Then he stopped abruptly, temporarily paralyzed with what he saw. The lock had been drilled. He glanced around to ensure that nothing outside the home looked out of place. He was dialing the police within seconds.

It only took minutes before two police had arrived. Garrick was still outside the house, not wanting to disturb anything, particularly since Alyssa was unaware that he even had access to the house. "Detective Taylor and Officer York," announced the detective as they approached Garrick who stood out in front of the house. "What's the situation, Garrick?" Most on the New Glory Police Department knew Garrick, although only the chief was aware of his involvement in private detective work.

"I was coming over to do some painting in the house. The key I have is for one of the back doors, and when I reached it, I saw it had been drilled. Nothing else appears out of the ordinary outside the home, but I haven't gone inside yet. Everything was fine when I left here yesterday around five thirty p.m."

"All right, let's have a look." Detective Taylor had been on the force for more than twenty-five years; Garrick could remember reading in the local paper about the celebration they had for him when he reached that milestone. He was the senior detective. Since there was not an excessive crime level in New Glory, he was, in fact, the only detective. He usually worked with one of the officers who had been on the force for a few years, giving them time to become familiar with their roles and with the community. Not all officers who worked in New Glory had been raised in the small town. Obviously, the aging law enforcement master was mentoring the handpicked Officer York.

They first checked the other entryways to ensure that they appeared secure. Everything was tightly locked. Moving to the door off the nook, they examined the compromised lock. Detective Taylor had his protégé dust the lock and doorway for fingerprints and take pictures. Once he was satisfied that they had gathered the information they needed from the back door, they moved inside the house.

From the serenity of the sun-drenched nook, the image before them was completely different. Facing the kitchen, every drawer was open, every cupboard door ajar, and every canister dumped. Fortunately, Alyssa had done a thorough job of discarding or giving away anything in the house that she did not want, so the contents were minimal, which meant the cleanup would be minimal but obviously not eliminated.

Off to the right, the only noticeable disturbance in the living room was the area rug, which was rolled up. Alyssa had given the furniture to a local charity, so nothing else was in that room. Garrick and the officers headed down the hallway into the north wing where the guest bedroom was. The chaos that had been prevalent in the kitchen was once again noticeable here. Closet doors were wide open, and built-in drawers and storage units were all askew as the intruders unmistakably searched for something.

The rest of the house conveyed the same scene. Nothing appeared to be missing; everything had just been rifled through as if an urgent quest had been underway. Since the house had just been swept thoroughly with a keep/store/donate/discard approach, there was not much left in the house, except for the study, which Alyssa had opted to leave until later.

The disarray when they opened the study doors was unbelievable. It would be near impossible to identify if anything was missing. Clearly, nothing had been left untouched. Even pictures were removed from the wall. What would the intruders be looking for that would involve removing wall hangings? Garrick became still as he had a thought. It would make sense since every possible storage cavity and crevice had been uncovered. Rugs and pictures potentially could have concealed access to other storage areas. They had to be looking for something specific—something the intruders felt would be hidden.

Did he know what? Could he guess whom? He just wasn't sure. Greg had been open on some topics and secretive on others, and Garrick really didn't know what types of valuables Greg would have kept at the house. After all, the princess-cut diamond ring that had belonged to his wife and left to June in the will was even stored in the vault at the store. Anything of any value could have easily been safely secured there.

Detective Taylor and Officer York were at the house for close to three hours. They asked several questions and then left to take the prints they had lifted in for identification. Garrick was positive the only prints they would turn up would be his, Alyssa's, and Greg's. Criminals that drill locks in suburban neighborhoods typically were sophisticated enough, on an illicit level, that they would have been wearing gloves.

The morning had been a complete waste of time. Hoping to salvage something out of the day, he drove to the store. He would be able to do the last-minute touch-ups today rather than leaving that until Saturday.

Main Street was busy. Each Friday, a group of seniors met for lunch at The Quarters. Those people who wanted to avoid the grocery store on Saturday would likely be in town today too.

Garrick was relieved to see the lock intact on the front door of New Glory Gems. He stepped inside and found some of the paint odor still lingered, so he propped the door open as he had done the morning before. A nice breeze gently blew in, freshening up the air quickly in the showroom.

Garrick did a quick walkthrough of the backrooms to placate himself that all was well there and then, returning to the main showroom, looked carefully at the walls and was pleased to see the paint looked fine as is. With a sigh, he decided to stop by the flower shop to see June and tell her about the break-in.

He walked down the street with too many things running through his head: news that Andrew had received word about being cut from the will, concerns over where his mother was now, separation anxiety over a woman he barely knew, and now the unsettling invasion at the house next to him. If he had not just found himself in a compulsory business arrangement, he was thinking a vacation somewhere remote would be sounding pretty good.

The door to Flourishing Flowers was being held open by a bountiful orange chrysanthemum plant potted in a large chocolate-brown pot. As he drew closer to the front window, he thought about ordering flowers for Alyssa's return the next day. He had his hands in his pockets as he walked past the display at the front, keeping his eyes focused on some of the arrangements.

Just as he reached the doorway, his head turned, and he had to retreat rapidly to avoid being trampled into the concrete sidewalk. One of June's deliverymen charged out, holding an enormous arrangement that had left him visually challenged.

Grateful to have arrived without serious injury, Garrick smiled as he walked into the cool, fragrant store and spotted June behind the counter talking to a lady. His eyes narrowed as he took in the woman. He wondered if he could back out without being noticed, but unfortunately, June looked past the tall woman, saw him, smiled, and nodded a greeting to him. He muttered to himself. He had hoped that she had left town but no such luck.

She wore black high heels, making her height even more pronounced. A wool wrap with bold geometric shapes of orange, red, brown, golden yellow, and lime green draped around her, and her dark hair was fastened up with a large gold clip.

Garrick did not approach the counter. He stood back, but because the space was small, he could not help but hear the conversation. "I think the arrangement with the light orange Asiatic lilies is the one I would like sent please."

"Certainly, it is a lovely seasonal bouquet with the various shades of orange, brown, and yellow, but it is really the red oak leaves that set it off. You said you would like it sent to the Waters Bed and Breakfast?" The woman nodded her confirmation, and to Garrick's astonishment, she pulled out a hundred-dollar bill and laid it on the counter.

"Oh, cash? So few people use cash these days, it seems odd to see it. Even in a small town like this, most people have taken to the credit and debit cards. Times do change, don't they?"

"Yes, and people change too." Garrick rolled his eyes, wondering if she was trying to convince herself of that. He had stood in the background long enough, moved forward to the counter, and leaned on it about a foot away from his mother.

"Hello, Jillian. I didn't expect to see you still in town. Thought you needed to get back to New York. Wouldn't want you to miss too many important appointments." He stared at her, daring her with his eyes to explain their relationship. Obviously, if he knew her name and that she was from New York, there was some sort of relationship.

She slowly turned sideways and sweetly smiled. Maybe she was right. He did not remember her ever being in control. "Garrick, how nice to see you again. New York will survive without me for a while. Don't worry yourself about me."

"Oh, I wasn't aware you knew anyone in New Glory? How do you two know each other?" June couldn't have delivered the ideal question any better if she had been reading a script. Garrick's gaze went from June as she finished speaking right back to Jillian.

"Wow, Jillian. It's been so long since we first met, I can honestly say I don't remember our first contact. But I am sure you do."

"Well, of course I do, Garrick." Addressing June then, she said, "It's a family connection, but not a close one, at least not anymore. I really should be on my way. Thank you again, June. Take care, Garrick." Just as she had floated from New Glory Gems at the beginning of the week, she now glided out of Flourishing Flowers.

Once she was out the door and far enough away to be out of earshot, June looked quizzically at Garrick. "How does a family connection become less close over time?"

"I don't want to talk about it, and you don't want to hear about it. Did she say if she was leaving town soon?"

"No, actually the exact opposite. She said she thought it was a wonderful location and that she could see herself becoming part of a community like this one." Garrick's mouth gaped open, and June's eyebrows rose.

Chapter 7

With a sense of relief, Alyssa passed the town limits sign welcoming her to New Glory, population 4,212. She had debated whether to go to her mom's place first to let her know she was back or just go straight to Garrick's house and call her mother from there. The traffic had not been heavy, so she had made good time on the road. The slowdown on the journey had been the flight from New York to Lexington and had certainly put her behind schedule. A last glance at the time helped her make the decision easily; she would let her mom know she was back once she got to Garrick's place.

The town was so colorful in shades of red, gold, orange, and brown, and a few leaves had started drifting to the ground in their graceful exit from life. Even now at sunset, it was a picture. The street that her new home and Garrick's house sat on was lined primarily with sugar maples and scarlet oak trees, although a couple of willow oaks were mixed in. The resulting fall color ranged from red to yellow with several spectacular blended shades in between. No wonder the street was duly named Autumn Wood Way.

By the time Alyssa pulled into Garrick's driveway, it was dark. When she climbed out of her Prius, she jumped when a hand reached out and took her arm. "It's just me," Garrick whispered as he pulled her close. This embrace was filled with pleasure and tenderness. "Missed ya," she heard him say into her hair.

"I missed you too. I thought I wasn't going to make our eight-o'clock date. My flight was late."

"I know. I checked online to see what time it landed. You made very good time once you hit the ground." He tried to look disapproving of the speed she obviously had driven. She ignored the dig.

"I didn't stop at Mom's, so I should call her to let her know I'm here."

"Sure, come in. You can call and then tell me about New York."

Entering Garrick's house, she went directly to the phone. Once she had assured her mother that she was safely settled back in New Glory, she went to sit on the couch with Garrick. She smiled as contentment overflowed.

"The movers should be here tomorrow afternoon. The apartment is empty and keys turned in. I am officially an ex–New Yorker!"

"You don't have to go back for anything else?"

"Nope. No more trips to the big city necessary." Allowing the relaxation to finally sink in brought the actual exhaustion she was experiencing out, and she leaned into him, resting her head on his chest. "How did things go around here?"

She sensed him flinch at the question and lifted her head to look at him. Garrick was trying to hide his "could we just avoid that subject" face. "I got the painting done at the store. We can open on Monday as planned if you like."

"Awesome. How does it look? Did the color turn out okay?" Alyssa was still skeptical about the wince she had detected, so she kept her eyes on him.

"Yes, I think you'll like it. Your mom stopped in, and she thought you would." Garrick paused and then let out a held breath before continuing. "Alyssa, something did happen while you were away, though." Garrick's expression had gone from easy to sullen.

"Oh, what?"

"Someone broke into your house."

"My house?" She was sitting upright now.

He nodded and sighed. "I might not have noticed if I hadn't been trying to surprise you. I got a key from your mom and went in and painted the master bedroom for you on Thursday afternoon."

"You did?" She felt a warm feeling engulf her.

"I went back on Friday with the intent of painting the living room, but when I got there, I found that someone had gone in and turned the place upside-down. It looks to me as if they were searching for something. The police came, and a report has been filed, although they'll likely want to get a statement from you as to where you were and if you can think of anyone that would want to break in."

She looked perplexed. "Why would anyone want to break in? I think the whole town knows I have pretty much cleared the house out. Why would anyone think there was something of value still there?"

Garrick shrugged. "I don't know. I got permission from the police to go in today and tidy up for you. So things are somewhat organized, considering the chaos of yesterday morning. I got the lock replaced on the door where they broke in too. You should have a look around and see if you notice anything missing."

"Oh, yes. Well, give me the bill, and I will pay you back for the lock. And thank you for painting and cleaning up the mess."

"There's probably something else I should tell you before you go out tomorrow and see people." He hesitated.

"What? Garrick, you might as well get it all out so I can just deal with it all at once."

"You and I are the subject of a certain amount of speculation round town these days."

"What do you mean?"

"I guess the fact that we sat together at church, had lunch, and then were spotted kissing on a local street, well…that sequence has resulted in some talk."

"Oh." Realization dawned on Alyssa. "I guess I have been away for quite a few years. I should have known that the chatter chain would be delighted with us."

"Chatter chain?"

She smiled. "Laura and I always got a kick out of how much gossip flew around here, so we had a few phrases to describe gossip like chatter chain, whispering wire, tale trail. We also had a couple of labels for those who participate in the recreational activity of gossiping: rumor reporters, news nuts, and—one my personal favorites—buzz babes. There were probably others, but I can't think of them right now."

Garrick gazed at her, amazed. "So it doesn't bother you?"

"No," she said with a laugh. "It will actually make good advertisement for New Glory Gems. Some people will actually come into the store just to see how you and I interact in order to assess for themselves if there is any truth to the stories. Always look for the positive, Garrick."

Sunday brought rain. Garrick selected a seat at church with Mark, Laura, and Jason, so when Alyssa and June came in, they sat in the seat ahead of Garrick. Alyssa suspected that he had intentionally sat somewhere there would not be enough room for her to join him. Perhaps he thought that would cause less talk, but in her mind it probably wouldn't matter at this point, since anything they did or didn't do would be conversation worthy.

She had lunch with him, but not in public. They had egg salad sandwiches at Garrick's place. After lunch, they played several games of backgammon. Alyssa could not remember when she had taken time to sit and just play. They were reasonably well matched, although in the end, Garrick won, four games to three. Until the moving truck arrived, they sat snuggled on the couch watching the movie remake of an old comedy and laughed at the absurd antics.

The movers pulled into Alyssa's driveway at 2:50 that afternoon and had unloaded and moved in the furniture and boxes as directed by 4:00 p.m. She was able to put her bedroom fully together and would pick up the clothes she had at her mom's house when she went over for dinner. Tonight she would be able to sleep in her very own house. A sense of giddiness threatened her stability. The idea that she was a homeowner was exciting, exhilarating, and overwhelming.

Garrick had decided to join June and Alyssa for dinner, so they drove over together. Since Alyssa had been busy with the house, she had not had time to make anything to take with them, so Garrick had taken up the baton and gone to the bakery. He bought a freshly baked pumpkin pie.

"Hi, Mom." Alyssa was audibly exhausted. Another good night's sleep was essential.

"Alyssa, Garrick. Come in. Oh, Garrick. Is that pumpkin pie? It smells good. Thank you for bringing it."

Garrick smiled and then said with a wink, "I baked it myself. Even brought whipped cream." The can of whipped cream made June smile.

"My, Garrick, this is a special treat. Did you milk the cow and skim the cream yourself too?" Alyssa chuckled at her mother. She loved to tease Garrick, and he loved to be teased by her. The two quipped back and forth for several minutes while Alyssa just sat back and quietly enjoyed the show.

Dinner was relaxing and lively. June told stories of some of the more interesting customers that she had dealt with at the flower shop. She had prepared the most beautiful bunch of long-stemmed red roses for a fiftieth wedding anniversary, more than a couple "I'm sorry" bouquets sent by people who would remain anonymous, one highly discreet "My wife can't find out about this" arrangement, and the highlight of the week was nineteen-year-old Trevor Daniels's selection of a special bouquet of white rosebuds for a first date.

"Oh, and I almost forgot." Looking at Alyssa, she added, "Garrick's relative who is staying at a bed and breakfast just outside of town was in on Friday too. Definitely an interesting week."

Alyssa tilted her head and narrowed her eyes. "You have a relative visiting in New Glory, Garrick? Why wouldn't they stay at your place? You have room, don't you?"

"By the time I knew she was in town, she was already settled in." Garrick seemed to shrug it off as unimportant and quickly moved on to another topic. That immediate subject change reminded Alyssa of her concerns over Garrick's reluctance to share personal information.

Monday, New Glory Gems opened at 10:00 a.m. There were several people in throughout the day. While most simply wanted to be neighborly, showing support and saying hi, a few people made purchases. That was a good sign. According to the extensive records that Alyssa's grandfather had kept, it seemed that Monday's sales had been relatively high.

Many people commented on how the store looked, praising Garrick on his painting skills. Alyssa had to admit he had done an excellent job on the painting in both the store and her bedroom.

Alyssa realized at about 2:30 p.m. that three-inch heels might not be the best shoe selection each day. She managed to wear them until they put the "closed" sign up, but she was moving much less fluidly than she had at the beginning of the day. She intended simply to stay at the store to work that evening, so she had brought comfortable clothes with her. She gave a silent prayer of thanks for God's direction on that as she kicked off the offending footwear at 4:01.

Around 4:30, as Alyssa cherished the comforting feel of her running shoes, she worked at pulling files from the cabinet in the backroom. Garrick, who had not left yet, emerged in the doorway. Leaning his left shoulder against the doorjamb, he crossed his arms and watched her. Looking sideways at him, she drew a deep breath.

He wore casual pants and a long-sleeved shirt. He had rolled the sleeves up, accentuating his muscular forearms. *He is so good looking. Why does he have to stand like that? It just makes him even more appealing.* "Are you leaving now?" she asked in a voice that admitted he was distracting her.

"In a minute." His voice seemed focused and his eyes were intent. He moved from the doorway, approaching the filing cabinet that she stood in front of. Perching an elbow on top of the tall filing cabinet, he looked down at Alyssa with extreme closeness. With his free arm, he reached out, pulling her in to him. A half-smile curved up on his shadowed face. "I didn't want to leave without saying good-bye." He did not move; he just gazed, taking her in.

"Very polite." Her eyes remained fixed on his.

"I try. Sometimes I overstep, though, and don't ask for permission when I probably should." He paused once again. Alyssa just waited through the silence. "For example, I don't plan on asking for your permission to kiss you here in the backroom of the store." His words were slow and so well articulated Alyssa should not have had any trouble following him, but she was getting lost in his eyes. Her senses were jolted back to full power when he leaned his head down to her and applied a gentle kiss to her lips. "May I call you after I get home from the seniors' program? I just want to make sure everything is okay at the house and that you made it home safely."

"It's not necessary." She smiled, aware that Garrick did not give everyone this level of protective care. "But you may." He kissed her forehead and left.

Alyssa could not understand what it was about him that affected her so. Max had often passionately kissed her, kisses that should have sent her into oblivion, and she never responded like this. All Garrick did was barely kiss her or simply put his arms around her, and she melted like a child's ice cream cone on a hot day.

By 6:00 p.m., her stomach was protesting, demanding food. She called down to Sarah's Café but found that they close early on

Mondays. So she called The Quarters, asking them to prepare her a soup and sandwich combo, which she would pick up. She returned the stack of folders that she had completed to the filing cabinet and grabbed another bundle. Setting them on the desk in the office, she moved around a bit to loosen up. She grabbed her jacket and headed over to The Quarters to get her meal.

Cream of broccoli tasted so good, and the turkey on cracked wheat bread was delicious. Food had several redeeming qualities, and in this case, it seemed to be literally bringing her back from near death to a productive state. Alyssa felt recharged and that she could work for hours.

She started to go through the laborious task and stopped short on the first folder. *Strange*, she thought. This folder's contents were similar to that other one that she could not explain. She tucked it in the bottom drawer with the first one and continued.

By nine thirty, she was wiped out, and although she had finished the first of the five filing cabinets, she now had not two folders on hold in the bottom drawer but five. Once the desk was cleared and all was tidied up, she pulled all five folders out. The dates on the five shipping invoices were all from 2009—January, February, June, August, and December. They were not spaced equally apart. They did not have similar gem profiles or similar quantities. The first one, dated January, had actually been the second one that Alyssa had uncovered. It was a small shipment of emeralds and tanzanite. The February shipment was the largest, with diamonds, sapphires, amethysts, rubies, and pearls. After that, they were small again and individual. The June shipment was all alexandrite, August was black opals, and finally December was jadeite.

She placed the documentation back in the drawer and left the store, ensuring it was secured before driving home.

Garrick called at ten to check on her. She hadn't been home long and wondered if he would have been alarmed if she had not yet returned. She didn't go into detail about the strange paperwork but did mention there had been a handful of invoices surface that were causing her some confusion. They decided to review them at the end of the day on Tuesday.

"How was the seniors' program tonight?" Alyssa inquired.

"Tonight was easy on me. I had Graham North in to speak and answer questions on estate planning. I had offered arts and crafts night to any of the folks who already had their estate adequately planned, but no one signed up for it, so I'll do that another night. Actually, I should have mentioned this before now, but I will be out of town on Columbus Day. I booked a seniors' bus trip for that Monday. Wasn't sure what you were planning concerning opening and closing on holidays."

"I will think about it. Of course, the big holidays we will definitely close. I guess we should see how business goes this week before we make that decision. Where is the bus trip to?"

"We're driving down to one of the dinner shows in Pigeon Forge. We have tickets for a lunchtime performance."

"Sounds like fun. Have you been to that show before?"

"No, we've done other dinner theater shows, but not this one. It'll be worth the drive, though. They always are. Well, I guess I'll see you in the morning, Alyssa."

"Yes, good night, Garrick." Alyssa went to bed with thoughts of Garrick fresh in her mind.

Tuesday after work, Alyssa steered Garrick in the direction of the office. She pulled out the five folders and showed him the details on them. He looked at them, dumbstruck. "There's no shipper information listed on these invoices. Where did the shipments come from?"

"I have no idea where they came from or what was done with them when they arrived, other than this piece of paper which was carefully filed. And look, each refers to vault B."

"These packing slips represent a significant value of gems. We need to figure out where vault B is. Have you asked June if she ever heard Greg mention anything about this?"

"No, I haven't, but I will."

They could hear a knock at the front door of the store. They had locked it at the end of the day before moving to the office to inspect the invoices.

"I'll go see who it is," Garrick offered. He quickened his steps as he saw June at the front door. "Hey, June. We were just talking about you. Come in."

"Should I be flattered or concerned that I was being talked about?"

"There is never anything bad to say about you. We were just curious if Greg had ever indicated that he had other vaults in which he might have stored stones? We're just having a challenge matching up a couple of receiving slips against the inventory here."

"The short answer to your question is no. Greg never mentioned any other vaults. However, I have just come from the bank."

"The bank? You didn't rob it, did you, June?" Garrick teased.

"I wouldn't have stopped here if I had. I would be nonstop to Brazil." She smirked and caught a glimpse of Alyssa snickering at the playful exchange. "Hi, Alyssa."

"Hi, Mom."

"I was just telling Garrick that I went to the bank, as I hadn't gone through your grandpa's safety deposit box yet. I found a couple of items in it that were not marked. I really don't know what they are, so I'm hoping you two will know."

"What was in there?" Alyssa asked.

"There is a key." June held up a door key on a simple key chain. "And this business card with numbers on the back. It must have been important for him to put it in the safety deposit box."

Alyssa took the key, and Garrick took the card. Alyssa turned and walked out of the showroom. She paused, looking at the rear space behind the showroom, hoping that the key would unlock one unanswered question. She walked to the fourth door that had remained unopened and tried the key in it. It slipped easily in, and turning it, she was able to turn the doorknob.

"Mom? Garrick?" Alyssa called, walking into the room.

Chapter 8

Garrick and June followed Alyssa's voice. He immediately recognized that the previously locked door was ajar, and stopping, he looked down at the numbers on the card and wondered if they could be a combination.

Peering in the small room, Garrick was surprised to see a small bedroom. Inside, Alyssa was looking around, appearing as confused as he felt. June entered right behind Garrick, and her voice broke the silence. "It's a bedroom?"

"Mmmhmm, it appears to be," Alyssa agreed. "Single bed, dresser, and wardrobe."

Garrick moved toward the furniture. Opening the drawers in the dresser, he found them empty. Drawer after drawer, he discovered the same thing—nothing. The wardrobe was empty too. The bed had linens on it and a comforter. "So he had an empty, furnished bedroom for one person in the back of his store and felt so compelled to keep the emptiness secure that he locked it and left the key in his safety deposit box. Does this make any sense to you, June?"

"No, it makes no sense."

"Garrick." Alyssa turned to him. "What was on the card that Mom handed you?"

"Numbers. I was hoping you were walking into a room with vault B and these numbers would be the combination. Now I have no idea what the numbers are. They had to be important, though, or he wouldn't have kept them at the bank."

"I don't think we are going to figure out this mystery right now, so until we do, let's keep the room locked and put the card in the main vault, Garrick." He agreed, and once they had locked the room, he put the seemingly meaningless items in the vault.

"I need to go. I have plans tonight," June said and was on her way. Garrick saw her out and locked the front door of the store before returning to the back where Alyssa had settled in the office chair.

She had another stack of folders on the desk and appeared to be prepared to work for a while. He stood in front of the medium-sized desk, Alyssa obviously unaware that he had even entered the room. He crossed his arms and stared down at her. Without looking up, in a loud voice intended to reach the showroom, she said, "Garrick?"

"Yes, Alyssa?" His voice was quiet but had the effect he was going for. Her head jerked up suddenly, letting out a small shriek of surprise. He smiled at her, his arms still crossed in front of his chest. Eyes closing and taking a deep breath, Alyssa calmed herself and then, opening her eyes to a narrow slit, glared up at him. Garrick's smile changed to pleasure-filled chortling. "You called me?"

"I don't remember why now," she explained in disgust.

Still smirking, he said, "Are you planning on working for a while?"

"Oh, yes, that's what I was going to say to you. I should work on the files for a while. If you have other plans for the evening, feel free to head out."

A thoughtful expression replaced the gleeful look he had pinned on her before. "There are a couple of problems with that scenario," he started. "First, you drove both of us to work this morning."

"Oh, carpool, right. Well, I trust you. Take my car. Do you think you could come back and pick me up later?" Her words sounded sheepish and pleading.

"Second, my plans for the evening included you, a movie, and some popcorn." Now he moved forward and placed his large hands flat on the desk and leaned over so that his face was within inches of hers. Taunting her, he dared, "How are you going solve that dilemma?"

"I wasn't aware we had plans together, Garrick."

"I was going to surprise you."

"You do that surprise trick a lot, don't you?"

"I like to keep life intriguing."

"Well, tell me, Garrick, who was the focus of all this unexpected intrigue before I got to town?"

"No one. I've been saving up!" At that, he noticed the corner of her mouth start to curve up. She rolled her eyes, and he knew he had her. "Come on. You need a break. I have a comedy all loaded and ready to go in the DVD player at my place. We will pick up pizza to go on the way home and relax for the entire evening."

She shifted her gaze from him to the folders and back to him again. "Okay. You tempted me. I will just put these back in the file cabinet and we can relax the evening away."

"Austin Powers? That's the movie we're going to watch?"

Garrick smiled at her surprise.

"Yep. We can watch all three if you want to. I don't watch them with very many women. I'm cautious of allowing females to compare me to the impressive mojo of the Man of Mystery."

Alyssa laughed at him. "Are you afraid you would come up short against Austin?"

"Wouldn't want to risk it."

Alyssa moved in closer. Reaching up, she placed her arms around his neck. "I don't think you have to worry." The feel of her pressed against him was making the process of thinking become more challenging. He wanted to give in and let the feelings lead him, but at the same time, he knew he needed to hold back.

"Do you not want to watch the movie?" he asked as his gaze focused on her face and the beautiful features framed by the long, dark hair. Garrick moved one hand through the hair and with the other arm pressed his hand on her lower back, bringing her even closer.

"Of course I want to watch the movie, but I am a multitasker." Garrick was losing his battle now. Between the long lashes, the moist lips, and the arms wrapped around him, he was fading fast.

He lowered his head and brushed his lips across hers. Sensations went rolling through him with one destination. She wore that same captivating scent that had distracted him at church, and she must have been wearing a flavored lipstick, because he could taste cherries despite the pizza they had just eaten. Her lips opened slightly, and recognizing that as an invitation, he deepened the kiss. He was losing control, and he knew it. His hand moved even lower, and he heard her sigh at the feel of him tightly pressing against her.

He allowed the kisses to grow passionately for long moments, but gradually he broke the embrace, putting just enough space between them to allow their breathing to settle to a rational speed. He pressed her head against his chest and kissed her hair, whispering, "I can't let this go any further, Alyssa. Not yet. Please understand?"

He released her enough that she could look up at him. "I do understand. I have boundaries too, Garrick. I won't let you cross them, but I will admit I am finding it more difficult respecting those limits with you than I have ever experienced with anyone else."

Those words sent a warm flush over Garrick, and his face became soft with emotion. "Then I think we are both experiencing deeper feelings than ever before." He ran his fingers down the side of her face and kissed her gently on the cheek. "Popcorn?"

She laughed. "Yeah, baby, yeah."

Garrick was surprised to hear his cell phone ring around 3:00 p.m. on Thursday. "Hello, Garrick Samuels."

"How are you, Garrick? I just got an update on Jillian."

"And?"

"She's back in New York. At least she was there for her parole meeting. She had an excuse for missing the week before, and apparently they bought it."

"When was the last meeting?"

"Last Thursday."

"She was in town here on Friday, expressing her intentions to become part of our little community. I'd be very interested to know how she is planning on paying for trips to New York each week."

"It does raise some questions, if she is back in Kentucky. She actually should be in New York today. I asked the parole officer to contact me if she doesn't show up, so I will let you know if I hear anything."

"I appreciate you keeping me in the loop."

"No problem. I'll be in touch."

"Thanks."

Friday by 6:00 p.m., Alyssa had completed the file cross-reference and transfer to her laptop. She had found another four packing slips not matching any inventory they had found. Each followed the same pattern, including a reference to vault B. She had compiled a separate listing of all the valuables listed on these receipts and printed a copy.

Garrick wanted to ask the police department if they could provide details on any jewel heists where the jewels were never recovered. He knew they would ask questions, however, and hated to implicate Greg Mason in anything. It would be far simpler if he had his PI license active, because then he would be able to operate with a bit more autonomy. The application and approval process was lengthy, though. He hoped everything would be resolved long before they could process a license.

After they closed the store Friday at eight o'clock, Garrick and Alyssa were expected at Mark and Laura's for the evening. Although both of them were tired, an evening with friends would be refreshing. Garrick knew that Alyssa would rather have gone over on Saturday night. She had a soft place in her heart for Jason, and by eight thirty, when they would arrive, the young man would already be off to bed.

"Hi, Laura." Alyssa's voice was smooth, although Garrick could detect the fatigue that hovered just below the surface. He wanted to just take her home and let her get the rest she really needed. An early night, he decided, regardless of Mark and Laura's arguments.

"Alyssa." Laura's voice was full of life as she wrapped her arms around her friend's neck. Garrick wondered if he would even get noticed standing just behind Alyssa, but then Laura's eyes focused on him. "Garrick." With the same level of enthusiasm, she moved the hug from Alyssa to Garrick. He should have known she wouldn't leave him out. "Mark? They're here."

"Yes, dear, I guessed that when I heard you exclaim 'Alyssa,' 'Garrick.'" Mark had joined his wife now at the door. They all laughed as Alyssa and Garrick moved into the house.

Mark gave Alyssa a hug and Garrick a firm, friendly handshake with the accompanying slap on the back. The four planned to play euchre.

Garrick was pleased to learn that Alyssa knew the game from her earlier years in New Glory, and tonight would make a handy refresher. He was planning a euchre tournament for the following month as a fundraiser for his seniors' program. Although the draw would be mostly an older crowd, he was hoping that Alyssa would join him at it. An interest in having her meet and get to know the people he spent his Monday nights with was growing, just as his interest in her was increasing.

"So, Alyssa, will it be men versus women?"

"Depends. Are you a good loser or a bad loser?" She looked straight at Garrick. Then, shifting her eyes toward Mark and Laura, she said, "You see, I didn't drive tonight, and if I play against Garrick and I win, which I have every intention of doing, I wouldn't want to be left without a ride home."

"I'll see you get home, partner," Laura said, directing Alyssa to the chair across from her.

Garrick knew she was joking, but he muttered under his breath just the same, "I am a gracious *winner*." He caught the smile on Alyssa's face, and the grin on his face grew as he took his seat at the card table.

The cards were dealt and they started playing. A few hands into the first game and the ladies had a healthy lead at six to two. There had been some fun back-and-forth chitchat, but then Mark carefully broached a subject that was typically off limits. "Garrick, I understand your mother's been in the area. I didn't realize she was still in touch with you."

Garrick paused, using the cards and his concentration on the game as an excuse. Finally he responded, "She hadn't been." Garrick really did not want the conversation to take this direction but wasn't sure how to shift it.

"So you have talked to her since she arrived?"

"As little as possible." No suit had been declared for the hand, and it was Garrick's turn to make it, if he chose to. Looking at his hand, which was made up of mostly hearts and diamonds, he said, "Spades *alone*." He glared at Mark. Eyebrows lifted slightly, Mark laid his cards down and pushed his chair back.

"Can I get anyone anything while my partner here cleans house?"

"I'll have another cranberry juice, please," Alyssa requested.

By the time Mark returned with Alyssa's drink and a Coke for himself, Laura could be heard needling Garrick. "Euchred you, yeah." Garrick had not taken a single trick, allowing the ladies to win that hand.

Mark looked at Garrick, shaking his head. "You did that on purpose, didn't you?" Garrick shrugged. "I got the message. No more discussions about your mother."

When the ladies ended up winning that game, naturally the men argued that it should not count since Garrick had thrown one hand. So they threw out that game and played two more, which the ladies also handily won. Alyssa and Laura claimed victory while Mark commiserated with Garrick. It didn't take the men long to lick their wounds and demand a rematch on another night. With the solidarity formed due to the loss, the obvious disagreement earlier was forgotten.

Garrick walked Alyssa to her door once he drove her home. He was cautious by nature and since the break-in at her house, he preferred to be overprotective rather than have something unnecessary happen. "Would you allow me to come in just to make sure everything is secure?"

"Of course." He knew her eyes followed him as he moved from one room to the next to ensure the house was undisturbed. "Garrick, did the program in criminal justice teach you how to *clear* a house?"

"How did you know about that?" Creases formed in his brow.

"Laura mentioned it."

Garrick's head dipped. He wondered what else Laura had said about him. "There were courses. I focused mainly on investigation, though."

"Where did you study?"

"John Jay College of Criminal Justice. I have a bachelor's in criminology with a minor in police studies."

"Did you ever use your education, or did you just show up in New Glory and wind your way into being a creative lapidary like your father?"

"I've used my education some." Garrick needed to make a decision. He wanted to build a lasting relationship with this woman. He was either about to lie about his past or fully disclose. "I actually went into business for myself right after college. I was doing pretty well, but then I ended up here and gradually just found myself working with your grandfather and really enjoying it."

"What was the business, Garrick?"

"Professional investigation."

Alyssa's face contorted as if trying to process his last response. Her eyes moved from left to right and then narrowed. "You were a private investigator?"

"Yeah, and since I've told you that much, I might as well let you know that I let my license run out, although I wish I had it right now. My mother is a walking investigative nightmare."

"Your mother? Is that the relative Mom mentioned was in the flower shop last Friday? Is she in some kind of trouble?"

"Yes, it's my mother who is in town, and no, she doesn't get in trouble. She *is* trouble. And that is probably all the soul baring I can indulge in for one night." Garrick moved up to her and wrapped his arms around her in a protective hug. "I promise I won't let her be trouble for you. I'm going to head home. Who's driving tomorrow?"

"My turn. I'll pick you up at nine thirty?"

The phone rang at 4:25 a.m., startling Garrick, and he struggled to shake free of the disorientation. "Hello?" he managed and listened as Police Chief Tom Dallas identified himself.

"Garrick Samuels?"

"Yeah?"

"There's been an incident downtown at New Glory Gems. Think you should come down here and determine what, if anything, is missing. I've contacted Alyssa Mason as well."

Garrick expelled a low moan. "Okay. I'm on my way."

He dialed Alyssa's home number regretfully.

"Hello?" Her voice was anxious.

"Alyssa. It's Garrick. I can go downtown and deal with whatever has happened. You don't need to worry about it."

"No, I'm coming."

Why he would think the conversation would have taken any other turn than that was beyond his comprehension. "I'll be by in five minutes to pick you up."

Arriving on Main Street, they discovered two police cars angle parked in front of New Glory Gems. The flashing lights on the vehicles still whirled, emitting that disturbing strobe effect. Garrick mused that the thrill of getting to turn the lights on was going to be the highlight of the NGPD Friday-night shift. New Glory was not a haven for crime or even for traffic violations. He was actually surprised that they had invested in vehicles with the emergency flashing lights.

"Alyssa, how about you stay here until I find out just what happened?"

"Not likely."

Smiling, he looked at her. "I thought it was worth a try."

"Come on. *We* need to find out what happened."

They approached an officer standing about ten feet from the front door. It was easy to get an initial idea of what had prompted the call. The glass in the front door was smashed. Garrick went back over the security features they had installed for the jewelry store. All the glass had break and shatter sensors, so as soon as the door's windowpane broke, an alarm would transmit through to the police department. He was certain this was the first time it had been put to use.

"Hi, Jasper. Broken window?" Garrick stated to the young police officer, Jasper Willows.

"Oh hey, Garrick, Miss Mason. Yes, sir, the alarm sounded at four twenty a.m. Frank and I got over here in record time. Nothin' much to slow us down at this hour. I called the police chief as soon as we got here, and I guess he must have called you directly after that. He's s'posed to be comin' down, but ya beat him." Jasper slipped that last remark in with a smirk. "Looks like someone just threw a brick through the door. Probably some kid, although not many New Glory kids would be out at this hour."

Garrick nodded, realizing that Jasper was right. The New Glory crowd was the epitome of law-abiding citizens. "Don't suppose there were any witnesses hanging around when you arrived, either?"

"Nope, notta one."

"Medium-sized brick by the looks of it. It would take a reasonable-sized kid to walk up carrying that, throw it, and then hightail it outta sight."

"Pro'bly."

"How long until Frank lets us in there to have a look around?"

"Shouldn't be long now. He hollered out, said none of the showcases was broken, but you two will have to confirm that nothin' was taken. Seems like just a prank to me, although we don't get many pranksters in town."

"No, not many. Might be another possibility, Jasper."

"Ya think? What would it be?"

Garrick smiled to himself. Jasper was a great kid and loved being a police officer, but his street smarts and investigative intuitions were still somewhat stunted. "Maybe someone was just testing to see what kind of security we had," Garrick suggested.

"What would they need to know that fer?" Garrick could see the expression on Alyssa's face from where he stood, and thankfully, Jasper could not.

"Maybe somebody is thinkin' bout breakin' in." Garrick had slowed his pace and modified his speech patterns now to match Jasper's. "Or maybe they wanted to know what kind of response time the police would have if there was an alarm."

"Geez, Garrick. That would mean that someone might be plannin' somethin'." Total shock covered Jasper's innocent face.

"Don't wanna rule it out, Jasper."

"If you folks want to come in and have a look to see if anything is missing, you can come in now," Frank said from just inside the store as the police chief drove up.

Garrick and Alyssa walked toward the store, but instead of walking in where the broken glass was still laying, Garrick suggested that Frank come around the back of the store with them. They could check to make sure there were no signs of forced entry back there and enter from the rear so as not to disturb anything until after the police chief had surveyed the scene.

Garrick and Alyssa had stopped parking on Main Street once they had reopened after Greg's death, to allow for as much parking in front of the shop as possible. At this hour, the small paved alcove behind New Glory Gems was dark and felt menacing. Garrick was relieved to see the lock at the back appeared secure. There was no sign of attempting to get through that door. It was solid. They would need some specialized equipment or a key to get through the back entrance.

The three entered together and carefully checked to make sure everything looked normal. Alyssa scooped up a list that she had printed showing their inventory by showcase, which would make the verification that everything was accounted for simple. However easy it would be, it still would take time and concentration. Garrick unlocked the fire door that separated the back area from the showroom, and they entered, beginning their inspection.

Two and half hours later, they had concluded that everything was there. Nothing had been taken. That was some consolation. The police had left to file their reports, and Garrick had left messages to get the necessary repairs made. In the meantime, one of them would need to stay at the store. Garrick volunteered to go down to Sarah's Café and get some breakfast for the two of them. They passed the time with coffee, bagels, croissants, and cleaning until they opened at 10:00 a.m.

Word spreads like the plague in a small town, so they had record numbers of people in on Saturday. However unfortunate the incident had been, it had been great for sales. Some of the purchases made before closing on Saturday overjoyed Alyssa. It had been so busy that they had not even had time to get lunch.

The new pane of glass and the installer arrived at 1:55. They asked him to wait the five minutes until they closed and let the last of the welcome patrons leave before the repairs began. They had been lucky on several counts. The weather had been pleasant. A rainstorm would have been disastrous with no front door. The installer was able to accommodate them perfectly. Given they needed the break-and-shatter glass cut to size and installed by the security company's installer, it had been remarkable to arrange on such short notice. And of course, nothing had been stolen.

Garrick sent Alyssa to the restaurant to grab a couple of sandwiches since the installer would be there for a while. Moments after she left, as the installer removed the remaining shards of glass from the doorframe, a man appeared in the doorway. Garrick's head was tilted down, looking at a newspaper, when he heard the installer say, "I think they're closed." Garrick looked up, and there standing at the entrance to New Glory Gems was a deliveryman with his arms full.

Garrick quickly moved to the man and accepted the floral delivery. Without thinking, he opened the unaddressed envelope and withdrew the card from inside. The color drained from his face as he read what it said: "First Responder in three minutes, nine seconds. Not bad."

Chapter 9

Alyssa paid for the sandwiches and turned to leave Sarah's Café, but before she reached the door, a woman stepped in front of her. Startled, she almost dropped the to-go bag and drinks but managed to mumble a "pardon me."

The woman was tall and well dressed. Alyssa noticed the clothes, the familiar New York style that she had gotten used to. This couldn't be a local resident. She was likely in her fifties, although Alyssa had never prided herself on being good at guessing ages. "It was my fault. Please forgive me." The voice was refined and seemed out of place in the café.

"I'm sorry; I don't recognize you. Are you from around here?" Alyssa was just now getting the right grip on the drinks and food after the near impact.

"Jillian Chadwick. I've been visiting, but think this town is charming. I'm considering relocating."

"Well, New Glory has always been very friendly. Are you staying with a friend or relative while you visit?"

"I've been staying at a bed and breakfast just outside of town. Very quiet. I think I am the only guest."

Alyssa paused briefly, remembering her mother's comment about a relative of Garrick's staying at a bed and breakfast just outside of

New Glory and the later connection she had made that Garrick had confirmed. This must be Garrick's mother. Although interested, she hesitated to involve herself in any way with this woman. Not yet at least. "Well, I really need to be leaving now, but it was nice to meet you, Ms. Chadwick. Perhaps we'll run into each other again."

"Yes, no doubt we will."

Alyssa slipped from the café and moved quickly down the street. That had taken much longer than she had planned on. Reaching the store, she managed to step past the worker without causing him inconvenience. She had expected to see Garrick in the showroom, but he wasn't there. Setting the food and drinks down on the counter, she went to the door leading to the back rooms and called for him.

"Be out in a minute," she heard him say gruffly. They had placed a couple of stools behind the main sales counter, so she pulled them up and unpackaged the food. Garrick appeared but looked distant.

"Hey, sorry I took so long. A woman almost ran me down in Sarah's Café. I just about dropped everything. She was obviously from out of town by the way she was dressed, although I never found out where she was from."

"Are you okay?" Garrick asked but without his normal concerned tone. "Did you actually collide with her?"

Alyssa laughed. "Oh no, it was just a *near* collision. She was tall; if there had been contact, I would have been flattened." She looked at Garrick with caring eyes. He may have asked a couple of involved questions, but he was not involved in this conversation the way he normally was. She wanted to confirm that she had been talking to his mother by finding out what she looked like. However, she sensed this was not the time to ask. "Is everything all right, Garrick? It seems like you have something on your mind."

"We got a delivery while you were out." He pointed to a corner of the store where he had set the bouquet, on the floor, out of the way.

"They're beautiful. Who sent them?" Alyssa asked.

"Don't know, but the way the card is worded, I'm guessing whoever is responsible for our early wake-up call today. They're not from your mom's shop. There's nothing to indicate what florist they came from." He handed her the card, and she looked at the words that were typed on it.

"Was someone timing the response to the alarm last night?"

"It sounds like it to me. I'll call the station and tell them. You know you don't have to sit here and wait with me. Why don't you go over and see your mom? I'll come by and get you as soon as I'm locked up." The suggestion sounded inviting to Alyssa.

Alyssa strolled into Flourishing Flowers and saw one of her mother's staff behind the counter. "Hi, Teri. Is Mom around?" She was anxious to have some time with her mother.

"Alyssa, nice to see you. No, your mother went home just after lunch today. I don't think she was feeling well."

"Was she okay when she got in this morning?" Apprehension gripped Alyssa. Her mother never got sick, other than the occasional migraine.

"Yes, she seemed fine. She even seemed fine after she heard all the details about the incident over at your store. We were reasonably busy but not overrun with work today. So she told me to take my time at lunch. When I got back, she seemed anxious and said she needed to go home, that she wasn't feeling well. I offered to close the shop long enough to drive her home, but she said she could drive fine and it was thoughtful but not necessary. I thought it might be one of those horrid migraines and she would need a ride. You know what she's like, though—always wanting to help others, but she feels uncomfortable about accepting any assistance from anyone."

"Yes, I know her well. Thanks, Teri. I'll give her a call and get over to check on her as soon as I can." Alyssa left the flower shop and walked down the street to one of the charming New Glory trademark benches.

Main Street in New Glory was attractive. Throughout the spring and summer months, hanging flowerpots lined the busy street, providing bold color to the enchanting shopping district. Even now, floral arrangements in fall colors adorned the sidewalk on either side of the characteristic park benches. Alyssa made her way to an empty bench, sat down, and pulled out her cell phone.

Dialing her mother's house, she heard the phone ring several times before the answering machine picked up. Alyssa ended the call. She tried her mom's cell phone, and it too went to voicemail. Alyssa was exhausted, and her reasoning powers were beginning to dull. Her eyes closed beneath the lack of sleep and concern, and she dropped her face into her hands.

Taking a deep breath, she lifted her head, knowing that she needed to go to her mom's and find out what was happening. She hoped she was just sleeping and letting the machine take the calls. It was probably a regular migraine, and she just didn't feel up to talking right now, but nevertheless Alyssa needed to make sure she was all right. As she opened her eyes, she struggled to focus in the afternoon sunshine on a person who stood directly in front of her.

"Alyssa, are you okay?" It was Mark, a friendly familiar voice.

"Mark, not really. I need to get to my mom's."

"Isn't Garrick at Gems?"

"Yes, the door is being repaired, so he can't leave, and I don't have a car here."

"Come on, sweetheart. You look like you are ready to drop. My truck's over here. I'll give you a lift and call Garrick to let him know." Alyssa went along willingly. She was angry with herself. She had never been any good on limited sleep. Even at college when everyone else was pulling all-nighters, she couldn't do it. She would be the token student who went to the exams on a full night's rest.

She was only registering about half of what was happening around her. It seemed to her that Mark had called Garrick and then they were driving. Within a matter of minutes, they were at her mom's house, and she had a sudden surge of energy. She jumped out of the truck with a "Thanks, Mark" and ran to the side door.

She knocked, but there was no answer. That was odd because the car was in the driveway. She tried the door and it was locked. She knew where the spare key was, so she retrieved it and let herself in. The side door brought her into the kitchen. It didn't appear as if any activity had occurred there since breakfast. She passed the dining room, and as she entered the living room, she saw her mother sitting in the glider rocker.

"Mom?" Alyssa's mother did not turn her head; she just maintained the steady rocking motion. "Mom. Are you all right?" She was moving over closer to her now, and when she got in front of her, she knelt down. June seemed absorbed in some other thought, to the absolute exclusion of what was happening around her. Alyssa placed her hand on her mother's arm, hoping that the contact would break through this barrier. "Mom?"

June seemed to awaken suddenly, even though she had not been asleep. She slowly moved her gaze to Alyssa and seemed startled that her daughter was right there with her. "Alyssa. Where did you come from?"

"Mom, I've been calling, but you didn't answer. I came over and I knocked, but you didn't come to the door, so I let myself in. Didn't you hear me calling your name when I came in the house?"

"Hmmm? I guess I didn't. I'm sorry. I have a lot on my mind."

"I stopped at the shop, and Teri told me you had gone home sick. How are you feeling now?" Alyssa talked slowly because it seemed that her mother needed time to regain her full awareness and comprehension.

"I felt fine when I drove to work this morning, but then I saw the damage at your place. That was upsetting. I'm glad nothing was taken and no one was hurt."

"So you didn't feel well after you saw what had happened at Gems?"

"No, I was fine after that too. Teri came in. I was expecting it to be busier today. Of course, everyone who came to town spent their time browsing at a jewelry store." Her comical teasing nature was returning, and that was a major relief to Alyssa.

"Yes, well, you know what the people in this town are like. They want to be able to say, 'I was there the day that New Glory Gems was vandalized.'"

June gave a halfhearted chuckle. "True. Small-town residents are a special breed, aren't they? I told Teri she might as well take her time over lunch since it was a bit on the slow side. So she left and then..." Her face turned doleful and took on a grey hue. "And then *he* called." She was staring again.

"*He* called?"

"Yes."

"Who called?" Alyssa could see that it was greatly troubling her mother.

June pulled herself from the stare once again and looked directly at Alyssa. "Andrew called."

"Uncle Andrew called? What did he say?" Alyssa was as surprised as her mother likely had been. Judging from the expression on her face, though, the conversation must not have been pleasant.

Then with near panic in her voice, June lifted out of the chair. "Where's Garrick?"

"New Glory Gems. Garrick speaking."

"Garrick. It's Alyssa. Is the installer almost done fixing the door?" Alyssa needed to assess the situation. She didn't want Garrick to bolt from the store, and she wasn't sure what his reaction was going to be.

"Actually, he is just cleaning up now. He should be out of here in five minutes or so. Mark told me he was dropping you off at your mom's house. Is everything okay there?" he asked.

"Not perfect. I was hoping you would come over as soon as you can lock up there. Mom had something unsettling happen today, and she wants to talk to both of us about it."

"I will come over as soon as I can leave here. Are you okay, Alyssa?"

"I'm fine. I'm more concerned about what Mom has to talk about right now."

"I'll be over shortly."

Within ten minutes, Garrick was tapping on the side door to June's house. Alyssa, having seen him pull into the drive, was at the door almost immediately. "Thanks for coming so quickly." Garrick nodded at her. She tried to hide her concern until they had both heard everything her mother had to say. However, she could tell that her expression was alarming Garrick more than her voice had on the phone.

"Mom, Garrick's here now. Can you tell us both what happened?"

Alyssa and Garrick sat on the chesterfield across from June and listened as she began.

"As I told Alyssa, I got a phone call at the shop over lunch hour today. It was from Andrew." Alyssa could see Garrick's eyes widen as she turned slightly so she would be able to read the reaction to what her mother was going to tell them. He was silent, though, allowing June to give the details in her way.

"When I answered the phone, I didn't recognize his voice at first. It's been years since I have spoken to him. He probably didn't recognize mine either, because he asked for June. When he realized he was talking to me, his tone changed. He became angry sounding." June had not gotten this far in retelling the conversation before Garrick had arrived, so both Alyssa and Garrick listened to this for the first time.

"He snapped the words out at me: 'This is the *disinherited* Andrew Mason' with a definite emphasis on disinherited. I guess he got the lawyer's letter."

"What did you say to him, Mom?"

"I didn't say anything. What could I say? However, he had lots to say. He told me that his father had always intended the store to be his someday. He didn't know how the three of us had convinced Greg to change the will, but he was sure that we were behind it. He continued by saying that even though we weren't aware of it, he had been investing in the business for a while, and he was going to recoup his investment. If any of us tried to stand in his way, he would not hesitate to eliminate any obstacle."

Both Garrick and Alyssa sat there in silence. "Then his voice changed and became very cordial, and he said to give his best to both of you."

"How certain are you of the words he used, June?" Garrick was concerned over what he had heard but wanted to make sure he wasn't analyzing a paraphrase instead of the actual wording.

"I may not have direct quotes on every bit of it, but I can tell you that 'recouping his investment' and 'eliminating any obstacles' are exact phrases."

"You never got caller ID on the florist shop's phone line, did you?" Garrick injected. June just shook her head. She had no idea what number he was calling from. "I've been through the books, June; there were no investments made to New Glory Gems by any outside person. Is he just referring to the time he worked in the store?"

"The way he worded it, Garrick, I got the impression that he felt there had been an ongoing and more recent investment," June explained. "Greg would never have knowingly accepted anything from him, though."

"From what Greg told me over the years, I would agree. We probably should report this to the police, June. Just in case." Garrick tried to make the suggestion as gently as possible.

"You're probably right." June looked so tired that Alyssa felt that asking her to make that call herself was demanding too much. She glanced at Garrick, who instinctively understood.

"How about I call the police station and have them send one of the guys over here and they can talk to you while Alyssa and I are still here?" June nodded, so Garrick made the call. It was about four o'clock before a police officer arrived to take the details concerning the call.

Alyssa ordered Chinese for the three of them. It arrived about a half hour after the police had left. Details had been documented and a report would be filed. In the meantime, she would make sure her mother was calm and well fed. That was really all she could do right now.

Monday morning Garrick was on his own at the store. Alyssa had decided to spend the morning with her mother, and Garrick had agreed to that wholeheartedly. After their record-breaking attendance on Saturday, things were quiet. Alyssa had suspected that would be the case, so it had been a good day for her to decide to spend some time with her mom. June typically took Mondays off unless it was close to Valentine's Day or in peak wedding season, in which case, many rental returns came back on Monday, making for a hectic beginning to the week.

Since it was so slow, Garrick was able to get a few things lined up. He researched a new laptop so Alyssa could have her personal one back. He also investigated some software options that were available for jewelry design. He had always sketched his designs by hand but was intrigued by some of the products the market had to offer.

Garrick had asked Alyssa if she would join him at the Monday night seniors' event he had planned. They were having a potluck dinner followed by a Crokinole party. She had a couple of reservations about the evening.

"I'm not sure what I will have time to prepare for the potluck."

"I wouldn't worry about that. These seniors have time, and they bring lots. I usually just take care of the tea and coffee, and there is always food left over—oodles of food." Garrick's reassurance did not remove the concern from Alyssa's face.

"And I have never played Crokinole. Is it easy?"

"There is not one of the folks who wouldn't be pleased to teach you and go over the rules with you. They love to show off what they know, and yes, it is easy. Unless you flick the wooden disc, and it hits one of the pegs. For some reason, that tends to hurt your finger, even though it doesn't hit it until after your finger is no longer involved in the shot." Garrick was shaking his head.

"Why did I not play it as a kid?"

"Don't know. Your grandfather enjoyed it, but maybe he didn't start playing it until later in life. The game has been around for well over a hundred years, though. There's even a World Crokinole Championship held annually in Canada."

"Really? Well in that case, I need to get up to speed." Alyssa's agreement to come made Garrick's day. Since he needed to start the coffee before everyone arrived, he and Alyssa headed straight to the community center from work. Alyssa set the tables with the placemats, napkins, and cutlery. They set the plates on the food table, and the cups went on the coffee and tea table.

By 6:00 p.m., all the regulars were pouring in with such an assortment of food that Garrick thought Alyssa would burst into laughter. "You were right. I didn't need to worry about bringing food."

Garrick stood back and watched a couple of older gentlemen give Alyssa instruction on the finer aspects of Crokinole. They explained how to shoot the wooden disc to avoid the pain to which Garrick had alluded. The rules were explained in detail, and with some practice shots, Alyssa began to show some real promise.

"Looks like we have a new Crokinole expert," Garrick commented as he stood behind her while she lined up a shot. She missed it and huffed, accusing Garrick of breaking her concentration with his unsolicited comments. Her complaints were made in jest, and he loved that she was enjoying herself with this special group of people.

Since they had brought separate cars in the morning, Garrick wouldn't have the opportunity to drive Alyssa home and give her the goodnight kiss that he so desperately wanted to. After everyone had left and the cleanup was complete, Garrick watched as Alyssa gave one last glance around to ensure everything was done. He was still gazing at her when her eyes passed back to him. "Did you enjoy yourself tonight?"

"Oh, are you kidding? Mr. Reynolds is a card. He had me in stitches the whole night." She walked to where he stood and added, "I like your friends."

"Yep, I've got good taste." The truth extended to people beyond the group of seniors. He tipped his head to the side and studied her lovely face. "I'm getting very attached to you."

"How do you know you are getting attached?" He reached out and wrapped his arms around her waist.

"Let's see. I can't wait to see you in the morning. I look forward to us working together each day. I'm anxious when we are apart. Oh, and I get a little jealous when Mr. Reynolds gets so much of your attention." Alyssa smiled at his joking.

He might not have ever let go of her had his cell phone not sounded. She pulled away from him to allow the phone to be answered. He glanced at the call display and didn't recognize the number. "Garrick Samuels."

"Garrick, dear, it's your mother." He immediately stiffened.

"How did you get this number?"

"Oh, that's not important. What is important is that I wanted to get together with you. We haven't had a chance to really resolve some of the past, and I want to make a fresh start with you." The sugary sweet voice was repulsive to Garrick. He knew he needed to keep his face from showing his reaction, but he was not sure if he was being successful.

"Is that right? Why now?"

"I mentioned to you that I have changed, and it's true. I was not a good mother before and I admit it, but I would like a second chance. Would you be willing to get together? I know you probably are not ready to have people recognize our relationship. If you would like, we could meet at your store. That would be more private. In a half hour say?"

"Tonight?"

"Why not? This is long overdue already."

"No, not tonight. Tomorrow night nine p.m."

"Very well. Tomorrow night." Garrick ended the call and looked at Alyssa.

"Just to let you know, partner, tomorrow we will be installing video surveillance equipment at Gems. It will be costly but, at this point, necessary."

"Who was on the phone, Garrick?" Alyssa was concerned by the side of the conversation she had been able to hear.

"Trouble. Time to go home."

"No, you don't. Who was on the phone?"

"My mother. She wants to do some bonding, so she says." There was extreme skepticism in his voice.

"And you don't believe her?"

"I don't believe anything she says."

"Okay. You are meeting with your mother tomorrow night at nine p.m. So why are we installing video surveillance at Gems?" Alyssa had not made the connection.

"That's where she wants to meet." Garrick stared at Alyssa waiting for her reaction.

"She wants to mend fences at your place of work?" Disbelief washed over her face.

With a flat laugh, Garrick shook his head. "No, she doesn't want to mend fences. Enough discussion about Jillian."

"Oh, I forgot to tell you." Alyssa paused and then said, "I think I met her on Saturday."

"Where?"

"She was the woman I almost collided with Saturday afternoon. She's tall, well dressed, well spoken, staying at a bed and breakfast outside of town, right?"

"What did she say to you, Alyssa?"

"Let me think." She slowly recalled the short conversation and then continued. "She said her name was Jillian *Chadwick*."

"Chadwick. That was my grandmother's maiden name. I wonder if she had it legally changed." Jillian had lived a life where normalcy had been refracted to deviance. Did she really expect him to believe that another hidden refraction could change her back? He paused, reigning in his thoughts of Jillian. "We should head home. I'm going to have an early day tomorrow, arranging for some good equipment."

"Does that mean you will be driving in on your own tomorrow?" Garrick could see there was a bit of disappointment in her face, and his expression softened.

"I can make most of the early arrangements from home. We can drive into work together. You are welcome to stick around and be completely bored watching me install the equipment after we close. Then I'll drive you home before I meet with Jillian." His hand had come up and rested on Alyssa's cheek, and he was sinking into her eyes.

"Would it be all right for me to stay at Gems while you talk to her?" Alyssa asked the question cautiously.

Garrick was against Jillian having any contact with Alyssa. "I would rather not have you there, but let me think about it." He was completely lost in her eyes, and he bent his head and kissed her. She was definitely getting under his skin.

The next morning Garrick started making his plans for the day. He determined what type of equipment he wanted and was on the phone to a couple of retailers by 8:30 a.m. He arranged for the required equipment to be couriered to Gems by four. There would be two cameras in the main showroom that would provide the necessary surveillance of the doors and the showcases. There would be another camera in the hallway of the back portion of the building that would capture any activity in or out of the four rooms and restroom.

Picking Alyssa up at 9:30, he drove down to Gems opening at the normal time to a limited business flow. While they busied themselves in the shop, Garrick joked with Alyssa, "You know after I install this equipment, we will have to limit our personal interactions to the rooms in the back. Otherwise, we will be recorded on camera." His eyebrows raised up and down in a teasing fashion.

She smiled and blushed. He hadn't seen her blush often, and he got a charge out of it. "Have you given any more thought to me staying here tonight while you talk with your mother?" Garrick's joking disposition disappeared, and she could see him physically stiffen.

"Let's call her Jillian. I don't think of her as my mother, and I don't want others in town to connect us like that."

"All right."

"Why do you want to be here?" Garrick had thought endlessly about the two women interacting. He had no idea what Alyssa's goal was in being part of the meeting.

"Well, I know this will sound absurd, but if she is as unscrupulous as you've suggested, I'm worried about you being here alone with her. I am a firm supporter of the 'safety in numbers' motto." He could see a wavering smile trying to form on her face. She was genuinely afraid for him. Did she really think she could protect him from Jillian?

With a pensive look, he stared at her without moving. "Would you be satisfied if someone other than you was here with me to meet with her?"

She hesitated, obviously wanting to be included and hear what was said, but he could see the resignation settling in her face. "All right, but who were you thinking of?"

"Let me call Mark. He knows some of Jillian's history, and you know he and I look out for one another. Plus, having an FBI special agent in the store while she is there is likely to discourage her from causing trouble." He went over and stood close to her, taking her hands in his. "I'll go call him right now and arrange it. I will drive you over there, leave you with Laura, and bring him back here with me tonight. Then when we're finished here, I'll take him home and pick you up. That way you can talk to me and see for yourself that I am fine, and I'll tell you everything about the meeting. I promise." He looked at her for approval with pleading eyes. She nodded in agreement, and he went to the office to call Mark.

Alyssa looked delighted as she entered the front door of Gems, involved in the clandestine testing of Garrick's newly installed surveillance cameras. Garrick watched on the monitors from the office and snickered at the way Alyssa slinked around the showroom trying to act like a disreputable suspect. She had to be the furthest thing from disreputable that he had ever come across.

As she walked through the doorway into the backrooms, Garrick switched from the two front monitors to the back hallway monitor and decided that for complete coverage, he would invest in one more camera and monitor. For the moment, though, they were protected, and all he needed to check now was that the images were taping properly.

It was time to get some food, though, so he and Alyssa scooted across to The Quarters for dinner. To their surprise, Mark, Laura, and Jason were just being seated in the restaurant. Laura spotted them almost immediately and quickly asked the hostess to seat them at a larger table to accommodate Garrick and Alyssa.

After dinner, it made sense for Alyssa to return with Laura and Jason to the house, and Mark joined Garrick over at Gems. They were able to confirm that the camera footage was taping, so Garrick was prepared for the evening's adventure.

"Exactly what is my role here tonight, Garr?" Mark had readily agreed to help him out but was looking for some clarification. "Am I playing good cop or bad cop?" He smiled at the thought.

"Alyssa just wants you playing protector," he said, enunciating each syllable in a robotic tone. "Nothing more involved than super-hero stuff."

"You know, I've never actually met Jillian. I would have accepted this invitation even if you wanted me to serve tea." The men were still exchanging wisecracks when the front door of Gems opened and in walked Jillian.

Chapter 10

The meeting with Jillian had been short. Mark's presence and his credentials had surprised her but had not alarmed her. Garrick had explained that Mark was there to assist him in testing the new surveillance equipment, drawing Jillian's attention to the added security.

She had played the part well, even congratulating Garrick on the new equipment. "You can never have too much security," she had said. There had been no bonding or rebuilding of the broken relationship. Clearly, Garrick was correct in his assessment that she was not interested in that at all.

Both Garrick and Alyssa looked forward to a few regular dull days since the last few had been perpetual commotion. That's what they got. In fact, the next two weeks were wonderfully normal. They spent days together at Gems except on the occasional day when Garrick needed to provide handyman expertise around town. Evenings were also spent together either at one of their homes, at June's, at Mark and Laura's, or with the seniors' group. Sundays they went to church together and then spent the rest of their day off enjoying each other's company.

There had been no further contact with Jillian. The men conjectured that she had been in the store just long enough to understand the security measures and figured there was no point in coming back.

Neither had there been any further contact from Andrew. No one knew whether to take that as a positive sign or just a warning of a predator lying in wait for its prey. Whatever the reasons for being drenched in uneventfulness, they were soaking it all in.

Columbus Day weekend had arrived, and Garrick was making final preparations for the seniors' trip to Pigeon Forge. After church on Sunday, both Alyssa and Garrick had a long list of items to do. Alyssa had put off going through everything in her grandfather's office, and it was time to take care of it. So, with an afternoon ahead of her and no planned interruptions, she attacked the one room in the house that scared her the most.

As she sat down behind the desk, she listened briefly to how extremely quiet the large house was. It was peaceful, but immediately her thoughts went to Garrick. She was captivated by him, a feeling she had never experienced with any other man. The sensations that overcame her when she pictured him or thought of the way he touched her were like electric circuits overloading. She planned to spend some time with him on Monday night after he got home from the bus trip, but in the meantime, she needed to focus on the duties at hand.

She started at the desk. Opening each drawer, she sorted and decided what was worth keeping versus what would be discarded. For the most part, her grandfather's desk was as organized as the paperwork had been at the store. There was little to throw out, as most everything had a purpose.

Behind the desk, there were built-in cabinets. Most shelves held reading materials. She remembered as a teenager being mesmerized by the scope of subject matter that he had accumulated. There were classics as well as contemporary fiction. Shelf after shelf was filled with nonfiction too. She had read some of them but had not even scratched the surface, so she would keep the extensive library intact.

Doors on the lower portion of the cabinets concealed deep drawers. These had probably been designed to eliminate the need for additional filing cabinets. Sizing them up, she suspected they would take the most time. Since everything had been pulled out and strewn around the room during the break-in when she was in New York, Garrick had gathered and stacked, but the contents were unlikely to be in any order. That would mean painfully going through everything page by page.

She started on the daunting task midafternoon. She emptied the shredding box four times before coming to the end of the drawers. There was nothing particularly interesting. She had come across receipts and tax documents that would have to be kept, but nothing of any other real significance. She adjusted a couple of the pictures on the walls, as they seemed a little crooked, and then glanced back at the bookshelves. Perhaps she would select a book and spend some time just reading.

As she scanned over the books, she pulled a couple out that looked interesting, and then something caught her eye. It was the hardcover edition of *The Adventures of Olive Outterridge*. She had loved the stories of Olive Outterridge when she was little. Her grandfather had read from that book to her on countless occasions. Thinking about it now, he must have bought it just for her because he had not had girls of his own and no other grandchildren.

Setting the other two books down on the desk behind her, she pulled it off the shelf and stared at it. She smiled as the memories flooded back, and she left the study with the children's book and went in search of the perfect comfortable couch to curl up in the corner of.

Alyssa sighed as she read the last page in the book. She still got a kick out of the adventures on which Olive found herself. Flipping the last page, she paused as she saw a diagram sketched on the inside of the back cover. "Odd." She looked closely at it. Although it was only cryptically labeled, it was obvious almost immediately that the diagram was a floor plan of New Glory Gems. She could pick out the showroom, the office, the two large backrooms and the other small room. The diagram had simply *A* beside it. The only other label on the diagram was in the small room that had been locked. Beside one wall was written *B*.

Alyssa was certain she had stopped breathing. Of course, there was no connection between this *B* and the *Vault B* on the mystery shipping slips. She snickered aloud. "No connection." And she shook her head. After all, she had been in the room, and there was no vault, much to their disappointment. She got up, returned the book to the study, and placed the other two books she had left on the desk back in place. It was getting late, and she prepared for bed.

After a quick call to Garrick to wish him a last-minute safe and enjoyable trip with his friends, she turned out the light to get to sleep.

Instead of sleeping, though, she kept seeing the sketch in the back of the Olive Outterridge book. After lying in bed for what seemed like hours, she must have finally fallen off to sleep, because she woke at 8:00 a.m., realizing that Garrick and crew would be about to pull out for their adventure.

She locked the front door of Gems with a smile. The day had been more profitable than she had anticipated. That was the way with retail ventures, of course. She could project sales and study trends, but when it came right down to it, the consumer had to put the money down and make the purchase. Consumers were predictable in large markets over short periods of time and in small ones like this over long periods of time, but the small market on a daily basis was up and down.

Alyssa moved to the back, intent on examining the small locked room after her discovery of the previous night. Obtaining the key from the vault, she unlocked the small bedroom and entered.

Standing in the doorway, she retrieved a mental image of the diagram in the book. From this position, the *B* would have been where the dresser sat. Her eyebrows dipped as she thought. Alyssa walked over to the dresser and tried to peer behind it, but could not see anything. It was set right up against the wall, which was not surprising since the room was as small as it was.

She managed to push the front corner enough for the back to inch out from the wall on one side. Still unable to see anything, she wrapped both hands around the back of the dresser and pulled it out farther from the wall. She did the same on the other side of the dresser, until it was out about two feet. Alyssa's eyes scanned the wall and then the floor. Her heart sped erratically as she saw the floor.

She needed to move the dresser just a little farther out to uncover fully what she had discovered. *There.* She stared down at a flush metal door in the floor with a recessed handle.

Slowly lifting the door, Alyssa saw a floor safe with a combination lock. "Vault B," she whispered to herself. She wished Garrick were here to share her excitement. Unable to contain her enthusiasm, she raced to get the card with the numbers on it from the main vault.

Carefully turning the combination lock to the numbers on the card, she tried the handle, and with a click, it turned. She opened it, and with eyes wide, Alyssa stared at a valuable cache of jewels.

"I'd be happy to come over and help out with the repairs to your back porch, Mrs. Sinclair. How about I call you tomorrow when I know what my schedule is like and we'll figure out a time?" Garrick was sitting in between Mrs. Sinclair and Mrs. Van De Laar at the Trail Ridge Restaurant for dinner on the way home from Pigeon Forge.

The day had been outstanding. The journey had been uneventful, exactly as everyone had hoped. The show was very entertaining, and the entire group was in a jovial mood, even the couple of souls that rarely allowed good humor to manifest.

"Oh, that would be wonderful, Garrick dear. Yes. Call me tomorrow, and we can set up a time. Say, have I ever mentioned my granddaughter Amy to you? She is sweet. You two would make a smart couple."

"Yes, Mrs. Sinclair. You have mentioned Amy before. I am seeing someone else right now, though."

"He's seeing that lovely Alyssa Mason." Mrs. Van De Laar leaned around Garrick and spoke to Mrs. Sinclair. Garrick smiled to himself. Mrs. Van De Laar's declining hearing was such a ruse.

"Alyssa Mason? Do I know her?" Mrs. Sinclair was yelling back around Garrick in consideration of Mrs. Van De Laar's poor hearing.

"Yes, Sadie, Garrick has brought her out to the seniors' program a few times."

"Really? I wonder how that slipped my mind." Garrick shook his head in delight.

Garrick's cell phone rang. "Excuse me, ladies." He moved away from the noisy table and answered his phone. "Garrick Samuels."

"Hey there. How's the day going?" The voice hit him hard with its sultry tone.

"It *was* going great. Now it is going even better. How has your day been, Alyssa?"

"It's been interesting actually. I made some sales that a certain co-owner of New Glory Gems will be delighted to hear about."

"I hope you are not going to suggest we start working on commission there, because you seem to have a way with the customers."

"No, of course not. We all have our small ways that we contribute. It just happens that I have contributed much today and you haven't."

He loved her teasing. "Tauntress," he shot back.

Alyssa giggled. "I was wondering if you would swing by the shop when you get back to town."

What is she up to? he wondered. He would have preferred to rendezvous at her place or his.

"I can do that. Is everything okay? You didn't have any problems today, did you?"

"No problems." Her voice sounded light and unconcerned.

"And you would tell me if there had been problems, right?"

With half a laugh, he heard her quietly say, "Eventually." Rolling his eyes, he gave up. She sounded in far too good of a mood to have had trouble crop up, so he would comply with her request without any further interrogation.

"Do you want me to call you when we pull in, or are you staying at Gems until I arrive?"

"Actually I think I might pop home, so if you can call me when you are about ten minutes out, I will meet you at the store."

He had no idea what would warrant her driving back to the store tonight when they could just go in a few minutes early tomorrow morning, but he was not going to dampen her upbeat disposition. "Okay, I'll call you later."

He returned to the table with a huge smile on his face. Mr. Jeffries sat across from him and saw the grin. "Was that your sweetie on the phone, Garrick?"

"Yes, sir, it was."

"You've been in New Glory for quite a few years now, haven't you, Garrick?"

"Yes, that's right, I have been."

"I don't recall you ever having taken to a young lady like this before."

"No, sir, I don't think I ever have."

"Well, you don't let her get away, ya hear?"

"I think that is excellent advice, Mr. Jeffries."

Garrick pulled out his phone and dialed Alyssa when they got close to home. He heard her sweet voice greet him, and he realized he could not wait to see her. How could he have become that attached to her? It had just been a day and a half since they had lunch together, and yet he felt as if they had been apart for ages. "Hey, sweetheart. We'll be pulling into New Glory in about ten minutes." Her voice was elated, and he was perplexed by what was up. "See you at the store. Bye."

Unable to keep the conversation private while on the bus, Garrick's traveling companions heard him mention the store. "Why would you go to the store at this time of night?" *They don't miss anything*, he thought, shaking his head.

"Just need to check on something before heading home. Nothing serious." If they only knew he was asking himself the very same question, they would have delved deeper into the possible reasons and expected a full report next time they saw him. It was just their way. They all thought of him as their adopted son, and that meant a great deal to Garrick.

Less than ten minutes later, they arrived. The bus pulled to a stop behind the town hall just off Glory Boulevard. Once all the folks had reached their cars or been picked up and the bus was driving out of the parking lot, Garrick climbed into his car and drove down Glory Boulevard to Jefferson Way so he could pull in behind New Glory Gems.

Alyssa's car was there, which did not surprise him, but did anger him. He had chosen to park back there for the very reason that he knew she would do the same. Parking in a dimly lit back parking lot at night instead of the brightly lit Main Street, where there would still be activity, was not the safest choice she could make. He would have to review small-town safety with her, although admittedly, the chances of anything happening in New Glory were remote.

"Alyssa?" Garrick called as he came through the back door. She poked her head out of the office and with a warm and enticing smile walked toward him.

She wrapped her arms around his neck and stretched up on her toes. "This probably sounds silly, but I really missed you." Her dark eyes had this power over him, and he felt as if he was losing himself in them. His arms had automatically encircled her, and he was bringing her in tight.

"Not silly." Garrick swallowed hard. "I hated not spending more time with you yesterday, and although today was great, I was counting the minutes until I would have you right here against me."

Alyssa's smile was one of gratification. Garrick bent his head, slowly shifting his gaze from her eyes to her lips, and then as his lips came in contact with her mouth, his eyes closed. The kiss was easy and gentle to start, communicating unspoken words. He heard a soft sigh, and that small sound seemed to release a passion he had been withholding. He turned and pressed her against the wall.

He could sense her surprise at the maneuver. He was surprised at it himself. The soft sounds she made pinned between the wall and his strong body did not reflect discomfort or distress, though. They communicated pleasure, a pleasure that was dangerous. He knew he had to pull back, but he was coming up short in gathering enough resolve to stop.

Alyssa's arms had dropped down, and her fingers gripped the front of his shirt. He cupped her cheek as he tilted his head to deepen the kiss from another angle. The heat between the two was smoldering, but he couldn't live with himself if he allowed this to continue any further.

Full of disappointment and regret, he slowly pulled back from her enough to gaze into those amazing eyes again. "Okay, so we are not going to be able to spend more than twelve hours apart from now on, because the reunion is just too volatile." He tried to show a partial smile. Watching Alyssa try to regain her composure was almost as painful as pulling away from her had been.

"You stopped. I'm not sure I wanted you to stop." The words came out choppy and breathless, and the admission almost shot flames up around them. They just stared into each other's eyes for the longest time, trying to regulate their breathing.

"So you had a good day," Alyssa began in an obvious attempt to get their minds on something else.

Garrick smiled. "Yes, it was quite a day." With an even wider grin, he added, "Mr. Jeffries doesn't think I should let you get away."

Alyssa blushed, and with a shy smile now, she answered, "Are you going to take his advice?" She was in a playful mood tonight.

"My father always told me I should respect my elders." He knew the implication would be clear to Alyssa without saying anything more, but he knew that a day was coming, sooner than he would have predicted, that he would make his intentions toward this woman crystal clear to her. "Enough teasing, Alyssa. Why did you want me to meet you here? I am sure it wasn't so you could assault me with your feminine wiles for the camera."

Alyssa's eyes grew several sizes, and then her head jerked automatically to the camera that was capturing every movement that they made. Garrick began to laugh, as he was certain she hadn't thought about that. "Garrick, can you erase it?" She sounded frantic and flustered. "Can you? Can you erase what the camera recorded?"

As Garrick saw it, he had two choices. He could tell her the truth that it could easily be erased and he would deal with it in the morning, or he could string her along a little. The devil really must have had his claws in him tonight because the idea of working her up really appealed to him. He let out some forced air and shook his head. "I got top-of-the-line equipment, Alyssa. Tamperproof. I could probably delete a section off our copy, but I wouldn't be able to touch the master copy."

"Master copy? There are two copies?"

"Well, yes, we have a copy, but there's a direct feed to the security company, so it would already have been copied onto their servers." Panic had settled in, and Garrick did not have the heart to further this deception. "Alyssa," he said with half a laugh, "I'm pulling your leg. There's no second copy, and I can erase the condemning evidence."

"You were joking?" Her eyes narrowed, and Garrick wondered if he should take cover.

"I'm sorry. Will you forgive me?"

With lips pursed, she said, "I'll have to think about it." She turned and walked into the office. Of course, Garrick followed. "All right, I guess I can forgive you. Have a seat. I want to show you something." Her smile was back. Finally, they must have gotten around to the reason he was here.

Alyssa continued as she pulled a children's book from behind the desk. "Yesterday after I had gone through Grandpa's office, I was looking over the books that he has, and this one caught my eye." She handed it to Garrick.

Garrick's eyes narrowed while he inspected Olive Outterridge and he shot her a questioning glance.

"Did you ever read Olive Outterridge when you were little, Garrick?" She had a delighted smile on her face. He shook his head. "Didn't expect so, since it is really a book directed toward young girls."

"So why did Greg have Olive Outterridge on his bookshelf?"

"He used to read it to me often when I was little. I loved it. So when I saw it, it brought back so many good memories. That's why I spent last evening reading the whole book cover to cover, all one hundred and sixty pages."

"Is that why you are in such a good mood? You've had your fix of Olive Outterridge?"

She chuckled at his questions. "When I got to the end of the book, I noticed that something had been sketched on the inside back cover." She nodded to Garrick to turn to the back and look for himself.

When he opened the book, he examined the drawing much the way Alyssa had. Since he was sitting in Gems, he actually turned the book so that the floor plan faced the same direction as the actual building. When he noticed the *B*, he shot her a quick understanding glance. "Come with me," she said.

She had the key to the room in her hand and, unlocking it, pushed it open and let Garrick walk in first. She had flicked the light for him so he would not walk into the dresser that was now sitting in the middle of the room. She had left the flush floor door lifted. Slipping by Garrick, she knelt and, as before, used the numbers on the small card to unlock the safe. Smiling proudly, she moved out of the way so Garrick could see for himself what she had discovered.

"You found them." He could now understand her elated mood.

Garrick stared at the cache of jewels almost as if in a trance. His smile started to grow as the news sunk in.

"We will have to match these against the shipping slips, but I expect it will be one of our easier tasks," Alyssa said. Garrick's eyes moved from the jewels to Alyssa, and his smile began to disappear. "What is it? What's wrong Garrick?"

"You're not planning on doing that tonight, are you?"

"Did you have other plans?" She was back to teasing him. He was back to smiling.

"As a matter of fact, I do have other plans." He closed down the safe and locked it, backed Alyssa out of the small room, and locked that door. As they exited out the back of New Glory Gems, Garrick began his lecture. "Now that we know where the jewels are and that they are safe, let's review safety rules for you and *parking at night*."

The rest of the week was busy. Garrick had to deal with Mrs. Sinclair's porch, as it was in worse shape than she had thought. Business had stayed brisk all week, which was a delight, but it meant that Alyssa was busy with customers and Garrick had to start working on some new pieces since their inventory was starting to diminish.

By Friday, they had not made much progress with the mysterious shipments. At 8:00 p.m. that night when they locked up, Garrick was anxious to talk to Alyssa. "Mark and Laura were supposed to get back today from their trip. Alyssa, I want to bring Mark in on tracking the origin of those jewels."

Alyssa looked pensive. "Why?"

"That many jewels had to have come across state lines, which makes it FBI jurisdiction. We won't get anywhere if we just involve the local police."

"All right, but you're not going to call him tonight about it, are you?"

"No, they need to get settled and spend some time with Jason. Are you okay with me talking to Mark about it?"

"I think I have to be. Regardless of whether Grandpa handled them the proper way or not, we have a responsibility to."

"Hey, how was the trip?" Garrick slid into the pew at church on Sunday beside Mark. Both Laura and Mark were tanned and looked relaxed. A week in St. Lucia must have been a great getaway for the couple.

"Garrick, it was fantastic. If it wasn't that we missed Jason so much, I'm not sure we would have come back."

"What? You didn't miss us?" Garrick joked with his good friend.

"Nothing personal, Garr, but you don't hold a candle to my beautiful wife on a secluded beach."

"Would the three of you like to come back to my place after the service for lunch? I've got something I was hoping to talk to you about before you get back to the office tomorrow."

"I'll ask my social director. Just one moment." As Mark turned and discussed lunch plans with his wife, Garrick glanced at Alyssa, who sat next to him. He was happier than he had ever been sitting here between his best friend and her. *Her.* He would not take the title of best friend away from Mark. However, the truth was Alyssa was his best friend now. She, however, was in a class of best friends that was separate from Mark Wilson. She was much more than a best friend. "She says our calendar is free and we would be happy to come over for a while." Nods confirmed the arrangements as the service began.

"That was wonderful, Garrick." Laura had a way of lifting anyone's spirits even if they were already high. Jason had crawled up on Mark's lap. It was obvious that he had missed his parents, although the reports were that the little guy had a great week with his grandparents.

"Thanks, Laura. I slaved all morning on this, so I expected you to appreciate it." He followed the comment with a wink. Turning to Mark, he said, "Mind if you and Jason and I take a walk? I wanted to talk something over with you."

Alyssa stood and started clearing the dishes from the table. "We'll clean up here while you men folk move along."

"Come on, Jason. It is time for us *men folk* to make our escape."

"It's not an escape when I just released you," Alyssa stated.

They had to get coats on, as the weather had turned colder overnight. The two men and the young boy ventured out under grey skies that threatened unfriendly conditions. Garrick began to tell Mark about some of the background concerning the hoard of jewels they had discovered stashed under the floor of one of the back rooms. "I don't see how all those jewels just materialized based on the paperwork we have. I also don't see how, if they are stolen, they were all lifted in state. Could you make a case for this to be a possible FBI investigation?"

They had arrived at the playground just down the street, and Jason was on the run to the slide. "I can't fault your logic on jurisdiction. That many jewels points to an organized crime ring that would never just operate within one state's boundaries. I'll talk to my field office manager first thing tomorrow. When I left on vacation, there were not any high-priority cases waiting for me, but that was a week ago. First, we'd need to investigate what records we have of unrecovered stolen gems that match your list. Do you have a complete list?"

"We worked late yesterday to finish it. I have a copy at the house. You can take it with you."

"Are the jewels secured?" Mark inquired.

With a slight chuckle, Garrick answered, "I would say so."

By midweek, Garrick had gotten word from Mark that a high-priority job had been waiting for him but that his field office manager was prepared to start looking into their case as soon as Mark finished this current assignment. Garrick had an uneasy feeling about the delay, but they would take whatever help they could when it was available at this point.

He was spending most of his days now working in the lapidary area on several pieces. He wanted to bolster the current offerings but also wanted some special pieces to start putting out closer to the holidays. People were typically willing to spend more on Christmas than some other occasions. He also had a custom engagement ring he was working on for a couple that lived not far from New Glory.

It was that custom job that had him thinking of other designs for engagement rings too. He would work up some designs, he decided, and see which ones he would create first.

At lunchtime, Alyssa came back to see his progress and was thrilled. She reflected on the enthusiasm she had felt when she would see her grandfather's new creations and delighted at feeling the same way now. "Is this for the engagement ring?" she asked as she lifted a design that sat next to a beautiful setting.

"Yes, it's going to be fantastic. Zoe is going to be swept off her feet when Kevin puts it on her finger." He was smiling, picturing the scene in his mind.

"Oh, Garrick, you are a romantic, aren't you?"

"Sort of have to be to create jewelry, don't you?"

"Are you going to want some lunch soon?"

"Probably need about a half hour to finish up what I am doing. Can you wait, or do you want to go ahead and get something now?"

"No, I can wait. I won't leave until you are freed up back here anyway. Otherwise, if a customer comes in, you would have to drop what you are doing."

Pausing, he looked at her. "Thanks, Alyssa. I won't be long."

Garrick could hear the front door open just after Alyssa returned to the main showroom. Perhaps she would make another sale before lunch, he mused. Not many minutes passed, however, and Alyssa appeared in the doorway once more. Her typical carefree smile that he was used to seeing was absent from her face. "What's wrong?"

Alyssa stood in the doorway, holding an opened envelope and a folded sheet of paper. "Garrick, the mail just arrived." Her eyebrows creased downward with concern, and her voice trembled. "I think you need to see this."

Garrick grew apprehensive studying the troubled look Alyssa cast. He gently set down the tools he was working with and stood from his work chair. Moving cautiously toward her and without saying a word, he took the paper from her. He unfolded the sheet and silently read the disturbing message that was printed on the paper.

> I'm back, and I want what is mine.
> Deny me, and you will lose everything.

Alyssa's voice was barely a whisper. "Is it from Uncle Andrew?" Garrick could see a shiver run through her body as she wrapped her arms around herself. He looked back at the note, continuing to try to make sense of the words. Now he reached over and carefully took the envelope from Alyssa. Postmarked right here in New Glory.

"I don't know. I think we should have lunch with your mother and see if she can think of anyone else that would feel they deserve a share of the estate."

Alyssa nodded. "All right. I'll go call her. Can we go now? It's been slow in here today. I am fine with closing for the day if we need to."

"I don't expect your mom will have that many ideas to share with us that it will take all afternoon." He tried to smile at her, and he drew his hand up to her cheek. He wanted to comfort her as much as possible, but he could quickly see she was not feeling very consolable at that moment.

Garrick could hear her first lock the front door and probably put up the *Closed* sign, and then he could hear her on the phone to her mother. He was still holding the paper and wondered if Mark was even reachable. He had no idea where this current assignment would have taken him. It would be completely "need to know," as all his work was. Laura wouldn't even know, but she might know if he could be reached by cell phone.

Pulling his cell out, he called Laura. "Laura, how's my girl?" He and Laura had been fast friends when they first met. That was one reason he had brought Mark to New Glory to meet her. He just had a feeling that they would be perfect together.

"Oh, Garrick. I'm fine. Is everything going okay with you and Alyssa?" Her lighthearted and easy tone was always genuine, and Garrick appreciated it even more when things were tense. He also got a kick out of the way she automatically grouped him and Alyssa together.

"Things are fine." He knew his voice had faltered on those words. "Laura, is Mark reachable by cell this week?"

There was a pause. "Yes, he is. Garrick, I can tell by your voice that not everything is fine. Can I do anything to help?"

"Nothing you can do or that you need to worry about. We're fine. I just need to ask Mark for some advice. Gotta run, Laura. Thanks."

Garrick immediately pulled up Mark's number and dialed. "Mark Wilson," he heard on the other end of the phone. He felt better already.

"Mark, we have a small issue at Gems. Do you have a couple of minutes?" Garrick knew he would be in the middle of some high-pressure situation this week and did not want to break in at a bad time.

"What's up?"

"We got an anonymous note in the mail postmarked New Glory." Garrick relayed the message and then added, "Mark, I'm not sure if we should notify the police or if we should wait for you to get back."

"That's easy; call the police immediately. That is a threatening note, and there is nothing to tie it to those mysterious jewels. This could be totally unrelated to what we will be investigating when I get back. Plus, it might be another ten days before I get home."

"Okay. I'll call them. Thanks, Mark." Alyssa was standing at the door, listening. She looked no less shell-shocked than she had moments earlier.

"Mom said she can meet us at The Quarters for a quick lunch if we go now. I didn't tell her what we are going to discuss. That was Mark on the phone?"

"Yeah. He said to call the police about the note. Let's go talk to your mom, and then I may just drop in at the police station." With a sigh, he walked to Alyssa and gave her a hug. "It's going to be okay. Let's go."

June sat staring at the page she held in her hands. She obviously was registering a great deal of concern over it as well. "What are your thoughts so far?" she hesitantly asked.

"My initial reaction was Uncle Andrew."

"Would there be anyone else, June, that you know of that would have a possible claim on Greg's estate?" June's shoulders slouched, her eyebrows dipped low, and she pursed her lips in deep thought.

"We haven't seen Andrew in twenty-five years. I have no idea what his life has been like or who he has spent it with. He could have six children or no children. I would have no idea." She paused for a moment. "Have you considered that it might not be related to the estate?"

Of course, that was possible. Garrick was not sure what scenario to consider first: the vengeful disinherited, the unacknowledged descendant, the jewel thief intent of retrieving his stash, or some scenario involving his less-than-angelic mother. With a defeated tone, Garrick answered, "June, anything is possible."

Chapter 11

"Garrick. Ah, Miss Mason. Pleasure to see ya both. It—it is a pleasure, right? Just a social call?" The officer lost his smile. "Y'all aren't here on police business, are ya?"

"Wish it was just a 'stop by and say hi' visit, but it's not. Is Detective Taylor working today?" Alyssa was perfectly content to allow Garrick to do all the talking in this arena. She would just answer any questions directed at her.

"Well, as a matter of fact, he was s'posed to be off today but had some work to finish up on, so he just arrived about half an hour ago. Is it urgent?"

"Yes, I'm afraid it could be. We need to see him."

Jasper Willows, the officer at the front desk, picked up the phone and dialed an extension. They could hear a gruff voice answer loudly, "What?" That was far from the disposition that Alyssa had experienced in any of the interactions they had had with the New Glory PD over the last few weeks, and there had been plenty.

"Garrick Samuels and Miss Mason are here, and they say it's urgent that they talk to you." More snarly sounding noises could be heard from the receiver the officer held. Jasper gave Garrick and Alyssa a sheepish smile while the sour tones continued, and he held the phone out from his ear a bit. Finally, Jasper said, "Okay, I'll tell 'em." He disconnected and turned to them. "He'll be happy to see ya. He said to go on back to his office."

Alyssa wanted to laugh. How could he possibly say the detective would be happy to see them after all the grumbling and growls they had heard? Garrick was fighting back a smile until they got out of sight of the front desk and were not yet to the detective's office. He turned to Alyssa, and she saw the huge grin displayed on his face. "It kind of makes you wonder who we should be more afraid of, this anonymous threat writer or the detective." At that, Alyssa did let a little snicker escape.

"Detective Taylor?" Garrick tapped on the door that had been left open into his office. "You must be ready to take over from the chief with an office like this." That drew a smile from the detective, and he leaned back in his chair.

"Not sure why they haven't given me a bedroom too. I spend enough nights here." Detective Taylor paused, held his bottom lip between his teeth, and then proceeded. "I am simply *afraid* to ask what the two of you are here to see me about." He closed a folder with the paperwork he had been catching up on and waited for the explanation.

Garrick pulled out the envelope and handed it to the detective. "That was delivered today around noon to Gems. Alyssa opened it and, after reading it, showed it to me. We met with her mother to see if she might have any ideas of who could be behind it. I also spoke with Mark Wilson, as he's about to start investigating an issue at Gems once he is done with his current assignment." Garrick paused. Alyssa could tell the detective needed to catch up, first with reading the brief note and then to absorb the fact that the FBI was soon going to be involved with something in his town.

As he read the note, first one eyebrow rose slightly and then both rose. "Well, I can see why we are talking today." He shook his head. "Miss Mason, did excitement like this hover around you in New York City?"

She closed her eyes briefly and then "No. Life was dull there compared to this. I always thought that people went to the big city to get their excitement quotient, but it seems to have worked in the reverse for me."

"Well, I guess we should start at the beginning. I'm going to take some notes so I don't forget any of the important details you're going to tell me. So first off, why would the FBI be investigating something at Gems?"

Garrick showed no surprise that the detective's first question related to news of FBI involvement. He proceeded to enlighten the detective on the unusual paperwork they had found when they first started inventorying the store. "We wanted to have an exact accounting of what we had in stock for sale, as well as the stones we had for creating new pieces of jewelry. However, these shipping slips were pointing at valuable resources that we couldn't account for."

"Could they just have been located somewhere else?"

"The problem was that there were no orders for the gems, no paper trail besides a shipping slip that indicated they had been received. There was no sender information either, so we had no way to follow the trail back to their origin. The paperwork also referenced a vault B, but no one, including the lawyer, had any knowledge of any other storage that Greg had. June found a key and a card with numbers on it that could have been a vault combination in Greg's safety deposit box. However, without a vault to try the combination on, it wasn't doing us much good."

"So if the FBI is getting involved, there must be good reason to think that these expensive jewels were stolen?"

"We didn't contact the FBI until we found them."

"You found them?"

"Yeah. Once we confirmed that what was recorded on the shipping slips was actually accounted for, I went to Mark with the list. The FBI is confident, after an initial review, that the jewels were stolen during a number of thefts, not only in Kentucky. Therefore, it's federal jurisdiction."

"So whoever sent them to Greg could be the one behind this threatening note." It was part statement and part question.

"Could be, but there are other possibilities too." Taylor nodded and took notes. He had been so captivated by the whole story that he was busily catching up on his notes. "What other options?"

"Well, Andrew Mason was cut from Greg's will a few years back. He could be upset about the disinheritance. Then there is the fact that we don't know where he has been or who he has been with over the last couple of decades. He could have offspring that are unhappy about the lack of inheritance."

Detective Taylor shook his head. "Well, that is three possibilities so far. We have a jewel theft ring, a disinherited son, and potentially disinherited descendants. Is that it?" His voice was bordering on sarcastic.

Alyssa believed those were the only options, so she was surprised to hear the hesitation in Garrick's voice.

"There is actually one more."

"Of course there is. Did you save the best for last?"

He ignored the detective's tone. "You might want to check on the whereabouts of Jillian Chadwick." Alyssa's head spun toward Garrick. He continued. "Jillian has been around town on and off for the last few weeks, staying at a bed and breakfast outside New Glory. She has a criminal record, is currently on probation, and should not be outside of New York State under the terms of that probation. Her criminal background is theft—high-end jewelry mainly." Alyssa drew in a silent gasp. She was unsure if the detective saw her shocked expression, though. Why hadn't Garrick told her? Did he not trust her? She continued to watch him carefully, never looking away.

"How do you know so much about this Jillian Chadwick?"

After a pause, Garrick answered, "She's my mother. The criminal record will likely show up under the name Jillian Samuels. Chadwick is a family name from a couple generations back."

"Had you considered reporting her to us, given she is breaking the law by being outside New York, or were you happy to have her around?"

"Happy? Not on your life. I was mortified when she showed up. I contacted my lawyer, and he reported it. She must be going back and forth, making excuses for the probation meetings she's missed. I don't know." He shook his head appearing disgusted.

"Okay, Miss Mason, do you have anything to add, or has Mr. Samuels covered it all?" There was no answer. Garrick turned now, seeing her still transfixed on him. Their eyes met, and in her eyes, the disappointment and hurt that he had not told her earlier would be evident.

Detective Taylor repeated his question. "Miss Mason, is there anything else you can tell me?"

"He's covered everything we know." Alyssa's tone was cold. He had covered more than she knew.

"Okay, we'll do some checks on those people that you are concerned about and see if we can eliminate a few of the possibilities. I'll be in touch."

Garrick and Alyssa moved silently from the detective's office. Once they were outside the station, Garrick turned to Alyssa. He reached out to stop her. Still she said nothing. "I can tell you are upset, Alyssa," Garrick said.

"Why hadn't you told me about your mother? I gave you several chances to tell me about her, but you said nothing. A jewel thief. She was a jewel thief and we own a jewelry store and you didn't tell me." The words were becoming more emotional.

Garrick clenched his jaw. "I'm sorry. I should have told you. I have been hiding everything about my mother for years from everyone, Alyssa. I was hoping she would leave and you would never need to know."

"Well, I know now. I also know that you could have told me and chose not to, which is as good as lying." She turned from Garrick and walked quickly away.

Monday, Detective Taylor stopped by Gems to see Garrick and Alyssa. He waited patiently while Alyssa finished with a customer. "Miss Mason. Would you and Mr. Samuels have a moment to talk with me?"

"Certainly. I'll just go call him." She opened the door between the showroom and the back section of the building. "Garrick, Detective Taylor is here."

"Be right out."

Once Garrick joined them in the front of the store, Detective Taylor got right down to business updating them on what progress had been made. "Jillian Chadwick was in New York last week, and she kept her scheduled meeting with her parole officer. We talked with the owners of the bed and breakfast that she had stayed at and confirmed that she had been in Kentucky for a number of nights. We reported that, and she will likely have some issues to deal with as a result. So, unless she had someone mail the letter for her, we can eliminate her as a suspect.

"That leaves Andrew Mason and potentially a couple of unidentified perpetrators. We located Mr. Mason, and it seems he was in Lexington last week on business. We have been able to verify that he was at least where he said he was from about 8:00 a.m. to 6:00 p.m. Do either of you know if there is anyone who might have been able to mail such a note on behalf of either of these suspects?" He looked from Alyssa to Garrick and waited.

"Well, actually," Garrick began, "there was some indication several years back that Andrew and Grace Emerson were connected in some way. The only people that were aware of that were Greg and I." Both Detective Taylor and Alyssa stared at Garrick.

"Any idea what type of connection?" Taylor asked as Alyssa just continued to stare at him. "And are there any other bits of information that you might be able to share that only you and Greg knew about?"

Garrick swallowed hard. "Never could pin down a solid connection. And, yeah, there's more, but June was also aware of some of the rest. Andrew has made threats before. It was about nine years ago. That's why I actually moved to New Glory. Greg hired me to do some investigative work because of the threats. He was concerned about his family."

With narrowed eyes, Detective Taylor poked at Garrick's admission. "Investigative work?" He waited for an explanation.

"I was doing professional investigation at that time. Strange thing was that as soon as I got to town, Andrew stopped contacting his father until three years ago, and even then, there were only two phone calls, but the second call was made from somewhere in New Glory. We opted not to inform June of that fact. No one heard anything more from him until he called June just recently."

"His threats had always been verbal over the phone?"

"As far as I know." Just then, a customer wandered into the store, and all three turned in the direction of the entryway. "I've got enough for now. I'll be in touch." Tipping his head to Alyssa and then the potential customer, Detective Taylor exited Gems.

"Kevin. Good to see you." Garrick was back to his usual self immediately. He had created a beautiful piece for Kevin to present to his girlfriend when he asked her to marry him. "Follow me. I'll show you what I've got in the back." Kevin grinned widely, and Alyssa could not help but smile back, although she found it difficult in light of the information that Garrick had just disclosed. That left Alyssa alone in the showroom. With a few minutes to think, she pondered some of the things that Garrick had just confessed. He had told her that he came to New Glory because of a girl, but in reality, it was because of her uncle. He had kept up the facade for eight years. Detective Taylor was even surprised to hear that Garrick had done investigative work. Evidently, Garrick was good at undercover work to keep his real purpose in New Glory so secretive. Mark must have known. He would have realized what Garrick was doing for a living when he first moved here.

What about these threats and the contact with her uncle over the years? It sounded like her mother had known about some of it, but she had never told Alyssa. She would chat with her mother about that. She didn't appreciate being kept in darkness, regardless of how ignorantly blissful it might have been. Her thoughts were interrupted by Garrick and Kevin returning from the back.

Alyssa smiled and asked how Kevin liked the ring. "It is perfect, just like Zoe." He almost appeared to be in a trance. Normally, Alyssa would have asked for details about the proposal and any plans the groom might have. Today, though, her heart wasn't in it. She needed to discuss a few things with Garrick.

"Kevin is going to bring Zoe in on Saturday to make sure the ring is the right size. I'll make any adjustments then. Until Friday, Kevin is going to guard that ring with his life."

"Garrick, did you want to handle this sale?" Alyssa asked.

"Oh yes, I will definitely 'ring' this one through myself." Smiling at Kevin, he pointed out that was a little bit of jewelry store humor.

As Kevin left the store, Garrick moved toward the back room. "Just a minute," Alyssa said. "I would like to talk to you."

"Yes, I sort of expected that." Garrick looked like a little boy who was expecting a stern reprimand.

"You neglected to tell me about your mother. You and Mom neglected to tell me about the threats Uncle Andrew made over the years. You *lied* about why you moved to New Glory. Have I missed anything?"

"No, that pretty much covers it. How angry are you?" Garrick asked sheepishly.

Alyssa shook her head for several seconds, not even able to look him in the eye. "I haven't decided yet."

Monday night was the long-awaited euchre tournament with the seniors. Alyssa had been brushing up on her skills, although she was really looking forward more to spending time with the diverse and entertaining crowd. Despite her disillusionment with Garrick, she didn't see why she should miss the evening's fun. This particular event was open to all ages, and the hope was that the tournament would draw out a sizable crowd. It would bring in some cash that Garrick could put toward other activities for the group.

They were not disappointed by the turnout, as they filled as many tables as they could set up. A little saddened, Alyssa had to stand on the sidelines as they had too many participants. It was fine, though. She could move from table to table and chat with everyone that way.

For an older circle of locals, Alyssa was always amazed at how late they stayed. Did people this age not need to get to bed early? They were never in a rush to clear out, so by the time the last of them had left, it was almost 11:00 p.m. Alyssa had stayed to say good night to everyone. She was preparing to leave when she noticed Garrick pull up short as he was clearing the reception table. Alyssa's heart sank, thinking that maybe some of the money they had collected as people arrived was missing, although she wasn't sure how he would know if a few dollars were gone.

"What's up, Garrick?" She didn't take her eyes off him and watched his shoulders lift as he drew in a deep breath. He wasn't answering her, so she moved toward him. His head dropped, and she could see that he had closed his eyes, now running a hand through his hair. By the time she reached him, he had placed both hands on the table for support as he gazed down at an envelope.

Alyssa heard herself make a small gasping sound as her eyes registered the envelope. She knew she was breathing but was not at all certain that enough oxygen was getting in. "Should I call the police, Garrick?"

He nodded. "They should dust it for prints before we touch it."

Typically, Garrick would make the call, but this sight seemed to have really shaken him, so Alyssa dialed.

"NGPD, Officer Willows speakin'." It was Jasper. Alyssa knew the reaction that Jasper would have to hearing her identify herself. She was singlehandedly going to justify them adding more officers to the force if this kept up much longer.

"Hi, Jasper. It's Alyssa Mason." She delivered the introduction with a tone full of trepidation. "We need you to send someone over to the community center."

"Miss Mason? What's happened?"

"It looks like we've received another note, and Garrick thinks before we open it someone should check the envelope for prints."

"All righty, Miss Mason. Now don't you fret. I'll have someone over there real quick."

"Thank you, Jasper."

To their surprise, two officers were there within five minutes, and Detective Taylor arrived just moments after that.

"Sorry to say it doesn't look like any fingerprints are on that envelope. Maybe we'll get lucky on the note inside once we open it. You're both positive it wasn't sitting here when you arrived tonight?"

"Wasn't on that table, and I was the first one to arrive." Garrick answered.

The detective nodded with regret.

"Were there any faces you didn't recognize here? It was a bigger group than usual for Monday nights, correct?"

"Yes, it was open to everyone, but I can't say that I noticed anyone I didn't know. The table is right beside the door, though, so I suppose it would be possible for someone to quickly come in, drop the envelope, and leave."

Detective Taylor was wearing Latex gloves as he carefully opened the envelope. Slowly pulling the page out that was inside, he unfolded it, and with Alyssa on one side of him and Garrick on the other, they read the note.

> You're wasting your time involving the police. They won't be able to help. The only solution is to give me what I want, and what I want is my share. If you don't...well, that would be unfortunate.

It was not much more to go on than the last note had provided. It was clear that whoever was writing them felt that they had a right to a part of something. Since the envelopes had both been addressed simply "Gems, New Glory," Alyssa pondered whom they were intended for. *Could the note refer to something in the store? Maybe it was about the hidden stash of jewels. Or was it intended for Garrick or me as individuals?*

"Whoever wrote these notes is meticulous in avoiding any sort of identification," Detective Taylor announced. The inside was as clear of prints as the exterior of the envelope had been. All Alyssa could think was that Mark would be back in a few days, and she hoped he would be able to discover something that the local police had not been able to find.

She and Garrick left the community center in downcast moods compared to the upbeat attitudes they had both been communicating all evening. She could tell Garrick was particularly agitated over tonight. "Garrick, is there anything I can do? You seem more upset about this than you were about the first note."

"I guess I am. When Andrew started contacting Greg years ago, the first calls were more specific than these notes are, but they were relatively calm. He got bolder, though, and the threats escalated."

"Are you concerned that these threats are going to escalate too?"

"I don't know. There is really no reason to escalate the threat until they tell us exactly what they want. If they want the jewels, then Mark can arrange for some sort of sting to catch them. If they're after a portion of the estate, that's a different can of worms. It's not as if you've received your inheritance and can just sign over half of it. We cannot afford for Mark to be delayed past this weekend. The locals are in over their heads on this one." Alyssa was concerned that Garrick was right about that.

Alyssa and Garrick had traveled separately to the community center. Alyssa said good night, and without offering a kiss, she climbed into her car. She suspected that Garrick would understand the discoveries of the last few days were still an issue for her and she needed some time to process everything in her mind.

What she was not expecting was to watch Garrick's car pull into her driveway behind her when she reached home. She wasn't ready to discuss her feelings about his lies—not yet. She took a deep breath, and as she opened her door, he was there.

"I know you are still upset with me, but let me check the house to make sure you are safe." Alyssa was exhausted, so she didn't argue, walking with him to the house in silence.

Garrick took the door key from her and unlocked it, entering the house ahead of her. "Are you going to sweep the house and issue the clear alert for me tonight before you leave?"

"Yeah, I'm going to check through the house, but I'm not leaving. Until we have this resolved, I won't be leaving you unattended." His authoritative tone tore through her.

"You what?" She could not have heard him correctly. It was thoughtful of him to want her safe, but he was not just deciding to remain in her house all night.

"You heard me. I'll sleep on the couch tonight."

"Garrick, it's inappropriate for you to stay here. The neighbors will…will talk."

"But won't it be good for business?" He shot her earlier sentiments back at her.

"That was just a *kiss* that was being gossiped about. This situation will infer much more," she retorted.

"All right, call all your neighbors and let them know that I am sleeping on an uncomfortable couch solely in the interest of your safety. That should ease their minds."

"If the couch is uncomfortable, go home." Alyssa was too tired to be civil. She wanted her privacy, she wanted to sleep, and she wanted to wake up to find this was nothing but a horrible dream.

Garrick had moved through the rest of the house, and everything seemed secure. "I'm going to bed." Alyssa's tone was full of disgust. Obviously, her preferences were not going to be considered. She walked in the direction of her bedroom, and as she passed by Garrick, he grabbed her arm.

"Don't go to bed mad." His eyes had softened. They were still so intense with feeling, though, her breath caught. She stood unable to pull her eyes away from his. She knew his breathing was accelerating. "I couldn't stand it if anything happened to you, Alyssa." With eyelids getting heavier, he allowed them to close as he moved in even closer. His lips gently caressed her cheek and slowly moved to her mouth.

Alyssa seemed unable to focus on her anger over Garrick's deception. As her legs liquefied beneath her, heat spread over her body, and her lips parted to Garrick's passionate kiss. His strong arms were around her now, and it was the only thing keeping her from melting to the floor. The emotional stress that both were feeling had been intense. They needed a release, but Alyssa would not compromise her beliefs. On several occasions, Garrick had been the one to pull back and keep control over their interactions, but she was not convinced that he was going to stop tonight. It seemed his reserve was completely used.

"Garrick, we need to stop this." She could hear the breathless words spoken between kisses, although she was uncertain if Garrick had heard them. It did not seem like it. He continued the carnal assault on her senses, and she was close to having no defenses left. "Please, Garrick, stop."

"Are you sure?" His voice sounded so rough, guttural, and almost primitive. She was not at all sure she wanted to stop, but she knew she had to.

"Yes, please stop." His eyes met hers. "This isn't right." His forehead came down and rested against hers as he slowed his breathing.

"I am not going to sleep at all tonight knowing you are here, within my reach. You are driving me to the edge, Alyssa." Her heart was heavy with concern over where their relationship was headed, while her body was focused on the intense cravings that just kept building with each day she spent with this man.

"The spare room is made up. You don't have to sleep on the couch."

He lifted his head from her forehead and took her face in his hands, still lost in her. "I know I didn't tell you everything I should have, but you *can* trust me. I love you, Alyssa." With that, he gently kissed her and then pulling away, walked her to the master bedroom and left her there alone.

Chapter 12

Garrick sat in the nook off Alyssa's kitchen early the next morning. He had not been back to his house yet, so he still wore the previous day's clothes, and a day's growth of stubble was shadowing his face. He wasn't sure what time she would wake up after the late night they had. Staring at the mug of coffee sitting in front of him, he tried to make sense of everything. Although he knew he should be focused on piecing together something about these arcane notes, his mind was filled with Alyssa and how close he had been to losing control with her the night before.

He had told her he loved her, and she had said nothing. *Can I blame her?* he thought. *She might never be able to trust me after I lied to her.* A couple hours of sleep were all that he had managed. Thoughts of her in his arms flooded his head. He took a gulp of coffee to try to shake the images away.

"Good morning." A tiny voice spoke from the entrance to the great room, which was positioned between the kitchen and Alyssa's bedroom. Garrick felt a low growl rumble through him as he took in the sight of her standing there.

"Good morning. I made coffee. Would you like a cup?" Garrick's expression was staid.

"Yes, please." Garrick handed a mug to her, and as she took it, her fingers brushed his hand. Even that sent a wave of arousal through him. He was in deep. "Did you get much sleep?" Alyssa asked.

"A bit. How 'bout you?"

"Not a lot. I guess I was doing a lot of thinking instead." She paused to take a sip of the coffee. "Mmmm. Good coffee. Thank you." She set the mug down on the kitchen counter and leaned against it. Garrick had remained close to Alyssa after pouring her coffee. Looking up at him, Alyssa began to speak. "About last night…I'm sorry about getting angry with you about staying here. It's not entirely what my neighbors will think that concerned me, Garrick.

"Obviously I don't want them to think that I am carrying on in some elicit fashion, but last night there were other reasons." Garrick continued to gaze at her, waiting patiently for her to say what she was evidently having a struggle to get out. "The truth is that I'm afraid to let you stay here, Garrick." His eyes narrowed, and his eyebrows creased low at her statement.

"You're afraid of me? Alyssa, I would never hurt you." He stepped closer, and she stepped back. "What have I done to make you frightened of me, sweetheart?"

She smiled at him. "I'm not afraid of *you*, Garrick. I'm afraid of *me*. I'm afraid of what I might allow to happen. You said last night that you loved me. I wanted to respond, but I am so confused. When I'm with you, when you touch me, I feel an intensity I am helpless to control. Yet the past few days—the details you withheld from me—I haven't been able to reconcile those in my mind." She paused and then continued. "I'm not sure I can."

He nodded, recognizing the damage his omissions had caused. "I've apologized, Alyssa. There won't be any more surprises. I understand you need time to determine if you *can* forgive me. However, it's not safe for you to stay alone until we get this issue with the notes straightened out, and I am not going to be comfortable with you just staying with your mother. I would suggest staying with Mark and

Laura if Mark was around, but with him gone, all we'd be doing is bringing potential trouble to their doorstep."

"I wouldn't want to endanger them."

"So what are we going to do that is going to keep both of us content?" With no resolution in place, the doorbell rang. Two heads synchronously turned in the direction of the front door. "Do you often have visitors at seven thirty in the morning?"

"No." He could see the apprehension on her face as she froze in her place.

"Let me get it." She did not even put up a battle; she just let him go to the front door. Opening it, he was surprised to see Alyssa's mother. "June?"

"Surprised to see me, Garrick? I would think I should be the one that is surprised to see you in my daughter's house at the crack of dawn." Garrick had never heard this tone from June before.

"Would you like to come in? It's chilly out there this morning." Stepping back out of the way, Garrick made room for June to move through the entryway, and he mused that the chill was now in the house. "Would you like a cup of coffee?"

"Where's my daughter?"

"She's—Well, she was in the kitchen. Now she's here to greet you. Alyssa, I'm going to pour your mother a cup of coffee, and the two of you can sit and chat. I need to run next door."

"Oh no, you don't. You will be sitting down with the two of us." Other than the recent reprimands from Alyssa about his lies, Garrick realized it had been a very long time since he felt like he was being scolded for anything. It felt strange and, in a funny way, loving. His mother had never cared that much about him to lecture him over anything.

"Am I in trouble, June?" The corner of Garrick's mouth tipped up. He wasn't sure if he dared make the smile any more pronounced.

"Verdict is still out." She glared at him. He felt as if the verdict might not be laid down by the most impartial judge. It did not help either that Alyssa was standing there looking guilty as sin.

"Hi, Mom. Come into the kitchen. We can talk in there."

Garrick got the promised coffee and hoped that would win him some points, but he was not holding his breath.

"I got three calls this morning between six thirty and seven fifteen from *your* neighbors, Alyssa." Garrick watched Alyssa roll her eyes. Knowing that her mother was watching her closely, he suspected that was not the right reaction to have.

"Mom, it's not what you think. It's not what *they* think."

"Well, let's get this out on the table then, shall we? What do you think they are thinking?"

"They are likely thinking that Garrick spent the night here and that resulted in inappropriate behavior for two unmarried adults."

"And is their thinking flawed?"

"Mom, Garrick stayed last night because there was another threat made and he didn't want me staying alone. He slept in the spare bedroom, and I slept in the master bedroom."

"Another threat? When? How? I was with both of you up until I left the community center at ten forty-five."

"June, we found it at the community center when we were cleaning up. We were there until midnight with the police. It was too late to call you, and besides, I'm not comfortable bringing whatever danger we are dealing with to anyone else. So you might as well know your daughter is likely going to have an overnight guest in her house until we get this resolved." He watched her face change from concern and confusion over the new threat back to disapproval. "We are talking about Alyssa's safety, June," he reminded her.

He could see she was still not happy about the situation. "Listen. Tell me what is bothering you. Do you not believe us that nothing happened last night, or are you only concerned with what the neighbors are saying?"

June looked a bit sheepish at the question. "I believe you." Glancing at both of them, she continued. "But it's not just what the neighbors are thinking. Last night nothing happened, but I see the way the two of you are together, and I am worried that something might happen."

"Fair enough. I cannot say anything to you, June, that is going to put your mind at rest completely. All I can say is that I deeply care about your daughter, and it is not my intention to allow anything improper to happen. As far as the neighbors, my car won't be parked here overnight again." Then, smiling at Alyssa, he added, "I just couldn't drive it home last night and trust that Alyssa wouldn't lock me out before I got back here." Turning to June, he concluded, "She wasn't happy about me staying. Seemed concerned about what the neighbors would think. I am going home for a shower, a shave, and some fresh clothes. I'll be back in a while without my car!" He winked and left.

The week seemed to drag. Both Alyssa and Garrick were anxious about what would happen next and about Mark getting back. Garrick stayed each night at Alyssa's house, and although certain things were on Garrick's mind, Alyssa's distance continued. Friday night after closing, they picked up pizza and drove back to Garrick's for the evening. He hoped some time to relax together would ease the divide that had developed between them. With a selection of movies and a large deluxe pizza, they did relax even if it was at opposite ends of the couch. After finishing just one movie, however, Alyssa announced she was heading home.

The frustration Garrick felt was overwhelming. He wanted to wrap her in his arms, to tell her how much he cared for her. He stood when she rose from the couch and walked toward her, but gazing into her eyes, he could tell there was still a significant barrier between them. Full of disappointment, he said, "Okay. I'll take you over. Just let me grab a couple of things."

Not only was his future with this woman being threatened by some unidentified danger, it was now clearly also in jeopardy because of his choices.

Saturday, Mark walked into Gems. Alyssa squealed in delight and wrapped enthusiastic arms around him. "Hey, this is a better reception than I got from Laura. Guess Garrick must not be here." He winked, and she playfully slapped his arm.

"Oh, stop it. I can pretty much imagine the welcome home you got from your loved ones, Mark. Garrick?" Garrick popped up from behind one of the showcases.

"Good thing you didn't make a play for my girl, or you would have been in serious trouble, my friend." Garrick noticed Alyssa's smile disappear. If Mark noticed, he didn't let on.

"Like you scare me. If I made a play for your girl, it would be Laura that I would need to be terrified of." The men laughed and headed into the back to be able to talk without interruptions.

"Did the assignment wind down the way you wanted?" Garrick was always fascinated with what tidbits Mark could tell him about the FBI investigations. It certainly wasn't much, but he could fill in his own scenarios for the privileged information.

"This one had a good ending. It just took longer to play out than we had hoped. What's the scoop here?"

"Two threatening notes so far. The police have both of them. No prints of any kind to run. My mother was in New York City at the time of the first note. Andrew Mason was in Lexington."

"Okay. Detective Taylor is handling it?"

"Yep."

"I'll get copies of the notes from him then. Do they know where Andrew was when the second note was delivered?"

"Sounded like he had the same alibi. He was in Lexington on business and could be accounted for during work hours."

"I'll get started on what I can today, but some things I won't get until Monday. What are you working on?" Mark nodded toward the collection of rings that were underway.

"It's a new engagement ring collection." The rings, in varying stages of completion, caused Garrick to reflect on how much he loved Alyssa.

"Oh? Which one is your favorite?"

"What makes you think I have a favorite?"

"The goofy way you're smirking. It's a dead giveaway. Don't need to be an FBI agent to spot that look."

"What look?" Garrick made sure there was no goofy smirk on his face now.

Mark grinned and then a small laugh escaped. "Look of love, Garr. You've got it bad." This comment soured as Garrick drew back to the image of Alyssa's frown over the simple "my girl" remark moments earlier.

"Get outta here. I have work to do."

"One last question. When will the best ring be done?"

"After you've resolved the jewel mystery and these threats."

"Okay. That sounds like incentive to me. Talk to you real soon." Garrick knew, though, it would take more than a solved mystery to place a ring on Alyssa's finger.

Garrick could hear Mark laughing as he passed through the showroom. "Sorry, Alyssa. I think I put him in a bad mood."

Sunday night, Garrick and Alyssa had dinner with June. They headed home early, and when Garrick turned Alyssa's car into her driveway, the headlights reflected off something odd. Getting out of the car, they walked around to the front of the house and stood in horror at what sat in front of them. White paint had been sprayed up the middle of the stone stairway leading to the front door. Garrick walked on one side of the paint strip and Alyssa on the other.

It continued on to the front door. Their eyes followed it up the middle of the wooden and glass double doors. Both of them were speechless. Alyssa turned and started walking around to the back of the house. Garrick was on her heels, and when they reached the backyard, they found a similar sight. Here, though, great effort had been expended to extend the paint strip up to the roofline. It stretched over elaborate stonework and windows and to the left of the paint strip was painted the word *yours* and to the right, the word *mine*.

"You don't suppose they got in the house, do you?" Alyssa looked shocked at what she was staring at.

"We're going to find out, but not until we have some backup." Garrick had already dialed his cell phone. "Mark, we've got trouble over at Alyssa's. Looks like someone is trying to stake a claim to half the house."

"You know that means that there might be two cases here. The notes are most likely from someone who is actually after the estate."

Nodding, Garrick agreed, "Yeah, that's right."

"Get the police over there."

"I'm going to call them now."

"I'm on my way."

"Thanks. See you in a few."

Next Garrick dialed the NGPD. "NGPD. Officer Travis speakin'."

"It's Garrick Samuels calling. We need Detective Taylor over at Alyssa Mason's home ASAP."

"I'll call him right now." Most of the police department recognized Garrick's voice at this stage. He probably didn't even need to announce himself.

An hour later, with a multitude of photographs and what prints they could find, they had entered the house. Much to everyone's relief, there was no sign that anyone had been inside. Alyssa was mortified at the exterior of her beautiful home. "I don't understand it, Garrick. If they think they should have half, why would they deface such a valuable asset?"

"I'll call someone first thing in the morning to come help me, and we'll get it cleaned up. If they really think they have a right to half of this house, they would have used water-soluble paint."

Tuesday morning, Mark was on their front door step at 7:00 a.m. "What are you doing here at this time? Is Laura okay?" In Garrick's rulebook, something had to be seriously wrong to show up unannounced at that time of day.

"I've got information, and you need to hear it. Get Alyssa up." Garrick just stood there. It was taking him time to process the two sentences that Mark had blurted out.

"Okay. *You* start coffee, and *I'll* get Alyssa up," Mark stated. That brought Garrick to life.

"I'll get her up. Move into the kitchen. We'll be there in a minute." He might be a good friend, but there were boundaries that Garrick would not let anyone cross.

He knocked at her door. He couldn't hear any movement from inside. He tried the door, and surprisingly, it wasn't locked. He mused that he would have to remember that she didn't lock her door and then promptly gave himself a firm reprimand. She was sound asleep. He hated to wake her, but it must be important for Mark to burst in like this. He walked over to the bed and sat on the edge.

"Alyssa? Alyssa, wake up." He touched her shoulder and gave her a very gentle shake. "Sweetheart, you need to wake up." Her eyes started to flutter, and slowly her breathing changed. Then there was a stretch, and her eyes opened and then closed again. "Sweetheart, Mark's here to talk to us."

Alyssa's eyes opened once again, and this time, Garrick's presence registered. Startled, she let out a gasp. "What are you doing in here?"

"I knocked, but you didn't hear me. You were sleeping really soundly. Mark arrived a few minutes ago and has something to tell us. Told me to get you to the kitchen. I'm sorry for scaring you. I should have waited outside." Alyssa nodded and looked away.

"I'll be there in a minute."

Garrick raised his hand to her cheek and softly trailed his fingers down to her chin. Swallowing hard, he got up from the bed and went to the kitchen.

"She'll be here soon," he told Mark. Alyssa took more than a couple of minutes, so by the time she emerged, the coffee was ready.

"Hello, Alyssa." Mark had always been a morning person. Normally Garrick wouldn't think morning was a bad thing either, but this one had started a little shaky. With coffee in front of each of them, Mark began to share the information he had uncovered.

"I took the inventory of the jewels in question and ran them against a database we have of jewel thefts with unrecovered gems. As you can imagine, it is a large database, but the good news is that we were able to match up certain portions of your collection against parts of specific thefts based on some of the unique pieces. Then, when we identified that the remainder of those burglaries could also be accounted for from your collection, we managed to match three separate thefts. Each of those thefts was believed to be connected, and of the other seven thefts that were suspected to be connected to the same group, we were able to completely account for all your jewels. It was actually unbelievable that we were able to get that close a match.

"Each of these thefts happened sometime between 1992 and 1997. Although the jewels were never recovered, arrests were made and three convictions were handed down."

"Where did the thefts take place?" Garrick asked.

"They were all over the eastern states, as far south as Georgia and as far north as Maine."

"So definitely FBI jurisdiction."

"Yep."

"How long were the sentences?"

"They each got five years and served about three of the five."

"You've got names?"

"Oh, I have names. Jeremy Raines, Andrew Mason, and Jillian Samuels."

Garrick sat motionless, trying to comprehend the implications of this. Alyssa looked from Garrick to Mark and back again.

"Uncle Andrew and your mother knew each other?" Alyssa's eyes narrowed as she looked at Garrick. "Did you know about this?" The question was accusatory, and Garrick wondered if Mark had noticed the tone of Alyssa's voice.

"I had no idea. Mark, do we have any information on the other guy, Jeremy Raines?"

"He's dead. He died in a car accident in Lexington about a week after Gregory Mason died." Alyssa gasped. "From every report I can find, that was the first time he had ever been in Lexington. Here's the really cool part. Andrew Mason was in Lexington at that time too."

Alyssa spoke up as the two men stared at each other, almost telepathically, sharing their thoughts on the possible connections. "If Jillian is after the jewels, why was she not being more secretive about her presence in town?"

"Likely because she thought she could weasel her way into my life and that might get her closer to the stash they planted at Gems. Andrew would know that he couldn't be that visible without a lot of history throwing up barriers."

Mark interjected, "I think we may be back to having a connection between the stolen jewels and the threatening notes."

"What are you thinking?"

"Who's the logical person to pick *Gems* as the cover for the stolen goods?"

"Andrew would be."

"Exactly. I did some checking. I talked with Sidney Frost, Greg's lawyer. It was a well-known fact years ago that Andrew was to inherit New Glory Gems. Only Gregory Mason and Sidney knew about the disinheritance and revised will that he put in place a few years ago. Andrew thought, up until that letter of disinheritance was sent to him, that he would inherit the store."

Alyssa looked confused. "But if he was holding them at Gems so he could get to them after Grandpa died, he might have been waiting for years yet. Grandpa wasn't extremely old, and he had been in good shape. If it wasn't for the car accident, he would—" Alyssa stopped as dreadful comprehension spread over her face. "Uncle Andrew couldn't have had anything to do with Grandpa's accident, could he?"

"I don't think we can rule out anything at this point." Mark regretted having to be so blunt with Alyssa. "Now, I'll apologize for coming over so early. I wanted you both to have a chance to digest all of this and have time to settle back down before getting to work this morning. I have to go into the office today and make some plans on how to proceed given what we've discovered.

"I'll be in touch, Garrick. Think about everything I've said, and try to think of any other connections that could help us get a tighter handle on exactly what's going on. And both of you be careful."

Chapter 13

Alyssa hurried down the street to Sarah's Café. She was meeting Laura and Jason for lunch after his morning at school. She enjoyed the time she spent with Laura and got a charge out of the little boy who had everyone wrapped around his finger.

The café was busy. Alyssa slipped into the restaurant, quickly scanning the clientele to spot her luncheon companions. As she strained her neck to look to the remote corner tables, she jumped as a "Boo" sounded from behind her.

Turning abruptly, she gasped. "Laura. You startled me." Alyssa's surprise quickly shifted to amusement. "I thought I was going to be late. I'm surprised you aren't already seated."

"Jason and I had a couple of stops to make after he got out of school, so we're just arriving. Are there any tables left?"

"Not many. Looks like one at the back." Turning to Sarah, she asked, "Is the table at the back available, Sarah?"

"Absolutely. Have a seat, and I will be right with you." How she kept up with the volumes she served was astounding. She did an amazing day business. Dinnertime was quieter, as the other eateries in town pulled more restaurant goers at that time of day.

It took the ladies a few minutes to set up Jason with a booster seat and sit down. They ordered their drinks. Both Alyssa and Laura ordered salads with grilled chicken, and Jason knew exactly what he wanted. "Two salads and a grilled cheese coming up," Sarah restated, and off she went to give their orders to the kitchen. When she returned with their drinks, Sarah also brought Jason crayons and a coloring sheet intended to entertain him fully while they waited for their meals. He had colored the same sheet many times before but never seemed to mind.

With the number of tables waiting for their meals, Alyssa knew they would be in for a longer lunch than she had planned, but Garrick had told her to take her time. Neither Alyssa nor Laura was in a rush, and Jason was always so content in this particular restaurant. They would make the most of the extra time. "So you must be thrilled to have Mark home."

"Oh, am I. He had to travel into the office today but said he expected he would be home early. We had a wonderful weekend, Alyssa. What about you and Garrick? Do I get an update on the romance of the decade?"

"Romance of the decade?" Alyssa asked without a smile.

"I would call it romance of the century, but Mark and I have that title nailed down. So the best you can do is decade!" She beamed and then recognized that Alyssa was not even looking at her. "Alyssa, what is it?" Laura asked.

"I wouldn't refer to it as the romance of the decade right now. In fact, I think *romance* might not be the most accurate word."

"What happened?" Laura looked as if someone had died.

"I'm just not sure that Garrick is trustworthy," she said quietly.

"Not trustworthy? Wow, I think you should explain that."

A quick update, without too many details, was all Alyssa was willing to provide.

Laura sat quietly listening, and when Alyssa finished, Laura said, "Well, I understand your position, but sometimes people withhold information out of love rather than any intentional deception."

Just as she finished her statement, Jason spoke up. "Mommy, what do you think of my picture that I drew?"

"You drew a great picture, Jason. Is it *Batman*?"

Big dimples dented his cheeks with the grin that appeared. He vigorously nodded. "Nah nah nah nah, nah nah nah nah, Batman."

"Jason has decided that for Halloween this year he will be Batman. Won't he be an awesome superhero?"

"Oh, I feel safer already," Alyssa declared with a small smile.

Laura sobered, looked directly at Alyssa, and said, "Batman, a man with a secret identity who helped people."

The conversation shifted to lighter topics once the food arrived, and as Alyssa had thought, it was over an hour before they were ready to leave. She sent Laura and Jason on their way, as she had planned on picking up the tab on their lunch today. As Alyssa walked up to the counter to pay their bills, Sarah was ringing through a large take-out order for one of the local NGPD.

"The police department must be having a party with all that food," Alyssa joked with Sarah when she stepped up to the cash register.

"Actually, he's taking it over to Detective Taylor and some of the other officers who got called to Grace's house about an hour ago. Sounds like they will be there awhile. I offered to run fresh coffee over to them midafternoon."

"Grace Emerson's?" Alyssa confirmed.

"Yes." Sarah leaned forward to Alyssa. "Grace called in about twelve fifteen. I guess when she got home for lunch, she found a man, dead, in her house."

The gasp was louder than Alyssa would have liked and then lowering her voice, she said, "Dead? Who?"

"I don't know, but I'm sure news will start to trickle out soon enough."

Astonished by the news, Alyssa slowly turned to leave. As she did, she called over her shoulder, "See you tomorrow, Sarah. Thanks for lunch."

Alyssa had hurried to get to the café for lunch, and now she hurried even faster to get back to the shop, not because she felt she was late, but because she wanted to tell Garrick about what she had just heard from Sarah. The immediate thoughts cascading through her mind were of her recent knowledge of Grace's relationship with her uncle. Although Garrick had not fully identified their connection, he had been certain a relationship existed.

Pushing through the front door of Gems, she found June standing talking to Garrick. She wondered if the news had already reached them and if they had any more details. "Hi. Sorry I am late getting back. It was crazy in at Sarah's."

"Pick up any good gossip in there today?" Garrick casually asked.

"A bit." Looking back and forth from one to the other, she decided they must not know based on their expressionless faces. "Neither of you have heard the news?"

Garrick's face drew in a little with concern unsure of what she meant. "What did you hear?"

"Grace Emerson found a man dead in her house at lunchtime."

Two shocked reactions were simultaneously blurted out. "What?" was June's immediate response, while Garrick asked, "Who?"

"I don't know anything else, other than Detective Taylor and some officers are at her place and will be there for a while. One of the officers was picking up take-out food at the café just as I was paying for lunch." Then, not able to control her nagging thoughts, she asked the question that continued to haunt her since Sarah had mentioned the death. "Do you think it could be Uncle Andrew?"

Garrick looked at June and June closed her eyes. "I don't know, Alyssa. Let's find out more before we start speculating."

That afternoon was the longest afternoon Alyssa could remember. Not only were there next to no customers in and out, but the anxiety of not knowing more details about what had happened at Grace's home made it seem like an eternity.

When they closed, they drove by Grace's house to see if the police were still there. There was only one police car remaining, but Mark's car was also parked on the street. Garrick pulled over and stopped the car. "I'll be right back. I'm just going to check in with Mark." Garrick jogged up to the front door of the Emerson home and knocked.

Alyssa watched from the car. She saw Mark come to the door and step out on the porch with Garrick. Sitting patiently waiting for a report was totally out of character for her, but for some reason it felt like the right thing to do. The men only spoke for a couple of minutes, and then Garrick was on his way back.

Once in the car, he buckled and pulled away from the curb. He said nothing and drove straight to his house. He turned the engine off and, looking straight ahead, spoke quietly. "We'll have dinner here tonight."

Walking to the house, Alyssa could feel her patience draining away. As soon as they were inside, she reached out and touching his arm broached the subject. "Garrick, what did Mark say?"

He turned, glancing at the hand that rested on his arm and then looked into her eyes. At first he said nothing, just covered her hand with his. "Come into the living room and sit down." They sat together on the couch in front of the fireplace, and Garrick began to relay what little information Mark had given him. "Grace went home for lunch. She arrived around ten minutes past noon. When she came in the house, she went to the study for something, and she found the body on the floor.

"He had been shot in the head at close range with his own gun. It was made to look like a suicide, but the initial investigation suggests that the angle of the shot couldn't have been self-inflicted. Alyssa, it was Andrew Mason."

Alyssa's shoulders slumped. She had no memory of the man and only knew that there had been serious enough issues to cause an unending rift in the family. Regardless of the conflict, he was still her father's brother, and she felt something. She just wasn't sure what it was. "I should call Mom."

"Mark said the police were going to stop by to tell her, so she may already have heard."

"You said they don't think the angle of the shot could have been self-inflicted. That would eliminate suicide and point to homicide?" The thought sent shivers through Alyssa. Murder. How bad had her uncle been that his life had ended in such a violent way? She suspected she would never know.

"Yes, Mark said it looks like murder. He mentioned there were some other pieces of information the police had shared with him, but he wasn't in a position to pass it along yet. They need to keep a few things under wraps or it could hinder the investigation."

"Do the police have any suspects?"

Garrick looked around the room. "I don't know for sure, but I would expect that Jillian would be near the top of the list."

"Why?" Alyssa's heart raced at the thought that Garrick's mother, however misdirected her life had been, would be capable of killing someone.

"Well, think about it. Three people were convicted on thefts involving a tremendous amount of unrecovered jewels. Two of the three are now dead. Who do you think would stand to gain the most from Andrew's death, assuming Jillian knows where the gems are?"

Not wanting to admit it, she recognized that people had killed for less. "What was he doing in Grace's house?"

"Mark said the police are being really tight lipped about the details. It might be awhile before we get any answers."

"Where does this leave Mark with the investigation of the jewels?"

"He said he would stop over here tonight to see us and discuss that, but my take on it is we have one less suspect in the mix. Hey, let me get some supper in the oven, and while I do that, you call your mom and make sure she is okay. In fact, invite her over for dinner. We'll eat around six o'clock." Alyssa nodded and reached for the phone that sat on the table beside her and, glancing at her watch, decided she would call Flourishing Flowers since her mom might still be there.

"Flourishing Flowers. Teri speaking. How may I help you?"

"Hey, Teri. It's Alyssa. Is Mom still there?"

"No, Alyssa. She went home about a half hour ago. She got some unsettling news and headed out right after that." The words were cautiously delivered, suggesting that Teri was trying to tread lightly in case Alyssa wasn't aware of what had happened.

"So the police were in to talk to her before she left?"

"Yes. You know what happened?"

"Well, I wouldn't say I know what happened; I know who it happened to. I'll give her a call at home. Thanks, Teri."

"No problem. Let me know if there is anything I can do for you."

She ended that call and immediately dialed her mom's place. "Hello?"

"Mom, are you all right?"

"I'm fine, dear. You've heard?"

"Yes. We drove by Grace's on the way home, and Mark was there. Garrick spoke to him for a couple of minutes. Hey, would you come over and have dinner with us at Garrick's place tonight? He says the dinner bell will ring at six p.m."

"I'm not sure I would be great company tonight, Alyssa."

"We may not be the best company either, but at least it will be company. If you want, I can come over, pick you up, and bring you here. Please say you will come."

"All right. I can drive myself, though. I'll come over around five thirty."

"Great. I will set the table for three. Bye."

A few minutes before five thirty, Garrick and Alyssa heard a car drive in. Expecting June, Alyssa went to the door. She opened it and was surprised to see someone else standing there. "Oh, hello." Recognition of the woman's identity took only seconds. It was Garrick's mother and possibly the number-one suspect in a murder case.

"Ms. Chadwick, isn't it?"

"Yes, that's correct. I'm here to see Garrick Samuels. I was sure I had the right house."

Both ladies turned in the direction of the kitchen doorway when they heard Garrick's voice. "June, come on out to the kitchen. I might need your help with something." The woman turned back to Alyssa and narrowed her eyes.

"Your name is June?" She looked confused.

"No, June is my mother. We were expecting her, so when we heard a car drive in we thought she had arrived. I'm Alyssa Mason." Comprehension began to spread over the woman's face, while she continued to stand in the doorway. Alyssa was becoming anxious about how to handle this woman's presence and quickly turned to call Garrick. There was no need to call him, though, as she watched him appear in the doorway.

His reaction was stupefied silence when his eyes focused on the woman who had taken another step into the house, closed the door, and stood in the foyer. "Hello, Garrick." His expression turned to stone, and after what seemed like a very long time, he moved toward her. Alyssa could hear another car drive in. This time she would check to see who it was before blindly opening the door.

"Jillian, I don't recall inviting you to my home." The tone was cold. Although she knew from experience that Garrick was capable of cooling his emotions where his mother was concerned, the degree tonight was extreme and unfamiliar to Alyssa. Suddenly Alyssa wished they had not invited June over to the house. She didn't want her mother's life jeopardized in any way, and what this woman was capable of was entirely unknown. "That is likely Mom," she said to Garrick, concern filling her voice.

"That's fine, Alyssa. June was invited and is welcome here, of course. Please let her in, and perhaps the two of you could take over in the kitchen while I deal with this situation."

The knock sounded, and Alyssa excused herself around Jillian to reach the door. "Hi, Mom. Come in." She stepped back, allowing June to enter. "Mom, this is Jillian, Garrick's mother."

Bewilderment was the only word that Alyssa could think of that described the look on June's face. "Oh, you were in the shop and ordered an arrangement a few weeks back." Then, looking at Garrick, she continued. "You came in too. Why didn't you tell me this was your mother?"

"Embarrassment." The word came out harshly. Alyssa cringed at it.

"Mom, Garrick's got some things on the stove that need to be watched. Would you be able to keep an eye on them?"

"Alyssa, maybe you should help your mother."

"No, I think I will stay here." Garrick growled under his breath at her obstinacy but decided to get on with the unpleasant discussion with this intruder.

"What are you doing back in town, Jillian?"

"Well, actually, I have a bit of a confession to make, Garrick." She paused briefly, maybe organizing her thoughts. "The only reason I came to New Glory in the first place was because Andrew Mason had stored some valuables of mine in New Glory Gems." She was quiet as she waited for Garrick to respond.

When Garrick offered no reply, she continued with a sigh. "I was hoping that I might be able to get access to them if I was to rebuild a relationship with you."

"I'm not really looking to rebuild anything with you, Jillian."

"I guess if I had been truthful with myself, I would have realized that. When I arrived, though, I really could see why you like it here. It is a wonderful small town."

"It's a little far from your parole officer, though, isn't it?"

"I managed to get the restrictions on my parole lightened up in order to see a doctor in Lexington."

"Are you sick, Jillian?" Garrick's voice remained unemotional, even with the suggestion that his mother might have some ailment.

She smiled. "No. I'm fine. I just needed a legal way to get to Kentucky to see you. They've officially transferred my parole meetings to a probation officer in Lexington starting this week."

Rolling his eyes, Garrick shot off a disgusted sounding "Great."

"I know you won't believe me, but once I was here and I had seen you again, the items I had been intent on retrieving lost interest for me. I realized how much I really would like to get to know you and try to apologize for all the anguish I put both you and your father through."

"Oh please, Jillian. You can't seriously think I am going to be taken in by that?"

With a wishful looking grin, she said, "No. I suppose not." The smile disappeared, and she continued. "I went back to New York a couple of weeks ago because a friend of mine had alerted me to a possible endangerment, but then I realized that I might not be the only one in danger, so I came back in order to warn you."

"Warn me about what?"

Jillian seemed to squirm right before their eyes. However, shaking her head slightly, she braced herself and proceeded. "You know I went to jail for theft several years ago. The jewels that had been stolen were never recovered. One of my co-conspirators had hidden them very well. Later, he moved them to another location in order to keep them safe and under the radar.

"I was quite close to the third member of our team. The plan had been that we would retrieve the jewels and divide them equally among the group much later. Much later arrived." Jillian was no longer maintaining eye contact with Garrick.

"Why don't we just cut to the chase here, Jillian, since my dinner is going to be ready soon? The two accomplices were Andrew Mason and Jeremy Raines. Let's just call them by name and skip this 'protect the hardly innocent' game."

"You're almost right. There was also a fourth member in our group—Gregory Mason. Andrew sent our take to him to stash in Gems."

A harsh gasp was heard from Alyssa. "What? How dare you accuse my grandfather of being involved in something like that? He would never do such a thing."

Jillian looked sympathetic. "I'm sorry, but it's true. He didn't take part in the actual burglaries, and that is how he managed to stay out of jail. His part was to store the jewels for a period time that Andrew would decide on.

"Andrew assured us that he was to inherit the jewelry store. That way, if anything happened to Greg, we would still be able to retrieve our portions. Then Andrew got greedy. He didn't like the thought of splitting the take four ways, so he manipulated Jeremy into arranging for Greg's death."

Two gasps were heard this time, as June stood at the doorway, now listening.

"After Andrew had Gregory Mason out of the way, he arranged for Jeremy's death. That would again increase his share. The red herring turned out to be that he didn't inherit New Glory Gems after all, which greatly complicated the retrieval process. I have no doubt that I would have been his next target if he had known of a way to get the jewels. He didn't, though, and since you, Garrick, had been conveniently positioned in the store, Andrew turned to me to see if I could get past you, find the jewels, and get them out.

"Unfortunately, between some top-of-the-line surveillance equipment and a nagging feeling in my stomach, I didn't complete the task as assigned.

"Jeremy's son had kept in contact with me, and just over two weeks ago, he reminded me that I was of little value to Andrew if I wasn't able to obtain the jewels and that my life might be in danger. That's why I left New Glory. If Andrew managed to get rid of me, he would get everything.

"Yesterday, Jeremy's son called to say that Andrew was in New Glory, and I immediately felt you might be in serious danger. Andrew won't stop at anything to get his property back. So I returned to tell you that Andrew is in town and you need to be very careful."

"Too late, Jillian."

"What do you mean?"

"Andrew was found dead today. Seems like *you* are the sole survivor, and I'm thinking that makes you a prime suspect in his death." Jillian went completely white. Alyssa thought she was going to pass out and quickly moved toward her. Garrick caught her arm, though, holding her back.

Jillian took an unsteady step backward and butted up to the door. She leaned against it, and one hand covered her mouth. Suddenly, a knock sounded loudly on the door that was supporting her, startling her into releasing a small cry.

It took Garrick and Alyssa by surprise too, as they had been so absorbed in Jillian's disclosure that they hadn't heard any vehicle arrive. Garrick checked through the side window and seeing Mark, promptly opened the door.

Garrick's sour expression stopped him short. "Do I have the wrong house? I thought a friend of mine lived here."

"Oh, you've got the right place. It's just getting a little crowded in here." Alyssa could read Garrick's hostile tone. He wanted to boot them all out. When Garrick stepped aside, Mark had a clear visual on Jillian.

Saying nothing, he simply stared for a moment. Alyssa hated uncomfortable silences. So she ended it. "Mark, I believe you met Jillian Samuels briefly one evening at the store?"

"It's Chadwick, actually. I had it changed. I haven't done everything legally over the years, but that one is legal."

Mark pursed his lips and then cautiously began. "I was expecting to spend some time with you, but not tonight, not here." He looked at Garrick for some explanation.

"Jillian arrived a little while ago and has been entertaining us with some interesting tales." Garrick's cynicism continued.

"I'm always up for a good tale. How would you like to tell a couple of the guys down at the police station the stories, Ms. Chadwick? You are actually being sought for questioning in relation to an incident that occurred earlier today."

"I suppose I should be calling a lawyer then?" Jillian seemed resigned to going in for an interrogation. Alyssa could only imagine it as being totally humiliating. She guessed it wasn't like the TV shows or the movies, and since it was only for questioning, she suspected there wouldn't be any fingerprinting or mug shots taken. Yet the idea was horrific to her. To Jillian, it seemed no different from going to the dentist.

"You can call your lawyer from the station." Turning to Garrick, he said, "I'll call you later. I had some things to talk to you about."

With Mark and Jillian out of the house, Garrick, Alyssa, and June were finally able to sit down to eat their meal. All three of them were downcast given the revelations that Jillian had unloaded. If it was all true, then Gregory Mason's death had not been an accident. Worse than that, though, was the unbelievable news that he had been an accomplice in the jewel theft ring and had stored the jewels in his own store. Some parts made sense as the three sorted through the details. Gregory had approached Garrick and hired him to deal with Andrew. The fact that he was related to Jillian was a connection they couldn't ignore. Perhaps he had thought it might serve a purpose in the end.

So much drama for such a typically quiet little place. Surely it would calm down soon. However, Alyssa couldn't help but picture Jillian's face when Garrick announced that Andrew was dead. There had been no previous knowledge of it. Jillian had displayed complete shock at the news. Alyssa really couldn't believe that Jillian had anything to do with Andrew's death.

If she had no involvement in Andrew's demise, then who was behind it? Alyssa knew she was jumping ahead of herself. The coroner still had to confirm that it was homicide before there was any need for a suspect.

Garrick had offered some input in the dinner conversation but for the most part had been unusually quiet throughout the meal. Alyssa hoped that he would open up later once June had gone home.

To her surprise, and quite possibly her displeasure, he took control of the conversation when dessert and coffee was sitting in front of them. "I know you won't be happy about this, but I feel it would be best if the two of you go shopping for a few days, somewhere far from here."

They both turned to look at Garrick. "Shopping?" June asked.

Alyssa narrowed her eyes. "Why?"

"Well, there are a few reasons. First of all, I have been told by reliable sources that shopping is very relaxing and therapeutic for women." He waited for confirmation, which came quickly. "Second, you both deserve a getaway and some time together." Raising his eyebrows in a questioning glance, he got another round of affirmative nods. "Third, it is probably going to be a few days until we get all this mess with Andrew sorted out, so there's no need for you to stick around because of that. You've both just gotten news that is going to take time to deal with. Take that time now.

"Teri can handle the flower shop, and I can handle Gems. Pick a city and do some good for the economy. I can't believe you would even question an offer to go shopping and update your wardrobes." *Oh, why did he have to suggest shopping? Not fair*, Alyssa thought. That was definitely her weakness. She knew her mother was probably due for a vacation.

"What do you say, Mom? Will we give him his wish and clear out of town for a few days?"

"Well, I would like to start some Christmas shopping, and a few new outfits would liven up my closet. Which city would we pick?"

"We could go to Louisville or Knoxville, or if you'd like we could drive to Cincinnati. Garrick, are you really going to let us go off by ourselves?"

"Yeah, you two go and have a good time."

June decided she should leave to go do some last-minute laundry, leaving Garrick and Alyssa alone. The quiet was amazing after the chaos of the earlier hours. Garrick sat down in the living room, and Alyssa walked toward him. She sat close to him on the couch but said nothing at first. He had shifted to allow her to lean into him, and she took advantage of that. What she was feeling was not entirely clear to her, but watching Jillian and Garrick interact had been eye opening. She was beginning to understand the depth of hostility he felt for his mother and why he had chosen to hide so much about his past. He might have been primarily protecting himself by concealing the truth, but he had also been protecting those he cared about most.

"This evening was difficult for you, wasn't it?" Alyssa started.

Garrick was silent but had turned his head and was looking down at her.

"Talking with your mother was difficult," she repeated.

"Yes, it was."

"I'm sorry. Before tonight, I didn't fully understand how you felt about her," Alyssa admitted.

"I don't want you to have to deal with her, Alyssa." Garrick pulled her in even tighter against him as they sat together.

"So why do you really want Mom and me to leave town right now? What are you concerned about?"

Garrick answered quietly, "I want you both out of harm's way. I don't know who to believe and who to trust right now. So please don't fight me on this. I need to know you are away from the danger, whatever it might be."

"I thought that was probably the reason. I will be calling you each day to check on you, because I don't feel good about you being in the vicinity of danger either." He nodded his understanding of her feelings and a small smile appeared on his face. "I suppose I should go home and pack too."

Garrick's voice had become low and a little rough. "No. You can pack tomorrow morning. I'm not going to see you for several days, so I'm going to need some extra time with you now, to hold me over." The question of forgiveness lingered behind those words. Alyssa wasn't yet sure of all her feelings for this man, but she did know she was ready to forgive him.

With one arm on the back of the couch, Garrick's other hand slid slowly over Alyssa's stomach and around to her back, encircling her waist. His eyes were intense, creating an intimate union. She was eager to lean in for this kiss, and as she did, the arm resting behind her pulled her in tight against him. The power this man had over her left her feeling defenseless, and yet she felt perfectly safe in his arms. She couldn't imagine anything endangering her here with him to protect her.

Chapter 14

Wednesday morning, Alyssa and her mother left for Cincinnati, Ohio. With plans to do major damage to the inventories of a number of their favorite boutiques, shops, and high-end fashion chains, they hit the road by midmorning. Garrick had opted to open Gems at 11:00 a.m. to allow him to be able to see them on their way out of New Glory and hopefully out of the way of potential harm.

He had no idea what the next few days would bring but wanted both ladies at a safe distance just in case. June had been a special woman to him for several years now, and Alyssa was just special in so many ways. He couldn't allow anything to happen to either of them.

By the time Garrick opened the store, news had quickly spread in the small community that Andrew Mason was dead. It did not seem as if word had gotten around that Jillian had been in for questioning, though. He was a bit surprised by that, although he wouldn't complain about lack of airtime. The more talk there was about Jillian, the more questions there would be about what her connection was to Andrew, to New Glory, and to anyone else here.

Garrick had some significant plans for this week, and they didn't involve murder and mysteries. He was more interested this week in forging paths to love and romance. Alyssa's words and actions the previous night had reignited Garrick's hope of a future with this woman. So he hoped that between Mark and the local police department, they would take care of solving all the puzzles that seemed to be accumulating. He had other things to deal with now that Alyssa was out of town.

Her presence in his life still seemed to be best described as a jolt. It had been a very pleasurable jolt, but nonetheless a jolt. He had remained contented with the occasional date before she had wandered back into New Glory. Now he was unable to think of anything or anyone else. She had completely monopolized his conscious state, likely even his unconscious state. The way she moved, the way she talked, the way she smelled stirred him up like no one else ever had.

He had picked out a stunning 1.06-carat round diamond, super ideal cut, and D color with VVS1 clarity. One of the rewards of this line of work was that you could have the pick of the very best at considerably less-than-retail pricing.

He had designed and created a beautiful setting already. If Alyssa had seen him working on it, she would have thought it was for the new line of engagement rings he was working on. This ring, however, would be one of a kind. He did not intend to duplicate the design to sell to others. The exquisite diamond would be set in platinum with small diamonds on either side of the profile. The band was smooth with delicate embellishments accented with diamonds. When he was done, this ring would epitomize romance.

He planned to finish the ring on Wednesday evening. That way, if Alyssa surprised him by returning home earlier than expected, he would not be caught with it unfinished.

There were other plans to make, though. Obviously, the ring was important to this event; however, just as a diamond needs its perfect setting, so too does the occasion need the perfect ambiance. So while he wasn't busy with customers, he sat in the showroom and began planning a very special evening. Pulling out the phone book, he found a caterer that he had heard great things about.

Garrick had just finished on the phone with the caterer when Mark walked through the front door of the store. "Garr, how did dinner turn out last night?"

"It was fine. My evening was probably more enjoyable than yours was."

Mark smirked and said, "We spent a while talking with Jillian—close to three hours, in fact."

"And?" Garrick asked.

"I don't know what further investigation is going to uncover, but right now, I don't think she had anything to do with Andrew's death."

Garrick didn't know whether to be relieved or disappointed by the assertion. On one hand, he didn't want to believe that his mother would be capable of murder. On the other hand, finding the culprit would put an end to the danger and allow New Glory and its residents to get back to normal. For Garrick it would mean being able to ask the woman he was in love with to marry him.

"So where does that leave us with the case?"

"It leaves us looking for a lead."

It also meant a murderer was still free.

After closing for the day, Garrick went to the back room and continued to work on the engagement ring band, polishing it to perfection. Then he placed the diamond in place and pinched the claws in to secure it. He cleaned and polished it one final time. He selected a ring box from their inventory and placed the stunning ring in it. He smiled to himself at what this small piece of jewelry represented. He closed the box and placed it in his jacket pocket. He would not update the records on this item until after the ring had been presented and accepted.

He was home by 8:00 p.m. and wondered how things were in Cincinnati. There was no reason he couldn't find out.

"Hey, sweetheart. I couldn't wait for your call. Hope I didn't catch you at a bad time."

"Of course not. Mom and I are playing cards right now, and I am overwhelming her with my Go Fish prowess. She will probably thank you for the interruption." Garrick could hear June moaning in the background and he smiled.

"How was the drive this morning?"

"It was good. We got here early in the afternoon and had a late lunch when we arrived. Then we did some serious credit card exercises for about four hours, at which point we both figured it would be wise if we just packed up and drove home before we spent any more money. Of course, it was too late to drive home so we are at the hotel."

Garrick teased, "Wow, sure am glad I don't see your credit card bills." They both laughed. "Did you do any Christmas shopping?"

"Mom did a little, but I'm just not in the mood yet."

"Do you have a store assault plan for tomorrow?"

"We thought we might try the outlet mall, but we really did shop ourselves out today, Garrick. I don't think we can shop for two more full days. Maybe I will talk Mom into a couple of hours at a spa."

Garrick could hear a squeal from June in the background. He knew they were having a great time together and that pleased him.

"How was your day, Garrick? Pick up those sales skills a bit, or should I be rushing home to keep us out of bankruptcy?"

"Haha. Well, I don't think we are headed to bankruptcy court just yet, but it was not record breaking either. I sold a couple of items over lunch, but beyond that, it was quiet. I should let the two of you get back to that scintillating game of Go Fish. Go easy on her. And, Alyssa?"

"Yes?"

"I love you, sweetheart."

When he heard her quietly say, "I love you too, Garrick," he was filled with an indescribable emotion.

Thursday morning, Garrick sat at the kitchen table at his home, looking over the newspaper, drinking his coffee, and thinking about

Alyssa. The sunshine was beaming in through the large window where he sat, and although the fall days had become considerably cooler, the sun still felt good as it flowed into his kitchen. The warmth made him think about where he would whisk Alyssa away to on a honeymoon. A tropical beach somewhere perhaps.

The ring of the phone startled him out of his daydream. Checking the caller ID, a smile stretched across his face. "Good morning, Alyssa."

"Good morning. It doesn't sound like I woke you up. You've already got your day started?"

"It is officially started now that I have heard from you."

"Garrick, I know you wanted us to stay away longer but I think we are going to come home tonight. I hope you aren't too upset about that." Garrick's forehead creased with concern. He admitted he wanted her close by, but he also needed her to be safe.

"Are you sure I can't convince you to shop just a little bit longer?" He tried to keep his voice lighthearted.

"Well, we are going to continue with the plans I mentioned last night. The outlet mall looks interesting, and we are both looking forward to a few hours of pampering at the spa, but we are planning to leave for home late afternoon. Would you be interested in a late dinner?"

"Actually, Mark twisted my arm into taking Chinese food over to their place tonight. Would you like to join us there around seven?

"Isn't Gems open until eight on a Thursday night, Garrick?" she asked with a teasing tone.

"Well, I think I will close at seven tonight. I will order the food to be ready for that time and then head straight over to Mark and Laura's place. That is, unless my boss decides to fire me for consecutive days of reduced hours, in which case I guess I could go over earlier."

"I could fire you, but I think you have the power to hire yourself back, so I'm not going to waste my time. Mom and I are going to do a little shopping and hit the spa, and then we will be on the road by the middle of the afternoon. We will meet you at Mark and Laura's for supper. So order enough for us, please."

"Oh boy, there goes my budget."

"You're not suggesting that Mom and I will eat that much, are you?"

"Not June. Nope." Then he laughed and admitted to himself that he was glad she was coming home two days early. "See ya around seven tonight."

"We'll be there." With that, he ended the call and had less than eleven hours until he could wrap his arms around her.

Garrick stood in Wok Culture waiting for his order to be packed up. The young lady working behind the counter brought out the bags of food. He grabbed the take-out order and drove to Mark and Laura's place, pulling into their driveway at about quarter past seven.

Immediately, his eyebrows creased low, as there was no sign of Alyssa's car. Garrick hurried to the door, and Laura, with her usual exuberance, welcomed him. Mark took the bags from Garrick, and Jason moved in at the table to start opening the various choices. Garrick gave Laura another hug. "I don't see you enough these days." Turning to Mark, he said, "Hope you don't mind, I invited Alyssa and June to join us."

Laura's eyes twinkled. "She called this morning, so we are expecting them too." She paused, studying Garrick. "You know you don't want to let her get away."

"Hmmm. You're not the first to hand out that particular piece of advice. And for the record, I don't intend to let her get away." He winked, and Laura smiled slyly at him.

"I am going to try not to ask for specifics on how you intend to do that, but just know that I really do want to know, and it is really hard for me to not ask!" Garrick laughed and, draping an arm around Laura, guided her to the table.

"Have you heard anything from Alyssa since she called this morning?" he asked cautiously, not wanting to let his concerns alarm them.

"No, but she had indicated she and June would be here by seven," Mark admitted, sending Garrick a concerned look.

"Excuse me then. I'll just go and call her cell to see where they are." Just as he pulled out his cell phone, lights reflected through the windows as a car drove up the driveway. Both Garrick and Mark peered out at the vehicle, and the outline of Alyssa's car put more relaxed expressions on their faces.

The mood was light during dinner, with lively stories filling the time together. Alyssa was really quite tired from the long drive, so she just transferred her luggage over to Garrick's car and sent June home with her car. They would get the vehicles swapped back the next day.

"I'm sorry we had to come back so soon, Garrick. I know you wanted us at a safe distance for longer than we were gone." He glanced over at her in the darkness of the car, lit only by the dashboard electronics. He wanted her safe, but right now, he couldn't help but be thankful that she was with him.

Stretching out his arm, he reached for her hand and held it as he drove the short distance to her house. "I'd be lying if I didn't admit I was happy to see you tonight. I missed you." She smiled, and even in the darkness, he could sense the blush on her cheeks.

He came to a stop in her driveway on Autumn Wood Way. "Let me get your bags inside, and then I will go hide my car at my house so June doesn't get any judgmental calls early tomorrow morning." Garrick walked up to the door with the luggage, and taking the key from Alyssa, he opened it, allowing her to go in ahead of him. He set her luggage inside the door and promised he would be right back. As he closed the door, he heard her phone ring.

Within five minutes, Garrick had returned to Alyssa's place. He let himself in and immediately noticed that she sat in the living room in near darkness. It didn't look as if she had turned any lights in the house on. The only illumination was from outside. He walked to her and, kneeling in front of her, looked into her eyes. What he saw was not the exhaustion he had expected to see, though. What he saw were tears rolling down her cheeks.

"Alyssa, what's wrong?" Then he noticed the phone that was in her hands. "What is it? Did someone call?" All Alyssa could do was nod while more tears streamed down her face, dripping off the edge of her chin.

Garrick removed the phone from her tight grip. He looked at the call history and saw that her mother had called just moments before he had walked in.

"Sweetheart? What did your mom call about?"

"It wasn't Mom who called." A look of absolute horror crept over her face. Struggling to say the words, she quietly explained. "Someone…someone called…from her house. They said they would hurt her if I didn't give them the jewels and some ridiculous amount of money." She buried her face in her hands. Garrick shut his eyes, trying to think with his head and not the angry emotions that were threatening to take over.

"Alyssa, was it a man or a woman?"

"Woman. I didn't recognize the voice."

"What exactly did the woman say?"

Alyssa concentrated, trying to remember the exact words. "I answered the phone, thinking it was Mom, but the woman said, 'Not Mom. June isn't able to come to the phone right now.' I asked who she was, and she said, 'Don't worry about who I am. What's more important is what I want from you.' So I asked what she wanted, and that's when she said, 'I want the jewels that were sent to Gregory Mason, and I want half of his estate. Let's just make it simple…two and a half million dollars is probably close enough to half.' I was dumbstruck by that amount and questioned her on it, but she said I would have to decide if Mom was 'worth it.'"

Garrick was furious but kept the rage in check. "Did she say when you had to give her the jewels and the money and how or where?"

"She said she expected the jewels by tomorrow at noon and the money was to be deposited into an account by the same time." Alyssa reached over and picked up a piece of paper with the banking information listed, but it was not in her handwriting. "Here's the account number."

"Who wrote this?"

Alyssa shrugged. "I guess she did. She told me while I was on the phone with her where to find the note with the information on it." She looked into Garrick's eyes. "She was here in the house sometime."

Garrick put the paper in his pocket.

"Did she let you talk to your mom?" Garrick's concern was growing.

She nodded and said, "I managed to ask if she was okay." Alyssa's voice was trembling now, and the words were coming out in sobs. "All I heard her say was my name. Then it was back to that woman."

"I need to call Mark."

"*No*. She specifically said, 'If you try to call that FBI guy or the police, June will regret it.'"

Garrick knew he needed Mark involved, but he also couldn't upset Alyssa any more than she already was. "Okay. Did she say how you were to get the jewels to her?"

"She just said to have the jewels ready and she would contact me to get them." Garrick sat on the couch beside Alyssa and wrapped his arms around her. He continued to hold her for several minutes, working out a plan in his mind as they sat in silence.

As her sobs were subsiding, Garrick heard her softly ask the question he was dreading: "What are the chances that woman is going to let Mom go at the end of this?"

"I don't know." Garrick had enough law enforcement training to know that the chances were not good.

"What are we going to do?" Alyssa asked as she looked at Garrick. He saw the fear overflowing from her eyes, along with the stream of tears.

"We're going to find a way to get June out safely. I just need time to think." He swallowed hard, wishing he had Mark here to work through a plan with.

Still sitting in the dark with only the street lights casting illumination into the room, both Garrick and Alyssa were startled when the phone rang. Garrick picked up the phone and answered, "Hello?"

"Garrick?"

"Yeah, it's me, Mark. What's up?"

"Hey, man, you don't sound like yourself. Is everything okay?"

"You caught me at a bad time."

There was a low rumble of laughter. "Did I catch you at a bad time, or did I catch at a good time?" The tone changed the entire meaning of the words, and Garrick was fully aware of the implied meaning.

"It's not like that, Mark. Why are you calling?"

"Tom Dallas just called." Garrick panicked, wondering what the police chief would be calling Mark for at this time of night. "They got a call earlier this evening about a body just outside of town. He was murdered, and they've already got an ID on him."

"Who was it?"

"Stephen *Raines*."

"Raines?"

"Yep. Jeremy's son." There was silence on both ends of the phone line. "Okay with you if I come over? Need to talk through a few scenarios."

"Ah, no actually, that might not be a good idea tonight."

"You can't put off what you were doing until tomorrow night?"

"It's not that." Garrick looked down at Alyssa, still tucked in close to him, with concern creasing her porcelain facial features. "We've got a situation that we can't involve you in." Alyssa's eyes grew large.

"A situation?" Mark slowly repeated.

"Yeah, that's right."

"And you can't involve me because of my law enforcement credentials?"

"Yeah."

"Okay, I'll butt out then. Call me when you can." Mark ended the call, and Garrick hung up.

Garrick knew if the woman they were dealing with had the smarts she could monitor text messages from his cell as well as any calls he made. What were the chances she would have every base covered, though? Would he risk June's well-being by taking the chance? He continued to think, holding on to the hope that Mark would do the opposite of butt out.

Garrick leaned down and as quietly as he could, whispered in Alyssa's ear, "Come with me." He stood and, taking her hand, led her out the back door onto the deck. He continued to speak in whispers, not knowing what type of surveillance could be in place.

"Mark called to tell me that Stephen Raines was found murdered just outside of town. He was Jeremy's son." Alyssa drew in a quick breath. "Mark will know from that call something is wrong. He may show up here, but if he does, you know it won't be by the front door, right?"

"What if she finds out?" Alyssa's words were hushed in return.

"Sweetheart, Mark is our best bet to get your mother out safely. We may have to take a chance on this."

"But she's my mother. How can I take a chance like that?" The tears were rolling down her cheeks again, and he wrapped his arms around her. "We shouldn't have come back. We should have stayed in Cincinnati like you wanted us to."

"Hey, don't think like that."

Garrick heard a slight rustling in the trees. He caught a glimpse of a figure toward the back of the yard. His heart pounded, but then the familiar outline registered.

Mark loomed in the shadows and became a welcome sight to his friend. He had parked a couple of streets away and maneuvered through backyards to avoid being seen arriving at Alyssa's house. Garrick directed Alyssa toward the back of the yard, keeping his arm protectively around her shoulders. "What is going on, Garr?" Mark instinctively knew to talk quietly. Surely, Alyssa's tear-streaked face was an indicator of potential trouble. "Some woman called demanding the jewels and two and half million dollars. She's holding June as insurance." Mark understood. Nothing more needed saying. Kidnapping or hostage situations often involved the FBI, and he knew all too well that they did not always end the way you would want. "Alyssa doesn't want to risk jeopardizing her mother by involving anyone. The woman told her no police and no *you*. She referred to you as 'that FBI guy.'"

"Did she give you a deadline?"

"Tomorrow noon," Garrick answered for Alyssa.

"Is there any way you can get your hands on that kind of money by then?"

"We just need to transfer it into what looks like an offshore account. Here, this is the account number. We'll need it back to make the transfer, but you may want to do some checking on it."

Mark smirked. "Good thing I showed up. Appears you were expecting me to."

"Sure was, and Mark? Whoever she is, she left the account number in the house. She was in this house at some point."

"Okay. The police are running all sorts of checks on people associated with Stephen Raines. I would bet that whoever this woman demanding the money is, she is connected to Raines. Just too many coincidences to be anything else since we can tie both of them, at least indirectly, to the jewels."

"Seems like there have been a lot of selfish people involved with those jewels."

"Valuables tend to bring out that side in people. I'll head over to the police station and let them know what is going on. I'll also alert my field office. We should have a negotiator on hand just in case. You'll be heading into Gems to retrieve the jewels, I presume?"

"Yeah, guess so. Not until tomorrow morning, though. We'll have to go to the bank about the transfer of funds. Problem is Alyssa doesn't have the money yet. June is the executor, so she and the lawyer are really the only ones that could authorize a funds transfer like that."

"Good." Mark turned to Alyssa and said, "Tell this woman that when she contacts you. Get June into the bank, and we can nab her before any of the exchange needs to happen." Garrick knew that Alyssa would not relax until this was behind them, but he sensed some relief wash over her hearing Mark's instructions.

Mark turned and was on his way out through the back to his car. Returning to the house, Garrick felt better now that he knew he had some backup and at least a sketchy plan to work with. "How about I make us some tea?" Garrick offered.

Alyssa nodded without speaking. She looked exhausted, but the likelihood of her sleeping tonight was slim.

Garrick and Alyssa walked through New Glory Gems to the office just after ten o'clock Friday morning. They prepared a case for the jewels and retrieved them from vault B.

Alyssa called the bank and spoke to the bank manager about what was required for her to transfer some of the money in her grandfather's estate to another bank account. As suspected, nothing could be done without June and the lawyer involved since the investments had not been transferred to Alyssa yet.

With Garrick beside her, she dialed her mother's home on speakerphone. June answered the phone tentatively. "Hello?"

"Mom, are you all right?"

"Yes, dear, I'm fine." That was all she had time to say, as the phone was taken from her and the woman's voice from the night before took over speaking.

"Do you have the jewels?"

Garrick nodded to Alyssa. "Yes, I have the jewels."

"Good. Have you made the transfer?" Garrick developed an odd look on his face but kept focused and indicated to Alyssa to explain the catch with the transfer.

"No. Since the estate hasn't settled yet, I don't have the money, and the only way to access Grandpa's investments and cash is by having my mother and the lawyer meet with the bank manager at the bank." There was complete silence. "Are you still there?"

"Why would June need to be there? Can't the lawyer handle it?" the woman demanded.

"Mom is the executor of the estate. They need her authorization," Alyssa answered.

Silence again delayed the exchange. Finally, the woman said, "I'll bring June to the bank at eleven a.m. Have the lawyer there. No police, or there'll be trouble." The call ended, and Garrick sat there with a stunned look on his face.

"What's wrong, Garrick?"

"It was Mary Emerson." Alyssa's face drew a blank briefly and then a frown as it registered.

"You mean Grace's daughter?"

"Yeah. Remember I said there was some connection between Grace and Andrew?" Alyssa nodded, and Garrick continued. "Whatever it was always eluded me. Now, Mary is claiming half of the estate." He looked at Alyssa with satisfaction and then smiled. "Mary is your cousin."

"But that would mean she is holding her aunt hostage in exchange for cash and valuables." Alyssa looked horrified.

Tipping his head to the side just slightly, he said, "Sweetheart, not everyone is as angelic as you."

"You knew her better than I did. What is she really capable of?" He shrugged and dialed the lawyer's office. Obviously, either the police or Mark had been in touch with Tyler, Lincoln, and Frost Law Associates, because little to no explanation was required when Garrick spoke to the lawyer.

At precisely eleven o'clock, Garrick and Alyssa entered the bank. Garrick scanned the small operation, and all looked as it should. Directly behind them was the lawyer, Sidney Frost. He leaned forward and whispered to Garrick, "Everything is under control." He knew that meant that backup was in place and this was simply a trap to ensnare a criminal whose identity would be a shock to the small-town community.

The bank manager, Aaron Hargrove, approached the three and escorted them to his office. Although they were separate from the main counter, Garrick was seated in the office in such a way he could watch what was happening.

Aaron Hargrove was in his mid-thirties. With early signs of hair loss, just a slight paunch, and average height, he had been a well-respected manager at the bank for about three years. He ensured that his staff were well trained, courteous, and discreet, resulting in no New Glory residents looking to bank elsewhere.

While they waited, Mr. Hargrove's phone rang. "New Glory Bank, Aaron Hargrove speaking." A puzzled look came over the man. "Yes, I have. Just give me a minute." His words had slowed as he glanced with concern at Garrick. He quickly wrote something on a memo pad, handed it to him, and then motioned for him to leave the office. Garrick realized as he was leaving that Hargrove had turned to his computer and had begun following instructions.

He read the note as soon as he was out the door. A sick feeling flooded over him. Mark was there immediately. Garrick handed the note over, and Mark's head dropped. "Sometimes technology is our worst enemy."

The note simply read "Video call and fax." Video calls allowed for visual conversations on the computer, providing the bank manager with the visual verification he would want of June's identity. They could also watch her sign the required documents and fax them back to the bank.

"Did you have them tailed when they left the house?"

"They haven't left the house yet, and obviously now she is not intending on leaving until the transfer is complete."

"How does she expect to get the jewels then?"

"Maybe she doesn't care about the jewels. That would eliminate any reason for her to come face-to-face with you and Alyssa or to return June to us alive. Once she sees the transfer is complete, she's probably expecting to slip out of town and no one will ever know who made off with the money."

"But I do know." Mark stared at Garrick. "I recognized the voice this morning on the phone. It's Mary Emerson. Mark, there's only one reason that she would be demanding half the estate and one way that she would have a good estimate of how much that was. She's got to be Andrew's daughter, and Grace would know from the lawyer's office the extent of his worth."

"You're sure it was Mary?"

"Positive."

"So tell me again why you didn't apply to the FBI?" Mark shook his head as he turned and first arranged for the police to pick up Grace Emerson. Second, he alerted the SWAT team that he had called in from Louisville, and finally the negotiator he had on standby from his field office.

Once he was off the phone, Garrick grabbed his attention. "Hey, I know you're thinking the jewels may not be a high priority to Mary, but if you still factor them into this scenario, does that potentially put Jillian at risk? Everyone else connected to those jewels has been eliminated except for her. Can we see where she is and make sure she is not being targeted too?"

Mark raised one eyebrow. "That's the first time I have ever heard you sound even the least bit concerned about Jillian."

"Yeah, well, let's hope it's not misplaced." Mark nodded that they would check on her.

The next forty minutes unfolded quickly but felt as if the events were being viewed in slow motion. The SWAT team positioned itself close but out of sight of June's house. The negotiator moved in closer. Police found Jillian at the bed and breakfast, having just arrived back from Lexington that morning, and Grace Emerson was taken by the police to where the negotiator waited.

Meanwhile, Aaron Hargrove had intentionally taken considerable time to get the video call running and was explaining the complexities of transferring funds from the estate to an account that was not in the name of a beneficiary listed in the will. His explanation was long and tedious, and Garrick could tell that Mary's patience was growing rigid.

"Fax us the form that needs to be signed," she finally snapped out, tired of the slow proceedings. Mary had carefully kept out of the camera feed so her identity would remain hidden. Mark nodded in the doorway to Mr. Hargrove, who then agreed to fax the document as demanded.

In the background at June's house, which was audible on the bank computer, Mark and Garrick could hear the negotiator making his first contact via a bullhorn. He had been instructed to distract Mary long enough to allow the SWAT team to get into position. Garrick had prepped them on access points to the house and its layout. That would give them the knowledge about the best way in and how long it would take them to be in position once inside.

Mark was able to converse with the negotiator and the SWAT team leader on June's location based on the visual they had through the video-call session.

Garrick could hear Mary's reaction to the negotiator. He knew they would have to move quickly since Mary was likely to panic now that she had been contacted. It would do her no good at this point to harm June, as she desperately needed her in order to get herself out safely. However, desperate people do desperate and often not well-thought-out things.

Mark motioned to Garrick that the SWAT team was inside the house. He was always impressed with the way those teams operated. They were inside, and yet it was obvious from the video-call feed that Mary was unaware of their presence.

Suddenly there was a flurry of bodies behind June. Three shots were fired, a scream was heard, and June had disappeared from the webcam shot. "Mom?" Alyssa practically pushed Aaron Hargrove off his chair, trying to get closer to the computer screen. "Mom?" She was terror stricken by what was happening. She had no way of knowing if anyone had been hit by the shots that sounded. No female voices were heard amid the commotion.

Alyssa rushed out of the bank manager's office and past Garrick and Mark, who hastily followed her. Garrick caught up and grabbed her arm. "Wait. Just wait until we get confirmation on what happened."

"I saw what happened!" she yelled. "Three shots were fired, and my mother is no longer sitting in front of the camera. I have to get to her."

Chapter 15

"Okay, we're going, but you're not driving."

"Alyssa, Garrick, you ride with me," Mark directed. They hurried out the back of the bank to the parking lot. That was where the police and FBI vehicles stationed at the bank had parked. In minutes, they were at June's house. An emergency response vehicle already sat in the driveway. "You can't go in until I give you the all clear. Do you understand?"

Regrettably, Alyssa nodded her understanding, and she and Garrick watched Mark enter the house. While they sat waiting for some sign from him, a stretcher emerged from the side door of the house. Alyssa gasped. From where they sat, there was no way to tell who was on the stretcher. She looked at Garrick with pleading eyes. He knew she wanted to get to the stretcher to find out if it was her mother or not, but he could not risk her well-being.

"Garrick, please. If they let the EMT in, it must be safe enough. I need to see her." His heart was breaking for her. What if the woman on the stretcher was Mary and June was still inside and no longer alive?

Thankfully, he didn't have to answer her, as Mark came out of the house and walked toward the car. Alyssa was out the door immediately. "Is she okay, Mark?"

"Calm down. June was knocked down in the confusion, and she hit her head on the desk. She's unconscious right now, Alyssa. That's why they are taking her to the hospital. The doctors will be in a better position to tell you exactly how she is when they've had a chance to examine her."

Garrick squeezed her hand. "We'll go to the hospital, sweetheart. I am sure we can get a ride from someone around here." Then turning to Mark, knowing that Grace Emerson remained outside the house, he asked another question. "What about Mary?"

"Two of the three shots hit her."

"And?"

"Don't think she'll make it." Then, nodding across the street toward the house, Mark said, "They're taking her out now. She was lucid for a while, but they had to give her morphine, so she's not coherent now."

"Did she say anything?"

"A bit. She was very bitter over Andrew. You were right about the connection. She said, 'Tell my mother I'm sorry about getting rid of Andrew, but it had to stop. I don't care if he was my father.'"

"So she admitted to killing Andrew. No mention of Stephen, though?"

"Nope, that's all we got. Hey, Jasper, can you run Garrick and Alyssa to their car so they can get to the hospital?"

"Yes, sir. Right this way."

Garrick and Alyssa sat in the emergency waiting room at the New Glory Hospital, waiting for word on June's condition. After two hours, still no doctor had shown up to give them an update. Even Garrick was getting impatient at this point.

"We should have heard something by now. They would know if it was just a concussion. What is taking so long?" Alyssa was on edge and clearly exhausted.

"She's in the best possible hands, Alyssa. We just need to keep the faith." Truthfully, however, Garrick had been entertaining the same thoughts. This seemed an unusually long time since she was taken into an exam room to be still waiting for word. "Let me see if I can find a vending machine around here. Maybe I can get us something to eat or drink."

He stood and walked down the hall out of a need to burn time and nervous energy and was immobilized as he watched Jillian walking toward him. He narrowed his eyes, not sure how to interpret her presence. Alyssa must have seen him stop because she was instantly by his side. "Your mother is here?"

"Seems so." Garrick said hesitantly.

"How is she?" Jillian's concern certainly came across as genuine, but Garrick still had reservations on her motives, so he remained cautious and said nothing.

"We don't know yet. It was thoughtful of you to come by to check." Alyssa was tentative too but did not have the history with Jillian that Garrick did. Jillian just nodded her understanding at them both.

"Ms. Mason?" A doctor, probably in his late forties approached the three of them.

"Yes, I'm Alyssa Mason. How is my mother?"

"She regained consciousness about a half hour ago. We've spent that time assessing her. We had done a CAT scan earlier, and from those results and her current condition, I am very optimistic that she will be just fine." The doctor managed to deliver a comforting smile at that point, which both Alyssa and Garrick needed. "We will be keeping her at least overnight to monitor her since she did sustain a serious enough concussion. If you would like to see her, I can take you in now. I would just prefer if you kept this visit short. You can come back after dinner tonight and see her again. We should have her in a room by then."

They followed him into the emergency exam room, and Alyssa sighed visibly at the sight of her mother's eyes open and a hint of a smile on her lips.

"Oh, Mom, I am so glad to see you. How do you feel?"

"My head hurts, but they are doing what they can to help that. Sounds like I am going to have another night away from home since they are refusing to let me leave the hospital until at least tomorrow. Would you mind terribly picking up a couple of things for me from the house and bringing them?" She sounded as if she were imposing and was reluctant to ask.

With a half laugh, Alyssa shook her head. "Of course I wouldn't mind. The doctor doesn't want us to stay long now. We'll come back after supper and bring whatever you need then."

"Oh, that would be so wonderful." June proceeded to list the few items she wanted, and Alyssa made a mental note of them. She gave her mother a gentle hug, and Garrick moved in to give June a smile and kiss on the cheek as well.

"See ya later, Mom."

Garrick's mother was sitting in the waiting room when they came out. He wandered over to where she was. "Jillian, June is doing much better. We're going to head out now, but thanks for coming by."

"Let me know if there is anything I can do to help Garrick. I mean it."

"Thanks." Turning to the exit, he and Alyssa left the hospital. He was stunned by how his mother was acting. Perhaps she really had changed.

Saturday morning, June was released from the hospital, so Alyssa and Garrick went to pick her up. When they arrived, they saw Mark walking into the hospital ahead of them.

By the time they reached June's room, Mark was already questioning her on anything that Mary Emerson might have said, or admitted to, of which he or the police were not aware. They paused outside the hospital room door while Mark asked his questions.

"Did she mention anything about a man named Stephen Raines?" Mark asked.

"Stephen? Well, we didn't exactly share personal information with each other, but I did hear her call her mother. She mentioned someone named Stephen. Should I know him?" June asked.

"No, you wouldn't know him," Mark answered.

"Obviously, I could only hear one side of the conversation, but she told her mother to get packed. With Andrew and Stephen out of the way they could leave and start over somewhere else."

"Was anything else mentioned during that phone call?"

"Not that I could make sense of with only hearing one side. I was mainly listening for anything that would indicate if I was going to be alive at the end of it all or not. However, nothing was really said about me."

"Well, you are alive and we are all relieved about that," Alyssa announced as she and Garrick walked in the room.

June's face lit up. "It's time for me to leave, Mark. Have you asked all your questions?"

"No more questions. Thanks, June. I believe Alyssa and Garrick have tried to straighten up your house, although it may need a few more repairs. We had to dig one bullet out of the wall," he stated with an apologetic half shrug.

"Yep, I'll take care of it next week, June," Garrick spoke up. Then turning to Mark, he continued. "What's the news on Mary Emerson?"

"Didn't make it through the surgery yesterday."

"And what about all these unsolved cases?"

"We'll have to finish up the paperwork, but based on June's statement, it's reasonable to conclude that Mary was behind both Andrew's and Stephen's deaths. Jillian provided us with information regarding Andrew's involvement in Jeremy's death and their combined role in Gregory's death, which is now regarded as a homicide. The unrecovered jewels that you and Alyssa discovered at New Glory Gems are in the hands of the FBI now.

"The police will be charging Grace with an accessory charge. She's already made a statement that June has just corroborated in part. She also made it clear that Gregory Mason was never voluntarily involved with the thefts. Andrew had been blackmailing him, so he really had no choice but to store the jewels when Andrew sent them to Gems."

"Blackmail?" Garrick's voice conveyed surprise.

"Apparently. Grace didn't know the specifics, but she knew Andrew had coerced Greg," Mark answered.

"I suppose we'll never know now. So we can actually put this behind us. From all the evidence, Jillian's only involvement was her recent knowledge of the first two deaths?" Garrick's question was directed at Mark.

"She's already done her time for the original thefts, and the only connection to the deaths was the information she brought forward to us. The district attorney has reviewed her statement and Grace's statement and has concluded that no charges are going to be brought against Jillian. She might be on the level this time, Garrick, when she claims to have turned over a new leaf."

With a quick lift of one eyebrow, Garrick said, "Well, that would be nice." Then turning to June, he said, "Come on, June. I have your carriage ready to escort you to the hospital exit."

"I'm not riding in a wheelchair. I am perfectly capable of walking out of here."

"Don't care what you say; it's hospital policy. So just play along and climb in."

The argument continued for a few more minutes, but in the end, Garrick won out. With a grumble, June complied, and they left the hospital, glad that the trepidation that had been plaguing all of them was finally in the past.

Garrick pulled Alyssa aside once they had her mother in the house. "I know you want to stay with your mother to keep an eye on her, but I was hoping to spend some time with you tonight. Would you please join me for dinner at my place at seven?" His eyes were telling in their depth. He wanted her to say yes, and yet there was a vague uneasiness that she might argue about staying with her mother.

He suspected she would want the time together as much as he did but was concerned her feelings of responsibility for her mother might be warring in her. He felt relief and excitement when she answered him. With a nod and an encouraging smile, she accepted his invitation. "I'd like that. I will get dinner for Mom around five thirty and then head home. What have you got planned, Mr. Samuels?" Obviously, she was intrigued by her curious tone.

"I was thinking of a special dinner tonight. We have lots to celebrate. After all, your mother is going to be fine, and for the first time in several weeks, I feel as if the danger is behind us."

She walked her fingers up the front of his shirt while moistening her lips. "What should I wear for this special dinner? Is it formal?" Her tone was teasing and probing.

Garrick's eyes were filled with passion. "Well," he started slowly, bringing his hand up to her cheek and stroking her cheekbone gently with his thumb. "I'm not wearing a tux, but if you would like to wear something…pretty…" His other hand cupped the opposite cheek now. He was leaning in closer to her. "Something…" But he didn't finish the thought because he was kissing her.

This kiss was not over quickly. He took his time, enjoying the moment. When he finally backed away from her, she appeared shaky and unbalanced. Drawing back to steadier ground, she replied to him breathlessly, "Okay, I will wear *something* then."

Smiling at her unsteady words, he reminded her, "Seven p.m. Don't be late." Alyssa nodded. Garrick was pleased, sensing she was still struggling to recover from the dazed condition he had left her in from the kiss. He walked from the room, anxious for the next few hours to pass with mach speed.

The time did pass, however slow it may have seemed to Garrick, and when Claude arrived from Traveling Chefs, all Garrick had to do was show him the kitchen, the area he planned to eat, and confirm the menu and arrangements. Then he disappeared to get ready for Alyssa's arrival. Claude would take care of setting the table including candles. He would also prepare and serve the meal. Garrick had opted for him to leave once dessert was served.

Alyssa stood at the front door at 7:00 p.m. Right on time, she thought as she rang the doorbell. It seemed odd to wait to be let in. She realized it had been some time since she had had any private time to speak of until this weekend. For so long now, Garrick had accompanied her everywhere.

She had put a coat on, as the weather had become quite chilly, but underneath that layer, she wore a cute little black dress with a tank bodice and v-neckline. It came into an empire waistline, and the short skirt was tan satin overlain with black organza covered in beaded embellishments. Alyssa wore her favorite black high heels and had pinned her hair up into a more formal style to complement the outfit she had selected.

She heard steps approaching the front door and took a deep breath before the door opened. There he was in the doorway, looking about as good as she had ever seen him. He was wearing brown pants and a brown suede sports jacket over a black shirt. She remembered the first time she had seen him. An automatic comparison with the males of New York had placed him in a different category than the men she had interacted with normally. He was completely different from them, and the qualities that made him distinctive had captured her attention.

His smile just about melted every fiber in her, and she automatically smiled back. He said nothing, just reached out for her hand and drew her inside. "May I take your coat?" The words came out so quietly that they seemed intimate.

She slipped the coat off and realized his breathing had changed. She smiled to herself. She had hoped for that very response. She had not turned to face him yet, and before she could, she felt his hands touch her bare arms and move up to her shoulders. He stepped closer and leaned in to whisper in her ear. "You look gorgeous." Then a hot kiss sizzled on her neck, and she realized now that her breathing was irregular too.

The aroma finally registered with her. "What are you making for dinner, Garrick? It smells wonderful."

"Hmmm. I can't take credit for any of it, but I agree it smells great. Can I get you something to drink?"

"Sure. Whatever you're having will be fine." He had taken her hand and led her into the living room.

"I'll be right back." He left a warm kiss on her cheek before leaving the room to get the drinks. She looked around and caught a glimpse of the dining room. The table was set beautifully. So entranced in thoughts of what the evening would be like, she did not notice him return.

"Alyssa?" He held out a champagne flute to her. Again, he had surprised her, and he smiled at her reaction. She realized he was pleased at her look of wonder.

"Champagne? Wow. Where did you get champagne in a dry county?" she suspiciously questioned.

"It's nonalcoholic." He smiled.

"Ah, you certainly know how to celebrate, don't you?"

"I get it right once in a while. I hope tonight will be one of those times."

She smiled and allowed a nervous laugh to escape. "So far so good." She held her glass as he proposed a toast.

"To a memorable night." She blinked and swallowed at the words and then lifted the glass to her lips and sipped. "I checked on dinner when I got the drinks. It will be ready to be served soon."

"Do you have a small army hidden in the kitchen, Garrick?" Her eyes sparkled with intrigue.

"I wouldn't call it an army."

"Excuse me, Mr. Samuels. If you would find your way to the dining room, dinner will be served shortly," Claude announced from the doorway to the kitchen. Alyssa stared at the small man who had spoken and then sent a questioning glance toward Garrick, who smiled at her curiosity.

"Alyssa, would you please join me in the dining room?" He held out his arm for her and led her to the dining room, which now had soft lighting and lit candles.

Garrick set his champagne glass down and then took hers and placed it on the table. He pulled out her chair, and Alyssa delightedly took a seat at the elegantly set table. "This is lovely, Garrick. Who was that man?"

Smiling, he answered, "I'll introduce you when he comes out. In the meantime, how was your mother when you left her?"

"Anxious to get rid of me. It kind of hurt." She feigned a dagger in the chest and then smirked. "She wanted some peace and quiet, and I can't blame her. She said she would like us to pick her up for church in the morning."

"We should be able to do that. You're not going back over there to spend the night at her place?"

"No, she made it quite clear that she would be fine without me and that she didn't want to see me until church time." Garrick simply laughed. Claude entered the dining room with two plates. "Your dinner is ready." He placed the meals in front of them, and again Alyssa's eyes grew large. Each plate was elegantly arranged with grilled tenderloins wrapped in bacon, steamed lobster with melted butter, a stuffed potato, and chilled mixed melon balls.

Garrick caught Claude before he left the table. "Alyssa, I would like to introduce Claude, our chef and server for this evening. Claude, this is Alyssa Mason."

"It is a great pleasure to meet you, Ms. Mason." A slight bow of his head made Alyssa feel like she was being treated royally.

"Thank you, and it is very nice to meet you also. This meal looks amazing."

"Enjoy your evening." Then he disappeared into the kitchen.

"Is he leaving now?" Alyssa queried.

"After he serves dessert, he'll be on his way."

"Dessert? I haven't been fasting for the last several days. You might have warned me I would need to bring a ravenous appetite with me."

The two talked, laughed, and thoroughly enjoyed each other and the food. When Claude removed their empty plates, he indicated that the dessert would be served momentarily.

When he brought it out, Alyssa was astonished to see the bananas foster. Garrick had truly made this evening one that would be unforgettable. She was absolutely speechless and simply gazed at him. Interrupting the silence, Claude said, "Mr. Samuels, Ms. Mason. I hope you will enjoy your dessert and the rest of your evening. I will let myself out."

"Thank you, Claude." Immediately, Garrick's attention returned to his guest. "Try it."

She closed her eyes briefly once it was in her mouth. "Oh my. That is delicious. I've never actually tried this before. I've been in New York restaurants that have it on the menu but never had it."

"The New York City restaurants would prepare it with alcohol and ignite it for a more dramatic dessert. Claude used a non-alcoholic recipe—no flames." He shrugged. Alyssa simply smiled at him.

After finishing, they took their refilled champagne glasses back to the living room. She should not have been surprised but still was. There in the living room, Claude had started a fire for them before leaving. The lighting was dimmed to set the mood. Garrick led her to the couch drawing her close to him; they sat and watched the flames dance in the fireplace.

"Garrick. This evening has been extraordinary."

"Any evening with you is extraordinary."

Alyssa blushed and gazed up into his eyes. "You make it so difficult for me to breathe, Garrick Samuels."

Holding her chin so that he could maintain the close eye contact, he allowed a small smile to show. "The day you and I met, my life changed, Alyssa. I didn't know it at the time, but I realized so quickly that I was interested in you for far more than your physical beauty.

"These past few weeks, we've had to spend an unusual amount of time together due to circumstances. For me—and I hope for you too—it's allowed my feelings for you to grow incredibly fast. We were brought together by your grandfather's death, and as sad an occasion as that was, it has made me as happy now as I have ever been.

"Until I met you, I never felt the need to have one person in my life for all time. Now I am seeing things differently. Alyssa, I need you in my life, and more than that, I want you in my life, always."

He moved, lowering himself to the floor on one knee. Alyssa was certain she was no longer breathing. "Alyssa, I would be honored if you would spend the rest of your life with me, as my wife. Will you marry me?"

Alyssa drew in a short harsh breath. "You're asking me to marry you?" Tears began to fill her eyes. She did not want to cry, but the emotions that his proposal elicited swelled the tears to overflowing. "Really?"

"Yes, I really am asking you to marry me." He was smiling a little now at her complete shock. He reached over to the end table beside the couch they sat on and pulled out the ring box he had carefully, strategically, placed there. "I would like you to wear this. It is my promise of the commitment that I will make to you on our wedding day. I don't want a long engagement, Alyssa. I want a long life with you as my wife. Will you marry me?"

She looked at the unopened box and then back at him. With tears streaming down her face, she frantically nodded and breathlessly whispered, "Yes, oh yes. I will marry you, Garrick. I will marry you."

He opened the box to show her the brilliant ring. The diamonds sparkled with the light from the fire, and the reflections flickered around the room. Alyssa could not help her reaction to the ring. With a small gasp, she whispered, "Garrick, it is…it is the most beautiful ring I have ever seen." Her eyes met his. "Is it one of your creations?"

He nodded. "It is my favorite, and it is one that I will never duplicate because the love I feel for you could never be matched." He moved back onto the couch beside her, and reaching for her left hand, he slid the ring into place. It fit perfectly and was dazzling. Drawing her gaze away from the ring by taking her face in his hands, he wiped away the tears that had streaked her cheeks.

"I love you, Alyssa Mason." He pressed his lips to hers, and a long and increasingly passionate kiss ignited between the two. When he finally allowed her to come up for air, she responded by telling him how much she loved him also.